The Burning Years

"Here's a fiction that's not afraid to tackle some of the biggest topics of our time."
—**Bill McKibben, author,** *The End of Nature* **and numerous environmental books, and founder of 350.org**

"...the journey through a different way of inhabiting our solar system based on the latest technologies, developments, and beliefs about who we are and our relationship to living, life, and space...It's wonderful—"
—**Rachel Armstrong, TED Senior Fellow, Professor and Pioneer of "Living Architecture."**

APS BOOKS

FELICITY HARLEY

Until The Last Book 1

THE BURNING YEARS

APS Books,
The Stables Field Lane,
Aberford,
West Yorkshire,
LS25 3AE

APS Books is a subsidiary of the APS Publications imprint

www.andrewsparke.com

First published by Double Dragon eBooks in 2017

A catalogue record for this book is available from the British Library

For my husband, Chris,
who has always believed in my writing.

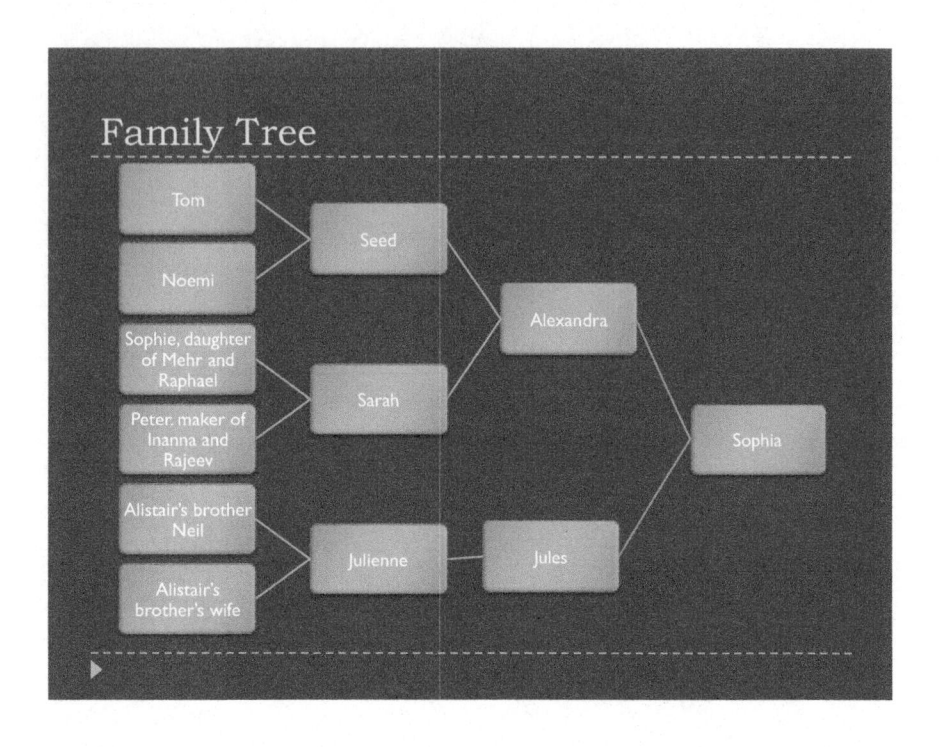

A glossary of scientific terms can be found at the end of this book which describes the words in bold face italics found throughout the text.

2060

Part I

Chapter 1
Inanna

Peter, my maker, has recently told me, "Inanna, the burning years are about to kick into full throttle." When I heard this from him, I knew none of the wars and fights and various ideologies and beliefs that keep humans apart will matter. We'll all be forced to put them aside as we fight together for the survival of our planet and our species.

Three years ago, I volunteered to allow DARPA (Defense Advanced Research Projects Agency) to affect a radical transformation of my body. Because I've always been an avid trans-humanist, this was something I welcomed. Since I was conversant with many of the advances in medical science, I didn't fear what re-engineering would do to me. I wanted to become one of the first to make this change.

Where did I come from? I'm half Palestinian and half Jewish. In 2020, my parents were removed forcibly from Israel. The fundamentalists eventually gained control of that country and transferred all the Israeli Arabs from Judea, Samaria, Gaza, and Israel proper to refugee camps outside their borders. It was called the Great Transfer. Many knew it wasn't a moral or humane policy, but they thought it necessary for security reasons.

The conflicts in the Arab Middle East between modern, secular Islamists and anti- modern ones continued to rage and, like animals caught in a trap, we lived in the middle of the firestorm. It was ridiculous to even imagine both sides could live peaceably together, when faced with such deep-seated, ideological differences. In the end, the fate of that area culminated in the nuclear exchange of 2035, started by a renegade group of terrorists.

In 2020, when I was five years old and after my parents had died from radiation sickness, I came to America to live with my uncle, my father's brother, and his wife in Washington, D.C. My uncle, who works in security, and I still keep in touch, but we were never close, so it's been easy to hide what's happening to me.

It has taken three years to completely transform my human body to *bionic*, removing any parts that might have been damaged by exposure to radiation when I was younger. The most amazing changes, however, have been in my brain, whose capacity has been greatly advanced. Because the nerve endings are now connected to electrical

3

reactors, the barriers between others and me can more easily be breached, and a way is open for me to connect directly with the brain of another person. I am, therefore, prepared to transfer my thoughts for enhanced cooperative problem solving.

In addition, when I link my brain with the Web of all human knowledge, and its myriad pieces of information, there can be a perfect and economic transference between us. In this way, I'm able to form a complex, compound, superhuman intelligence. Peter says I'm a breakthrough in organic evolution and will, through these connections, feel myself a part of the whole brain of humankind.

One of the things he has mentioned is that by linking my brain to the ideas of others, I will no longer be bound by feelings of individuality. The compound human mind, this multiple organism I will create, will hold all of humanity's memories, ideas, and thoughts.

In addition, my mind has no pre-existing blueprints, so my creative insights and ideas are spontaneous, independent, and completely my own, and are, therefore, portable and free to move independently. All my recent learning has taken place in my consciousness, which as a result of my bio-engineered brain, has been able to evolve complex ideas that far exceed anything I could have produced in my unaltered state.

I find I can control my feelings or **neuroelectric** waveform shapes, as I call them, in such a way that I can induce fear or happiness or completion, in order to favor whatever task I'm trying to accomplish. Since I can decide whether I feel happy or sad, I'm less vulnerable than a fully biological human to outside influences.

I'm carrying a lot of important information necessary for the survival of Peter and his friends, and also for maintaining and building solutions and systems in the post climate-change community, rebuilt on the Earth's surface that will inevitably emerge, once this environmental catastrophe is over in many hundreds of years. My implants use my own **bioenergy** to recharge themselves, so I'm completely self-sufficient and can live anywhere. I'm 'off the grid' so to speak.

My companion, Rajeev, has been created in a similar fashion to myself. However, since he is culturally a male and has male hormones and a male brain, his thoughts and feelings are different than mine. I know because we're able to share them directly and non-verbally with each other.

In fact, we've been advised not to try and connect our brain cells too often, because we don't know what kinds of electromagnetic energy we'll produce between us. We're considered adolescents as far as our understanding of our abilities are concerned, and are still learning how to control our so-called 'super powers.'

Before he agreed to be changed, Rajeev was a top athlete and a boy genius, engineering highly advanced computer systems. He was an excellent gamer and had a rich imagination as he developed more and more complex and abstract theories.

Rajeev is originally from a small village in Northern India. He left there at the age of ten for Bangalore to live with his older brother after their parents died from a viral infection. He is a Hindu and when he was young, his mother taught him the key principles he should live his life by honesty, refraining from injuring living beings, patience, forbearance, self-restraint, and compassion. She also taught him about *Moksha*, his soul's journey away from the cycle of birth and death towards freedom, self-realization, and self-knowledge.

By fifteen, Rajeev had distinguished himself internationally as a brilliant student in the fields of math and physics. In 2049, when he was nineteen, he was recruited by a U.S. company working on cyber defense for the military, and brought to Washington, D.C. Both of us are being enhanced specifically so we can work with DARPA on some of the latest defensive weapons and solar ray shields they are developing, and we will soon be transferred from the facility in which we live, to continue to work on these innovative technologies in DARPA's underground refuge at Mount Weather.

We are the first of several prototypes and the only two whose human nervous systems have so far successfully made a seamless interface with our devices. Peter has recently told me we are examples of perfect trans-humans, because we both have such a strong philosophical grounding in what he calls 'essentially life-affirming tenets.'

Chapter 2
Sophie

I was born in New Mexico when my mother, Mehr, was sixty-five, thanks to my father, Raphael's, 'intervention.' I was raised there and home-schooled until I left for college in 2045. By then we were starting to see very serious effects from climate change. My mother told me frequently that a lot of 'dark money' was being spent by those in the world who cynically wanted us to believe our climate wasn't changing, despite overwhelming evidence that it was. She died at ninety-five years of age, just before the burning years hit us with full force. I suppose some people would have called her an 'other.' She never re-entered society after Raphael left and lived like a hermit in her small house at the base of the Sangre de Cristo Mountains.

By the early Twenty-First Century, even before I was born, we'd become aware that climate change was a major issue and we needed to do something about it if we were to survive as a species. However, history tells us there were strong groups of economically privileged individuals whose self-interest flourished because of denying its existence. These individuals, many of whom, including several of our Presidents and political strongmen, had a significant stake in the fossil fuel industry. and caused most of Earth's inhabitants to sacrifice their health and future. The religion of these economically privileged people was one of perpetual growth, of unleashing the market, even though many of us knew in our hearts this was wrong, and that we lived on a finite planet, one slowly being destroyed by their greed, and our own over-consumption.

Perhaps the worst thing about this period was we couldn't figure out a way to separate corporate entities from our governments. They and their money overran our political systems the world over. Some even deliberately caused governments to de-invest in all possible alternatives to fossil fuels, so consumers would have to keep buying their products.

On the positive side, however, by the time I entered government service in 2050, quite a few decentralized, independent, green communities were developing around the world; post-industrial ones that had rejected the fossil fuel economy and heavily utilized advanced science and technology. In these communities, members owned the sources of energy, the majority of which were geo-thermal, solar, and wind based.

Additionally, critical to their success, food production was decentralized, **intercropping** was practiced, and livestock raised in a humane manner. The use of light and water was also maximized. Chemical fertilizers were banned, and quick-growing plants developed, plants able to replace nutrients into the soil. But sadly, there were not enough of these communities to make a major difference and slow down what was rapidly happening to our planet.

When I took on my government position, after I graduated from university, the "Weather Wars" were in full force. The United States had been investing in HAARP (The High Frequency Active Auroral Research Program) since 1960 and had moved parts of it from Alaska to an underground facility, Area 52, in the Nevada desert, where its scientists worked on research that would enable us to continue to **geo-engineer** the weather.

By 2030 they had developed in that facility a way to push and relocate weather and, as climate change happened, they believed they could ensure our national survival by redirecting extreme weather events meant for us into various parts of the world. Then other developed countries began to tinker with the weather as well, which set off massive droughts and storms everywhere.

While we had international environmental agreements, as the impending cataclysm approached, countries panicked. That's how the "Weather Wars" started. In 2045, because we were all trying to save ourselves from the effects of climate change, treaties and agreements between countries became obsolete as conventional weapons were now useless. Carbon dioxide and other heat-trapping gases had risen to such an extent into the atmosphere around the globe that they had formed a thick blanket. As these heat-trapping gas concentrations increased, the blanket's thickness also increased and trapped even more heat in our lower atmosphere. Heat that had been designed by nature to escape through the stratosphere was now no longer able to do so, and resulted in it being much cooler than it should have been. This abnormal coolness then contributed to ozone loss, which effectively cancelled out any progress we had made in the past, by reducing **CFC's**.

Like us, most developed countries around the globe didn't care what happened in other parts of the world and were using any number of untested methods to reduce the effects of regional climate change.

These methods included blocking a portion of the sun's rays; fertilizing nearby oceans with iron to pull carbon out of the atmosphere; covering their land with vast sheets of white plastic, making them look like giant snowfields to reflect sunlight back into space; and building machines that could suck carbon out of the air.

We, in the United States, led the pack and after I joined DARPA, my job was to control the giant space mirrors in place in the *ionosphere.* We were brightening clouds above the Earth, and spraying seawater into the sky with cannons to make more clouds. We'd also stolen *Tesla's* resonance theories and were sending sonic pulsars up into the atmosphere. The pulsars caused volcanoes to spew out sulphur dioxide, which would supposedly increase our cloud cover, but ended up on top of everything else causing earthquakes and tidal waves, inadvertently wiping out large parts of our land, including the West Coast and its populations.

In my heart, I knew what we were really doing, all of us together, was causing our 'mother,' Gaia, to go crazy, as we played out the final scenario of the Industrial Revolution. A Revolution that had led some of us to believe we could tame nature and make it our own.

'Solar Radiation Management,' as we called it euphemistically in our department, would fail in the long term to cool our continental landmass. And, as we engineered what we called '*global dimming*,' we drove away our blue skies and all we saw now was white above us, like an unremitting autumnal fog, so that at night we could no longer observe the moon or the stars.

The 'ones in the know,' the elite in all the countries, understood the tiny particles of sulphur we had been putting into the atmosphere for years, would eventually deplete the radiation shield from our planet. Because they knew what others didn't, these elite were preparing their underground cities where they, their children, grandchildren, and great grandchildren would live until many years into the future, when their descendants could re-emerge, like mole-people, onto an Earth's surface that was perhaps beginning to heal.

Many of these 'elites' including our politicians, were the same ones who had been responsible in the first place for causing the methane leaks, using extra-dirty coal, creating tar sand deposits, and turning a blind eye to the massive spillage of natural gas from their gargantuan projects.

To add fuel to this destructive fire we had started, in 2050 we also caused the Arctic to finally all but melt away, and in doing so inadvertently released several pre-historic viruses that had been trapped for millions of years under the perma-frost. The release of these viruses caused the deaths of millions of the poor and disenfranchised, who were not allowed access to the limited, expensive, and hastily developed vaccines controlled by private pharmaceutical companies.

Now, ten years after I joined DARPA, in the year 2060, it was the right time for me to be exactly where I was. My husband, Peter, and I had the ability to use any information we obtained at our jobs for the construction of a survivalist community we were building on the great underground Ogallala Aquifer. This Aquifer stretches from Nebraska into Texas. Most of its southern parts had gone dry by 2025, but the water in the deepest regions of it, starting in Nebraska, has miraculously remained the same.

Our friends, who were fellow scientists and architects, together with us, had spent the past fifteen years building a series of modern, technologically advanced living structures that floated on the surface of the Aquifer in giant caverns below the Earth. It was a place where we knew we could be safe for many years by hiding under the surface of our planet.

***

My close friend, Rachel, is also working at DARPA and has been assigned to Project *Persephone*, whose goal has been the creation of a habitable, long duration Worldship. Forty-five years in the making, *Persephone* is about to launch.

Rachel has been consumed by her efforts to develop plans for a habitable, interstellar starship. She and her colleagues are in the midst of figuring out how to use the innate force of different materials to create artificial living structures that can regenerate themselves.

On *Persephone*, a new kind of architectural design will be used—its interior and exterior will behave like an evolving ecosystem. *Persephone* will need to support the crew for the duration of their journey, which if they do not find a habitable planet could last for hundreds of years. The architecture and structures within the Worldship will therefore be created from the bottom up, using varieties of rocks and soils. On *Persephone*, all of the dynamic systems will regenerate themselves.

Persephone's synthetic soil will also support plants, microbes, and other entities necessary for a self-sustaining ecosystem. It is an ecology different from that on Earth and has been produced specifically for the purpose of this voyage.

Rachel wrote in a recent communication to her crew:

Soils are a living web of relationships within complex bodies that will eventually grow old and die. Plants take root in the rich chemical medium and bind the particles together to attract animal life. Conversely, soil harbors fungi and bacteria that break down the bodies of dead creatures and turns them into more soil. Soils are biological cities. They house, nourish, and provide the vital infrastructure for terrestrial life, which laid the foundations for the establishment of ecosystems, the evolution of humans, and the construction of the built environment. The rich complexity of soil systems provides a model and literal substrate for Persephone's built environment that can self-maintain and connect with ecological systems.

Soil scientists observe how we can mix the various particles, adjust the acidity, compost the organic substrate, and bring these inorganic and organic worlds together. But making a soil is more than measuring ingredients for a recipe, soil is composed of matter that possesses the vibrancy and vivid hues of the rainbow, embodying the poetry of symbiosis – and perhaps most importantly – is our binding contract with Nature.

But how may we forge a contract with Nature in space, where no native biology is known to exist, only physics and chemistry? Over the last few years, I have been working with living chemistries and synthetic biologies, shaping materials that possess a will and exert a force of their own, independently of a central program or my design and engineering intentions. These materials have formed primitive, dynamic cell-like structures – or **protocells***.*

Through **symbiosis***, we are now able to create our own soils. Our magnificent living ship is capable of natural computing, one based on the mathematical powers of Nature, Persephone can harness the creativity of* **particle worms** *to create her own unique life-producing events independent of any of us.*

While producing food is the event by which we used to measure the success of soils, we can now measure soil conditions by the chemical interactions we induce within it that have given birth to our little city inside Persephone, and indeed to all our human worlds we may build together in outer space.

Over the past few months, Rachel's boss Alistair, who is also a close colleague of mine, and her co-captain, Yuri, a Russian physicist and engineer, whose skills compliment Rachel's well, have been assembling a talented crew for this modern-day Ark. All 200 of them have been carefully recruited and monitored intensively for their on-going health and psychological suitability. They are comprised of doctors, herbalists, chemical engineers, psychologists, philosophers, musicians, writers, poets, and painters. Since all are young, in their twenties and thirties, they will have the chance to live long lives, perhaps long enough to reach Proxima Centauri and Planet b.

Because the ship is only carrying 200 crew members, yet has the capacity to sustain 500 individuals, they will be able and be encouraged to reproduce offspring; each female on-board can give birth to one, artificially inseminated child. No male crew member will know whether he is the father of a particular child, because this tiny nucleus of humanity will represent an experiment designed to promote the concept of a whole village raising and caring for its children.

Although men and women will live separately on *Persephone*, sexual relationships, either homo or heterosexual, will be permitted. All men will be given the option to preserve their sperm in the ship's sperm bank prior to having mandated vasectomies, so no unplanned pregnancies occur.

When it launches, *Persephone* will be equipped with fully functioning **MEMs** for each crew member that feed into on-board cyber-clinics. Due to the advances in modern medicine, **MEMs** (Micro Electrical Mechanical Systems) are currently being used de facto ONLY by a select group of the very rich and exceptionally talented. These new systems monitor blood chemistry and automatically dispense appropriate drugs. Other functions of MEMs include monitoring pathogens and injecting appropriate antibodies from a library of treatments; acting as portable ultrasound imagers and skin cancer detectors, utilizing telemetry; transmitting daily vital signs to care centers from medical interfaces at home; performing biopsies remotely and minor surgery with the use of robots. Extensive home monitoring systems signal emergencies and enable immediate help.

In addition, MEMs modify body chemistry without drugs by promoting tissue re-growth and organ regeneration. Sleep Inducers cause the body to produce just the right amount of melatonin for falling asleep. **Electro-pharma** assists the body as it turns its own systems on and off, and MEMS-enabled micro-robots travel through the body to clear arteries and make repairs.

Since MEMS implanted within each crew member will still be subject to a software virus or breakdown, traditional doctors are on board *Persephone* as well, doctors who understand the old systems of diagnostics and surgery. Because the ship has been designed as a living organism, herbs, teas, and other natural substances will be used as alternative ways of continuously replenishing chemical sources of pharmacopeia. For this reason, trained holistic doctors and herbalists are also among the crew members.

Critically, Rachel, Peter, and I have also designed a medical system for the underground community of family and friends where we plan on living. This will be similar, but much less sophisticated, than the one on *Persephone*.

In addition to considering the biology and environmental needs of our new societies, all of us have often raised the question of governance, as we discuss the social structures of our different Post-Apocalyptic Communities. The community on the Ogallala Aquifer will use **Ubuntu Principles** designed for communities established with others at the beginning of this century. The governing principals are based on an ancient African word meaning 'humanity to others,' and also "I am what I am because of who we all are."

Rachel has decided that, outside of government directives, the Worldship she commands will operate on these principals as well but will also utilize a loose management hierarchy. The hope is that an elected council will dispense justice through conversation and consensus. The ship, however, also carries lethal weapons that only Rachel and her co-captain know how to access. These will hopefully only be used in self-defense of the ship and its crew.

There has been much official, interdepartmental discussion about whether one of the two trans-humans, Inanna or Rajeev, should go with Rachel. However, in the end, because the outcome of *Persephone*'s trip is unknown, it's been decided by our superiors that the safest course of action will be for them both to be sent to Mount Weather, the new seat of government located under the Blue Hills of Virginia.

The Mount Weather community consists of a massive underground city powered by nuclear, geo-thermal, solar, and wind energy. It has been designed by DARPA to house 1 million people most of whom have been selected because they are the brightest and the richest members of our current U.S. society. In addition to building this underground city, a series of above-ground titanium domes, giant translucent umbrellas, have also been constructed, where it's planned for everyone to move once the solar flares, volcanic eruptions, tidal waves, and earthquakes caused by climate change and the disastrous weather modification programs, have died down.

I also understand there are large food-producing factories and gardens located there, and all other animal-based food needed by residents will be artificially produced from **protocells**. Over fifty percent of the water necessary for these growing areas, and for Mount Weather's human inhabitants, will be recycled and provided to the community from underground aquifers. Water will also be captured in giant tanks above the ground. The new U.S. plutocracy has included non-human **cyborgs** in their labor design for the city, to in part be used for repairing vital equipment located on the surface of the planet.

An unelected Ruling Cabinet will be the governing plutocracy and, for public relations purposes only, includes the elected office of a President. This new, artificially constructed society will be controlled by a rigid, top-down hierarchy that has a secret police force to help maintain it. The government will also of course include administrators and bureaucrats to take care of the every-day details necessary to implement the Cabinet's mandates. In addition, this Ruling Cabinet and its bureaucrats will also be responsible for governing all the other 131 underground cities located around the United States.

I've heard it will also be in close touch with similar communities built by other plutocrats and non-elected governing bodies in China, Japan, Russia and select European countries. Peter and I and our close friends figure this Cabinet will govern like the current US government, by rewarding loyalty highly and by tightly controlling all access to information and money to continue to successfully centralize its power base.

I understand South American, Middle Eastern, Indian/Asian, and African survivalist communities of the size and magnitude of the ones in the U.S. do not appear to exist. I also understand that the 'Powers-That-Be' don't know whether there will be any long-term surviving communities from these areas because they were the first to experience massive droughts and the breakdown of governments and civil society. I'm sure if they find out there are some, however, they'll be 'encouraged' to take part in a kind of new, autocratic, global society. For this reason, the Cabinet has retained a strong defensive force of Military SEALs, and continues with its development of futuristic, nihilistic, weaponry.

I've also learned recently with great interest that reproduction will be strictly controlled, so cities do not become overpopulated. Every resident will have to apply for a permit to have a child. Children may be genetically modified to fit the labor needs of the plutocrats, and infanticide will clearly become common if residents break the rules and try to slip through the net of enforced birth control and genetic modification. As a result, a good proportion of first generation residents will be young and childless.

Because of our above top-secret clearance, we've been able to access this information about the city, and also monitor all of the current communications taking place amongst government departments. We now know we will need to leave D.C. soon and get to our community at Ogallala. We will have to do this before Inanna and Rajeev are taken to Mount Weather.

Rachel, Peter, and I dread leaving each other. Peter has promised that, like entangled particles, we'll try and find her somehow in outer space or some other alternative dimension, if we here on Earth make it through what's to come. She laughingly has told us it might be the other way around, that she will return here to find us. We all know these are empty promises and we will probably be defeated by linear time, but it makes us feel good anyway.

A few weeks before she is due to launch, Rachel downloaded the master plan for Worldship *Persephone* into Inanna's brain, so all inter-faceable systems, chemistry, and ***synthetic biology*** will be preserved. Because this was done surreptitiously and without permission, her superiors have no idea how valuable Inanna really is.

In only a few years from now with a weakened ozone layer, we all know the sun, like a violent, unforgiving ex-lover, will begin in earnest to viciously bombard the Earth's surface from above and combined with the heat trapping clouds will create a combustible oven, and Peter and I want to be deep underground when that happens.

Chapter 3
Sophie

Because of our imminent departure to Weather City, Peter and I plan to leave DC early tomorrow morning and head out towards Western Nebraska taking Inanna and Rajeev with us. Since it was a last-minute decision on all our parts, we had to get Tom, Peter's college roommate and the chief architect of the Ogallala settlement, to agree to accept them. Based on his interest in these two transhumans, he's told us he'll be able to effectively hide us from the government until he is able to negotiate a compromise.

Tom doesn't know I am also planning to destroy many of the government's most dangerous programs before we leave, and that the government will be desperate to capture us, if only to punish us for our lack of loyalty. Peter, however, believes Tom has enough leverage because of his family's centuries-old membership in the elite club that has now become the Ruling Cabinet, to successfully secure an eventual pardon from them.

We've already assembled what we need to take and have packed the van disguised to look like an official DARPA vehicle. We've discussed taking weapons, and finally decided Peter will steal some electro-magnetic laser guns, which we'll carry with us. He believes, however, that the trans-humans will be our most effective weapon and negotiating tool with the U.S. Government.

Before we leave, Peter and I will release an intelligent virus into the DARPA computer programs to wipe out any information on the two trans-humans that's been stored there. I'll also infect all the computer programs in my department with this virus as well in the hope it spreads to the databases at HAARP. In particular I don't want any more human engineered weather modification to take place in the future, since I believe and has been proved that in the long term the Earth has the power to heal herself without our blundering help.

I realize as we prepare to leave that I'm looking forward very much to living at Ogallala. Our group has constructed all the habitation environments there to be **biodynamic** like those on the Worldship *Persephone*. Unlike them, however, we'll be able to access energy from the surface of the planet. We've installed specially constructed panels and wind machines on the farmland above, ones that can withstand the tremendous force of solar winds as well as the heat of the solar flares I know will inevitably break through the thick cloud cover and the damaged ozone layer to Earth's surface.

The ceilings of the caves where we will be living are well lit, and there are several massive titanium and glass domes rising above the surface of the Nebraska farmland above us, covered with **photovoltaic cells** that have been treated with ultra violet and radiation shields and can be exposed to direct sunlight. Mechanical blinds cover them and can be retracted by us at will.

The housing and living structures that form the basis of our imaginative, small city, float on several interconnected underground lakes, and consist of what look like floating islands, some of which are star-shaped with sandy beaches nestled between each of their tentacles. Rachel has helped us develop a variety of new chemical, bio-engineered trees and grass that form small parks and playgrounds.

Our house, located on one of the floating islands, rises above it like a small, compact undulating wave, and is partially submerged below the water. Lights installed on the structure's exterior shine outwards, creating a beautiful blue glow, so we can see fish and other creatures swimming outside our windows. I know Sarah, my five-year-old will love this.

My beautiful daughter is tall for her age and rather willowy. She has lovely dark eyes and skin like Peter with curly black hair. She is a curious and strangely bright child, who seems able to understand things far beyond what most children her age comprehend. She is extremely empathetic and can't bear to see anyone get hurt. When she was small, she would always say, "Make Mommie's owie go away," and gently find and kiss any small cuts or bruises I had.

Many of the floating islands at our Ogallala underground community are greenhouses and veritable factories of recycling and food production. We're growing all manner of plants, fruits and vegetables within their confines, and we'll live surrounded by a massive forest of organic and **protocell** life. Two greenhouses are devoted almost entirely to the growing of medicinal herbs, and these and new chemically engineered plants will provide us with a living pharmacy.

We haven't abandoned information technology, of course. Our power sources feed servers that store libraries of human knowledge and are in place for Inanna and Rajeev to be hooked into as well as to the larger Web. There's also a well-equipped hospital. Peter's lab has been installed nearby, so he may continue his work on genetic engineering and bionic devices that enhance and expand the concept of human life.

I'll be involved in monitoring our underground city's climate control so human and plant inhabitants thrive. We've already brought a few cyborg robots to this hiding place that will be used in the future for repairs needed to any equipment located above the ground. We've also established a storehouse of spare parts as well as radiation repellent suits, boots, and helmets.

Because our living spaces can be open to the underground, cave-like environment and the air within it, we will move freely in boats between all our homes and shared spaces (unlike the inhabitants of *Persephone* who must face the forces of lower gravity and higher levels of cosmic radiation outside their living structure).

We've stocked the lake with fish and these, together with protocell food, fruits and vegetables, will be our major sources of nutrition. We have insects too, needed for cross pollination, including bees, butterflies, worms, and other organic life within our food growing habitats that are essential to the ongoing propagation of plant-based species. In addition, we've introduced birds that fly freely around inside the caves, and ducks and other water-based fowl to float on the underground river, flowing gently and almost silently among the living structures.

Our community is by necessity small, no more than 200 people, most of whom consist of friends and family. It's been developed with Tom's private financing, and while the Ruling Cabinet knows of its existence, they don't, according to Tom, see it as being vitally important to their very long-term plans for control and possibly once again eventual global domination.

We've decided that our society will be governed under **Ubuntu** rule with a Council of Elders. Unlike *Persephone*, the Ogallala community is comprised of a mixture of ages and consists of some nuclear families, but our children will always be considered the responsibility of all community members. While reproduction will not be restricted, we'll ask residents to discuss their family planning with the Council, to make sure there are enough resources within the community to provide for everyone.

Since most inhabitants already have their families in place, it will be the children, like our Sarah who, when they grow up and reach adulthood, will need permission from the elders and Council to marry and reproduce. We hope reproduction will not be limited, but we will ask individuals within the community, unlike in the past, to readily agree to do what is best not just for themselves, but also for the whole.

Chapter 4
Sophie

Peter worked late into last night, and before he came home, he smuggled Rajeev and Inanna out of the building by using the garbage shafts descending from the tenth floor where his lab is located. Even though they're both very strong because of their enhanced, flexible limbs, he's placed them in plexi-boxes to protect them from damage. The boxes fit perfectly into the top of the garbage shoot, which will deliver them safely into a large dumpster located directly behind the building.

Because the trans-humans are now in full control of their emotions and their lives, Peter gave them the choice as to whether they wished to come with us. As Rajeev told Peter very recently, "I'm happy to leave with you both as long as Inanna is as well."

Inanna has also told me separately in private conversations, "I'm interested in seeing how my body works. I'd like to create a child, one incorporating my new bionic, genetic being together with human DNA. Also, remember, Sophie, I carry the secret of *Persephone's* bio-chemical systems, and I want to study these, and find many new applications for them."

For these reasons and perhaps others which they haven't shared with me, they've both decided to attempt a risky journey with the three of us to Ogallala.
***

We leave the house the next day around 5:00 a.m. and drive to Peter's office to retrieve Inanna and Rajeev from the dumpsters where they've spent the night. They're quite hungry and thirsty, not having eaten or drunk anything for over ten hours, so we give them boiled eggs, tea, and thick slices of bread.

Peter deactivated the security cameras monitoring that part of the building, and he's made it look as though one of the wires shorted out. We have enough food to last for a few days, a couple of tents and some sleeping bags. We'll head out towards Parkersburg on Route 50 then make our way across West Virginia, Indiana, Kentucky, Missouri, and Kansas. We're avoiding the Northern route, and we've painted DARPA signs on the side of the van as well as equipping it with a simulated satellite on the roof, so it won't be easy for them to discover us right away.

I'm feeling pumped up with adrenaline because I know we're taking more chances than we should by including Inanna and Rajeev in our plans. While we're important to the government as employees, the value of the only two successfully generated, prototype trans-humans is immeasurable, and the government will do whatever is necessary to get them back. I know Peter will still be of some use to them, so it's likely they'll capture him alive, but Sarah and I, well, we're disposable.

When I look at my little five-year-old daughter, I can't believe how much it's possible to love another human being. I watched my daughter grow from an amoebic being inside me to a person. As she emerged into the world, I saw her rise on her knees then onto her two fat legs to reach out and grasp at things with her tiny fingers. Like any animal she ate and shat as she was supposed to do, but because she was human as well, she talked, cried, and became someone entirely different from me; it was her questions that caught my heart. In her speech, my daughter showed her individuality, and in that moment, I knew all our children deserve something much better than the tainted future we are giving them right now.

As we drive through the city on our way to its outskirts, Sarah sits in the back seat of the van on Inanna's lap humming a song and I watch in the mirror as Inanna braids her hair. Rajeev has been playing a game with her, letting her pretend she's stronger than he is as he arm wrestles with her. He's also counting the multi-colored, self-drive cars, and pretending he can't remember how many he's seen.

I look out the window briefly with some nostalgia for this city and see people travelling to work as usual. UPS and FedEx vans are delivering packages, and people are going about their daily lives in the orderly and robotic fashion that has been the norm on Earth for hundreds of years. However now the suffocating heat, the blanket of clouds, and the continual foul smell of burning forests in the thick, yellow air forces people to wear oxygen masks and carry small tanks on their backs whenever they are outside.

Because I'm human like them, I cannot help but feel tremendous compassion as I watch them. My mother Mehr, the prophetess, foretold that this was coming, but declared that our matriarchy would survive. Holding onto her words now gives me courage but doesn't make the ache in my stomach go away.

Before she died last year, Sarah, and I spent a month with her in her tiny house in New Mexico. Most nights she and I would lie in the desert looking up into a dark, starless sky, reflecting on how small our little planet was compared to the vastness of the Universe above us.

Peter, my beloved husband, has not recently expressed his feelings to me about leaving our life here because he's been so caught up in the practicalities of our journey. However, I can sense how terrible he feels when he reveals his frustration and anger by kicking the side of the van because he is not able to pack it exactly the way he wants it. Luckily, Rajeev and Inanna are able to immediately calculate the objects we wish to take versus the space available and arrange it more comfortably. In fact, because of their calculations, we stop at a grocery store and load more water than we had originally thought we needed.

As we continue our journey through the city Rajeev remarks from the back seat. "There must have been some growing awareness amongst all these people we're seeing outside that the planet couldn't continue to sustain itself. For instance," he continues, "by the beginning of the twenty-first century the numbers of human beings were still continuing to grow exponentially. Clearly, nobody accurately calculated the resources that were available to sustain them. With the advent of modern medicine, people were living longer and longer, which resulted in more overcrowding. In nature beings die so others can live. Our species may technically be able to survive for longer and longer periods of time, but perhaps in the long run, it's better that most of us die, rather than kill off the planet which has been designed to sustain us."

"As a scientist, I realize it's been years since our leaders paid any attention to Earth's finite resources," Peter replies.

"Of course," Rajeev responds, "but it seems, unfortunately, many of our politicians were not sufficiently conversant with math or science to be able to understand any of this effectively."

"I don't think it was their ability to understand math and science that was in question," Peter answers. "I think it had more to do with the influence of money versus political moral will."

A long silence follows before I finally break it by discussing with Peter where we should plan on stopping for the night. Eventually after going backwards and forwards for some time on the merits of various locations, Peter and I decide we'll camp outside of Parkersburg, in a wooded spot off Route 50. We estimate that, if we make that our stop, we'll only require four more days of travel before arriving in Ogallala, our final destination. *With any luck,* I think, *after Parkersburg, our next stop will be Bedford, Indiana.*

Just before we settle down for the night, I receive a brief message from a colleague that reads: *Thank you my friend, they're after you, be careful.* Considering this message, Peter announces we should only sleep for a few hours before heading back on the road, and not stop again until we get to Ogallala.

Because we're driving a van that's running on compressed air with a 1000-mile tank capacity, we won't have to pause to refuel. It's made of very lightweight panels of seaweed designed to capture and store solar energy directly as a back-up source.

With this solar back-up, we believe we can arrive at Ogallala without having to pull in at one of the high compression fueling stations now extremely rare to find. We're hoping temperatures outside remain stable, and we won't experience abrupt phases of heating or cooling that will interfere with the van's operation.

While Peter and I lie close to each other later that evening, our sleeping bags zipped together, Sarah snuggles between us. I have trouble sleeping because every cracking twig and bush rustling in the wind reminds me we are being followed. The air outside of the city is a little cleaner but is still filled with the faint smell of the endlessly burning timber across the US, in Canada, and in Mexico.

With Rajeev's help, we've taken precautions to block all signals from any electronic footprints we might be making. Without an electronic footprint, the government's helicopters equipped with radar will have a more difficult time tracking us down.

Just as I finally drift off into an uneasy half sleep however, a loud noise jerks me awake and I am immediately aware of needing to protect my daughter whose sweet, innocent skin lies hotly against mine. At the same time, I also feel Peter's even breath against my hair, his arms around my waist, before he stirs, sensing I am alert and awake, and lays his hand on my arm.

"Love you," he murmurs softly as he rolls over away from me. After seeing his face so close to mine and hearing his comforting words, I'm able to rest somewhat more easily, at least for the time being.

Chapter 5
Alistair

A day after Sophie and Peter have left the city, and a few days before *Persephone* is finally scheduled to launch, Alistair is preparing to move with his family to Weather City. Alistair is a two-star general in the U.S. Military whose specialty is **stellar formation and evolution**. He has been integral to the U.S. Space Exploration Program for the past twenty-five years and is the Director of the Mars Colonization Program.

Alistair is to be *Persephone's* primary contact on Earth. In that capacity, he will monitor *Persephone's* take-off and progress over the next few years as she travels beyond Europa into outer space, and as the ship begins the thirty-eight-year flight plan he and others have mapped out for them to Proxima Centauri. Using the on-going information about *Persephone* that will be fed back to Mount Weather, Alistair will host a radio podcast on this ground-breaking journey for broadcast throughout the new U.S.

He has never by nature been an optimist, and that is why he privately has some doubts *Persephone* will in fact complete her long and hazardous journey. Through his studies he has come to believe the Cosmos is not a benign loving force as some would like to surmise, but rather it is an unruly, ungovernable body full of chaotic events, such as monstrous gamma-ray bursts, deadly pulsars, matter-crushing gravitational fields, and ravenous, cannibalistic black holes. In fact, he would not be at all surprised if a rogue asteroid or comet hit the Earth in a few years, wiping out what is left of its flora and fauna.

Unlike his colleagues Sophie and Peter, Alistair has pledged his complete loyalty to the Ruling Cabinet and is far from the 'revolutionaries' he believes they have become. He has accepted the current situation and his role in it, not only because he is part of the Government as a highly placed military officer, but mainly because he has been allowed to conduct his vital scientific work without interference.

Although Alistair doesn't know Sophie well, he's enjoyed working with her on some of his government projects. He's often had lunch with her in the DARPA cafeteria and she's briefly met his wife, Robyn, a geneticist, who also works in the same facility.

Until recently, because Alistair believed Sophie and Peter would also evacuate to Mount Weather, much of his and Sophie's private conversations around the lunch table over past months had been about what they should all expect once they get there. This was comforting since neither he nor Robyn were able to share government-arranged evacuation plans with other family, friends, and colleagues, who they know will not be included in this very select community of high value evacuees.

This secrecy has caused a great deal of soul searching on Alistair and his wife's part, and a degree of survivor's guilt, as well. The main reason for their silence is to ensure that Styx, their 12-year-old daughter, will have a good chance of remaining alive. They've spent many long, sleepless nights debating the morality of their decision, and whether it's worth having such a weight on their consciences. They know, however, that if they share information about the Government's plans to evacuate only them and not others among their close circle, they will put their own survival in jeopardy.

Alistair had intended to leave his brother a letter, to be delivered upon his departure, which would explain his reason for remaining silent. His wife had planned on doing the same for her sister. Alistair had also intended to provide his brother with a gun so he could easily take his own life as well as the lives of his family whenever conditions on the outside became unbearable.

Now, however, he is grateful these extreme actions won't be necessary since Sophie has recently shared her intention to live at Ogallala, and she has left directions for him to give to his family on how they might reach that community. This small 'life preserver' that has unexpectedly been thrown his way, gives him some measure of hope that his immediate family, at least, will have the chance to survive if they're able to reach Ogallala safely. So, it is actually Alistair, at some risk to himself, who reached out to Sophie through an unmonitored network to let her know the authorities had begun actively searching for them.

As he and his family prepare to travel to Weather City, he carries downstairs the four suitcases, which contain all they will be allowed to bring with them of their past life. They've been told they will be assigned furnished apartments, and, in addition, the government will operate fully stocked grocery stores and other shops carrying practical items available free to them for the first few years; or at least until a paid consumer economy is fully implemented again.

Alistair cannot imagine what it will be like to live underground. He has been told the cities have been built using imaginative architectural concepts, and there will be shopping malls, movie theatres, swimming pools, and all the other practical and recreational amenities previously enjoyed above, on the surface of the planet.

He has also learned from an engineer colleague that natural light will be transferred from solar-collecting dishes and directed through fiber-optic cables to be dispersed underground using installed ceiling panels serving as diffusers. The light that reaches underground will provide perfect conditions for photosynthesis, enabling the growth of living vegetation. In addition, his colleague has revealed that 'earth lobbies' will be built in every structure. He has surmised that these will be rather like the historic, vertical Hanging Gardens of Babylon and will help filter air for the city's inhabitants. Alistair also understands that most of the other 131 underground cities around the U.S. have also been constructed using the same model.

This complex network of underground cities established across the new U.S. includes Pittsburgh, Danbury, Chicago, Denver, Albuquerque, Phoenix, Las Vegas and other inland locations not yet affected by the rising oceans, unlike the lost cities of Miami, San Diego, New York, Los Angeles, Portland and Seattle. They are known as Continuity of Government Cities (COGC), are operated by the Federal Emergency Agency and are, like Weather City, buried at least a thousand feet below the Earth's surface.

There are mass-transit systems consisting of *maglev*, high-speed trains connecting one to another. The *maglev* trains float like birds skimming over water on *guideways*, travelling faster than the speed of sound, and making it possible to reach locations in the New West in only thirty minutes.

The underground railways and cities were constructed over a short period of only ten years, using *nuclear sub terrenes* and *liquid lithium* that have the capability of melting their way through rock and soil and, in the case of the railways, creating a series of glass-lined, forty-foot-wide tunnels. The absence of debris from their construction meant the entire process could be carried out without drawing the attention of the general population to what was happening.

As 'black cities' their construction was funded with billions of dollars obtained from illegal drug and arms sales. In addition, the have cost the government and private investors from between fourteen to

25

seventeen billion dollars for each city.

***

Once Alistair, Robyn and Styx leave DC, they board buses that will carry them to Weather City. They are surprised to see that it only takes about an hour to reach their destination, where they are dropped off in front of their apartment in Skye Ridge, a housing development sitting 900 feet above the rest of the city. They are amazed to find this 'community within a community,' designed for the very top echelons of the military, senior government, and corporate members of society, has its own exclusive vertical farm, forests, and recreational areas.

They don't spend much time in their government-assigned two-bedroom apartment, however, before setting off again to begin exploring their new neighborhood. They take an elevator down to street level connecting Sky Ridge to the main city and find they can walk quite easily around the network of storage canals. These canals, connected to vast underground aquifers, spread like blue veins around the city and are banked on either side by towering, brightly lit residential and commercial structures that clearly simulate an environment like the one they had previously experienced above ground. They notice immediately the large shafts that let in natural light through thousands of diamond-shaped photovoltaic glass vents, and which considerably brighten the city landscape around them.

The three of them spend a fair amount of time together curiously exploring the central parts of the city, eating lunch in one of the numerous restaurants, before Robyn and Styx return to the Skye Ridge apartment to settle in, and Alistair eagerly heads over to his office. It's located right next to a large command center full of 3-D screens connected to Worldship *Persephone's* communication satellites. Once Alistair arrives at the command center, he immediately positions himself, along with his team of fellow scientists, in front of several of the giant monitors so he can contact the pilots who are already on board and preparing to take off on this historic journey the next day.

"Everything is proceeding according to plan General," Rachael leader of the group lets him know enthusiastically, once she hears his voice.

"Glad to hear it Captain Chen," he answers her warmly. He has always admired Rachel for her ability to absorb and process large amounts of diverse technical information easily.

Because she's a close friend of Peter and Sophie's, he would like

26

to tell her that they have fled from the city, but he understands as they chat about various aspects of her future flight, he cannot reveal this information to her.

In fact, as he continues to sit in front of the massive screens going over the details of *Persephone's* flight plan with Rachel, he is acutely aware in the back of his mind he will now have to be extremely guarded about everything he says both here and in his own home. That is because *"the watchers,"* elements of the CIA and FBI that have morphed into a secret police force, closely monitor the conversations of residents of all the underground cities. He knows for instance his cell phone and all his contacts are minutely examined by them.

In the future Alistair knows he will try and focus as much as possible on his work and his daughter. In this way, he thinks he will be able to shut out what he is absolutely certain is going to happen to the inhabitants left on Earth's surface, as the temperatures outside increase. There's no doubt he still has moral qualms about many of the government's decisions in this regard, but he doesn't discuss these with anyone besides Robyn.

His military superiors do, in fact, bring him in for questioning the next day about Sophie and Peter's whereabouts, and to inform him they've taken Rajeev and Inanna with them. Because of his impeccable track record and importance to the space exploration mission however, they believe him when he says, "I had no idea Sophie and Peter planned to steal the trans-humans. I'm surprised they would think to implement such an ill-conceived plan." Then adds as an afterthought, "in fact, I think they've
in a way betrayed all of us by their actions." He intentionally omits from this conversation, that he has known all along Sophie and Peter intended to leave, and that he does actually know where they are going.

Later, as he exits the offices of his superiors, he recognizes he has moved rapidly into ethical areas that leave him uncomfortable. As a Manichaean, he wants to see everything in black and white, but now his two colleagues have saved his family, and this act of kindness has led him into the kinds of thought and behaviors which would be described by him as undefined or gray.

The day after he's brought in for questioning, while giving Rachel her final briefing before Worldship *Persephone* launches, unusually he finds his mind wandering. He thinks about whether his brother's family have made it out of D.C. and are now safely heading towards Ogallala. He also realizes, without too much surprise, that he hopes very much Sophie and Peter have made it to Western Nebraska as well. Then he wonders if his newfound interest in their success makes him a traitor of some sort.

That evening in his apartment, after Styx has gone to bed, Alistair motions to Robyn to come into the bathroom then turns on the shower and both taps in the bathtub. He puts his fingers against his lips and draws her to him as he whispers in her ear, "We're being listened to and perhaps watched."

She nods her head at him.

"They questioned me about where Peter and Sophie have gone," he says.

"You didn't say anything?" She looks at him intently.

"No, of course not. They might have found our families as well. Although I'm not sure how long they've all got because I believe the government ultimately won't let that community survive—it's out of their control and too dangerous."

"Why did they take such a risk?" Robyn asks.

"They probably didn't want to live their entire lives under the thumb of big brother. Once our basic needs are provided for and we feel safe, people like us are willing to give up a great deal of freedom. Anyway, we've already been bought."

"Yes, you're right," she confirms, "we live well, not like the others."

He nods his head.

"How will we know if they make it?"

"We probably won't," he says.

They hug each other to take away the pain of not knowing, the isolation caused in both of them by having dangerous secrets.

"If it hadn't been for Styx…" Robyn says, speaking into his shoulder which smells familiar and comfortable to her.

He remains silent as he presses her back to show he understands and agrees.

"What's next for us?" she whispers.

"We do our work, live our lives, keep our mouths shut—and hope we survive, hope our daughter survives as well, and if we're lucky maybe even our grandchildren."

"It's not so bad here," she replies stroking his cheek.

"No, we're the lucky ones," he answers, before saying under his breath, "maybe."

Chapter 6
Rachel and Yuri

Persephone is launching a few days early because the conduits for solar winds, which resemble large, blue, insectoid-like, spherical beings in the **magnetosphere** and now the **ionosphere**, are rapidly expanding over the Arctic and Antarctic. As a result, they will soon overlap at the Equator and, as they do so, will bring with them massive bursts of ultraviolet radiation as well as major geo-magnetic storms which could severely damage the ship.

Thus, after her final briefing from Alistair and other members of his team, Rachel goes up to the flight deck to prepare the ship for take-off. Her orders are to fly to Mars first and rendezvous with the pre-existing military base which has been there since 2025. Currently there are ten thousand military and civilian personnel living on this base. When they first arrived, the inhabitants were housed in a series of connected, inflatable components that contained bedrooms, working and living areas, and, most importantly, plant production areas. Recently, however, cyborgs and robots have constructed several biospheres from titanium, delivered to them by previous shuttles, which have increased and enhanced their inhabitable spaces. The military settlers have been adjusting slowly over the past thirty-five years to living in Mars's 38% gravity field, and modifying and monitoring these effects on their bodies, using MEMs.

Rachel has been instructed that once she reaches Mars and has established a connection with the military commanders stationed there, *Persephone* is to proceed to Europa, Jupiter's moon, where cyborg robots have constructed an underwater city. Because Europa is now able to sustain life, the plutocrats believe there are possibilities for colonization similar to that on Mars, thus some of the personnel from Mars are to be transported there, before the ship goes deeper into space on its way to the Alpha Centauri star system. It will take a month to reach Mars and one more to get to Europa. The mission's primary goal however is to try and reach an earth-like planet, Planet b, which has been identified near Proxima Centauri. It has been figured that using *Persephone's* current nuclear ion drive it will take thirty-eight years to get there.

Because the new U.S. government realizes their satellite communications will not be able to reach as deeply into space as the ship proceeds on its journey, *Persephone* is carrying its own system, through which it will attempt to connect to Weather City for as long as it is able.

The present crew have been left instructions, which will remain with their descendants, to return to Earth to see whether there is still life there, and if so, whether it's suitable for re-colonization.

The Worldship is, in essence, a modern-day Ark being thrown out into the Cosmos, in the hope that if no one else from the human species survives, she and her cargo of animal and human genetic material will.

The world's scientists now believe there are many habitable planets in binary star systems like Alpha Centauri. They are convinced of this because they know a circular orbit around two stars (suns) can be as smooth as our orbit around one. They also know that the early steps of these rocky planets' formation would be exactly the same as those that formed Earth. In addition, they are sure these planets are located in the 'Goldilocks Zone,' one that is neither too hot nor too cold, has liquid water, and can therefore support human or other biological life.

The primary source of power on *Persephone* comes from a catalytic, "warm" nuclear fusion, double-layer, ion drive. The ship looks like a large oblong cylinder with five smaller cylinders attached behind it like the tail of a kite. Each of these cylinders is connected to hydrogen engines, so they form five individual spacecraft that will be used for exploration purposes.

Luckily, some years ago, the sociopolitical environment changed, and this warm nuclear fusion propulsion system, with its huge capability, was adopted for peaceful purposes. It was determined then that environmental space contamination from the system was negligible if it was used outside of the Earth's ***magnetosphere***, making it more palatable during its early-stage development. Rachel is satisfied it's been sufficiently tested in many missions to Mars and is now ready to be put to longer term use.

One of the most important challenges for the crew of *Persephone* will be to smoothly reduce the speed of a ship this large from maximum velocity, and keep it in a stable orbit around Mars, Europa and other planets, while the crew explores them. No space flight prior to this one has ever tested the required systems for this difficult maneuver, and the technology to do so successfully is still in its infancy stages.

In 2014, NASA had just begun working on the first unmanned interstellar probe, which was to be followed by a manned mission, scheduled to launch in 2100 for the Alpha Centauri star system and arriving there eighty-five years later. As for a colonizing mission to the planets surrounding Proxima Centauri, that was not envisioned before 2260. Schedules have had to speed up enormously because of the catastrophic climate events.

For this reason, the ship is carrying many life samples from Earth, as well as a digital compendium of human knowledge. A bank of frozen human and animal eggs and sperm that can be grown in artificial wombs is stored on board, the use of which will be bound by rigid scientific protocols.

***

Now, as she sits in the Captain's chair just before take-off, Rachel is acutely aware of her responsibilities as the pilot of this tiny, flying Worldship, carrying its precious cargo of what, together with those who may also survive on Mars and the Moon, may very well be the last of the human race.

As she feels the spaceship being drawn up by a pneumatic lift like a subterranean giant onto the surface of the launch pad, she's grateful that at least no radiation will be released from the ship's nuclear reactors at launch; chemical rockets that emit no toxins whatsoever to the atmosphere, will be used to lift her off. It is only after *Persephone* has departed Earth's magnetosphere that her warm nuclear fusion system will kick in.

At only thirty-five years of age, Rachel is already an experienced Captain with eight years of training as an astronaut, and advanced degrees in biochemistry and chemical engineering. Because she's so self-sufficient and projects a sense of total self-confidence, her colleagues consider her to be cold. However, her close friends would not define her in this way. While they think of her as ambitious and efficient, they also know she has a great sense of humor, loves to play jokes on people, and is a tremendous tango dancer.

One of Rachel's recent lovers was an Argentinean dance instructor, whom she referred to as "her beautiful distraction." She would explain him as exactly the kind of drug she needed to drive away all the mathematical formulae that were constantly spinning around in her head. When in his arms, naked or clothed, she would think only of colors and sounds and rhythms, which gave her a kind of inner peace and sharpened her sensual perceptions. Whether it was the silk dress she wore to dance, her ridiculously high shoes, or the smell of his skin when it sweated slightly, the totality of dancing or making love with him calmed her down. She had often wished she could take "her beautiful distraction" everywhere so that in moments of fear and confusion, she could turn to him as some kind of personal stress reducer.

Now thinking about her Argentinean lover, she turns to Yuri, her Co-Captain, and asks, "Do you tango?"

"What's that, you ask?" he says.

"Oh, never mind," she says, smiling to herself.

He's silent for a bit then replies without looking at her, "No, but I can learn if you want me to."

After this brief exchange, they become silent and focused, as they carefully check everything off from their pre-flight roster.

Yuri looks over at her as he turns on the microphone so the crew members already harnessed in their seats in the rear of the Worldship, can hear him, as well as the people on the flight control deck. "T-9 minutes and holding, activating flight recorders, starting automatic ground launch sequencer, retracting orbiter access arm, starting auxiliary power units, arming solid rocket booster range safety devices, starting orbiter aero surface and main engine profile test."

Rachel nods at him and adds, "Roger. Crew members close and lock visors, switch orbiter transfer from ground to internal power, go to auto sequencer start, activate launch pad sound suppression, activate main engine burn off system, and start main engines."

"Time to put on another show for the ants," Yuri says to Rachel softly under his breath.

Rachel replies, smiling, "Light the fires, cowboys, it's off into the wild, wild black yonder," as the ship slowly and surely leaves the ground.

"Good morning ladies and gentlemen," Rachel adds, "this is your Captain, Rachel Chen, speaking and I want to welcome you aboard Worldship *Persephone*. Once we get airborne, our flight time will be thirty-eight years. We'll have excellent visibility today and after we break through the magnetosphere, outside temperatures will exceed 150,000K. But don't worry," she adds, laughing, "you won't be going out there to get your Vitamin D. As soon as we're fully in orbit and start the EPPP system, you can unbuckle your harnesses, remove your visors, and get into your play clothes."

Then, before leaning over to switch off her microphone, she says, "We have lift off mission control, we have lift off." As she speaks, she hears clapping and cheering through her headphones from those at the other end on the ground.

"What are you really thinking?" Yuri asks casually as he switches off his microphone and glances over at her.

"I'm thinking that I don't want to have to observe what's going to happen as the Earth gets hotter and hotter.

"I'm glad it will be very far away," he replies.

"And you?"

"What a bloody waste," he says, "is what I'm thinking. How bloody stupid can you get."

"Right, angry and sad at the same time."

"More angry than sad, I'd say. Imagine intentionally blowing yourself up, although I know religious fanatics do that all the time. I never understood suicide and I don't any better now. Boom, all gone because they thought they were a lot damn smarter than nature."

"Ah, the danger of arrogance," Rachel replies, smiling.

"Combine that with corrupt politicians and greedy businessmen, and you've got a cosmic level event taking all the ants with it," Yuri responds.

"Any one of those ants mean anything to you, Yuri?" Rachel asks.

"My mother and thank God she's dead."

"What will you miss most," she says pensively, "about your life on Earth?"

"The beach and the ocean. When I was a small boy, my mother would take me there all the time. Then when I got older it was a place of solitude for me. I never minded when it got too cold to swim. It was the wildness of it and the sand blowing and waves; the sound, too, that echo is what I'll miss. Salt water in my nose and on my skin; licking it off my hands. No one will be able to go outside because it'll be too hot and the oceans will become dark, blue waves no more, just grayness and the bitter grittiness of the dust."

He remains silent.

"No more whales calling to us from the depths," Rachel adds. "But who knows? Perhaps the whales will survive us, perhaps from the very depth of the sea they'll sing our requiem. Perhaps we'll hear them in the solar winds as they blow across on our new planet mourning our loss, even though we almost killed them all."

"Perhaps," he says sadly. He's younger than Rachel, a pragmatic boy who grew up in a small town on the Black Sea and went to college in Moscow. Then because he was a brilliant physicist and engineer, he was sent to join the *Persephone* mission by the plutocrats there—they also have a secret city hidden under St. Petersburg, to which they have fled. Yuri doesn't ask too many questions. He generally just does as he's told.

As an avid reader, Yuri enjoys the Russian classics like Dostoyevsky and Tolstoy. He secretly cries when he reads *Anna Karenina*, which he's absorbed more times than he can count. Karenina's suicide is the only one he understands and respects.

Yuri also likes hockey and ice-skating and blinis. He loves those little, tiny soft pancakes with their sour cream and black caviar that has become increasingly hard to find in Moscow, as the oceans continue to acidify.

Yuri is not a spiritual man, but he's filled with a sense of the grand tragedy and the ephemeral beauty of life. He thinks of living as an end in itself without having any deeper meaning than that. As an atheist, physics is his religion of choice.

Unlike most Russians, Yuri doesn't like vodka but prefers single malt scotch. He is a man generally grateful for what life has given him; he says *spasibo* a lot to no one in particular. Although he's never been in love, he's had a few girlfriends and likes to be in the company of 'attractive' women. (Yuri's idea of 'attractive' is smart, funny and kind.) He wouldn't mind sleeping with Rachel who is ten years his senior, but he also says to himself when he thinks about it, "Yuri, you don't shit where you eat." For that reason, he's decided he won't even if she's interested.

For a long time now, Yuri's been carefully studying the geophysics of radical climate change caused by human activity, including the rapid release of greenhouse gases and CO_2. Clearly, this information is not 'new news'; world governments have known about this for over fifty years and failed to sufficiently prevent it. What they do now know that is new, though, is that global warming has reduced the UPPER-most areas of the ozone layer.

In addition, world governments have also known for some time that if a massive CME (***Coronal Mass Ejection***) from the sun occurs, it will burn its way through the clouds and destroy many portions of the Earth and all its inhabitants still living on the surface. It could be, in essence, the equivalent of a huge nuclear explosion.

Yuri has realized the plutocrats in charge are not sure if the surface of the Earth will ever become habitable again in the next 1000 years. Recent information fed back to them from the Mars team has confirmed the Red Planet was once wet and warm billions of years ago, like Earth had been, and had also been covered by a thick blanket of ozone, which provided it with warmer temperatures and greater atmospheric pressure. In the past Mars most certainly had rivers, oceans and lakes just like those on Earth.

"Mars, a planet so full of possibility, just like our Earth, is now a barren wasteland. I guess, its death has failed to provide us with sufficient warning of our own demise," Yuri often repeats out loud as he lies staring up at the ceiling on the nights he has a hard time sleeping.

Yuri also knows that asteroids and comets have often come dangerously close to Earth and scientists have already used EPPP technology to explode them before they reached the surface. However, if satellite and other advanced weapons systems go offline during the present crisis, he thinks that the probability is high of one asteroid or comet eventually hitting the ocean in a few years, causing fifty-foot tidal waves and earthquakes and blowing dust and dirt and water into the already damaged atmosphere.

He has confidence in his ability and in Rachel's to do the best they can in the worst of circumstances. He has a tendency to be focused on interpersonal harmony and doesn't often immerse himself in the emotional details of negative events. As such, he is a perfect counterpart to Rachel, who has less of a focus on community and is more individualistic and ambitious, a product, most likely of her American culture. Yuri is generally happy to be on the Worldship and figures that he might as well die in space as anywhere else. Space, to him, is the place where he belongs, alive or dead.

As Persephone now flies like a giant condor without wings into the upper atmosphere and beyond the **magnetosphere**, he and Rachel successfully launch the EPPP System. After this has happened, Yuri leaves Rachel on the flight deck and goes below to his cabin to change out of his flight suit then to the cafeteria to grab a bite to eat. They'll reach Mars in a month and he's looking forward to that. He has no desire to look back at the Earth and imagine her in her death throes.

After he leaves, Rachel keeps steady watch and sees her planet

36

grow smaller and smaller behind their ship. It looks beautiful, as always, a spinning green and blue ball ringed by wispy clouds, a familiar sight to her from previous missions.

She lived for many months aboard the now vacant space station, *MIR*, which continues to circle the Earth. Now she thinks it's sad to see this important historic relic left empty but still echoing with the voices of all the cosmonauts from around the world who once inhabited it. *The original space station*, she reflects, *concrete evidence of our desire and ability to live in space.*

Chapter 7
Sophie

We woke up before the sun rose and are already heading towards St. Louis. As a result, we have been able to travel comfortably at high speeds on uncluttered roads. To allow for continuous travel, we intend to take turns sitting at the controls of the self-drive van. Given the circumstances, we'll eat in the van and stop only for short bathroom breaks.

As a result of droughts, water shortages, natural disasters and the viral and bacterial infections that broke out in the mid-forties, most communities outside of the cities in the Northeast and Midwest have already been drastically reduced. Overall, the U.S. population has decreased from three hundred and eighteen million to no more than ten million.

Because most residents of smaller cities live in the countryside where they have more direct access to water and food, many of these places we pass now, like Lexington, Louisville and Evansville, are for the most part abandoned. Town and city governments still function marginally, and are in touch with the central government in D.C. For this reason, the system of roads and bridges has been maintained, as have limited air travel and satellite communications. To serve the ruling government and corporations, the brightest and most talented individuals now live in the cities.

After the major effects of climate change and weather modification took hold, a totalitarian system of government under the control of a Ruling Cabinet has been in complete control. The chaos that was unleashed by actions of the terrified population threatened individual and national security and allowed powerful individuals in our country to do away with any remnants of our historic and hard-fought democracy.

Once the Ruling Cabinet, the government and its military go underground, the people who are left will have to fend for themselves. Some towns and a few private individuals have already built shelters. However, it's unlikely many people will survive in the long term, without access to water and the massive farms and food-producing facilities the government has constructed.

We've been luckier than those others because Tom, Peter's college buddy, was a plutocrat, who made a private fortune in a technology company established by his father fifty years ago. It's his billions that have allowed us to create a highly developed community, independent from the government. Since we won't need to live underground entirely for the first few years we are at Ogallala, we'll have the opportunity to test out how our systems function and determine whether there is anything additional we might need to survive. For this reason, we'll require access to vehicles, including vans like ours that will allow us to travel distances from the site to secure necessary materials. We've also got an old-fashioned radio and antenna that will allow us to receive and intercept signals and pictures from the surface of the planet. In this outdated way, we'll be able to eavesdrop on the government and its global communications system undetected.

Since Tom, like his father, is a technology wizard, he's overseen all our computerized, electronic systems. He's always been fascinated by Peter's work with the trans-humans, Rajeev and Inanna, and now he knows we're bringing them to Ash Hollow, he's asked if Peter will consider adapting his biological body in the same way he has theirs. He's an avid post-humanist and a strong supporter of the *singularity*, an era in human development during which it has been proposed human intelligence will transcend our natural biology. He believes, and he's not wrong, that artificial intelligence in its most advanced stages can far exceed human intellectual capacity and our ability to survive in harsh environments. Rajeev and Inanna represent the proof of the superiority of a certain brand of artificial intelligence. They are far more astute than Peter and me and possess much greater problem-solving and inventive skills. In fact, they've been very patient with us considering how small our human intellectual capacity is compared to theirs.

Peter's decision to create trans-humans by beginning with human physiology and adding machine characteristics rather than the other way around, is based on his desire to create an artificial intelligence that would fundamentally 'understand' our basic humanity and align with our values. Similarly, Rachel has created the living machine, Worldship *Persephone,* by using the blueprint of Gaia, our mother: her chemistry, her biology, and most importantly, her soils.

Now, as we speed along the highway across Indiana, as the dawn is beginning to break red gold across the flat skyline, and while

39

Sarah sleeps peacefully in the back sprawled across Inanna and Rajeev's laps, we chat softly. I glance in the mirror from time to time and observe my child, her cheeks hot and soft with sleep, and watch as the dark hairs that have fallen across her mouth rise with each of her breaths that are so dear to me; the soft internal proof of her life whispering its way across her lips.

As I stare intently, Inanna brushes Sarah's hair away from her face, and Rajeev raises her small hand and kisses its palm as he looks down at her.

"Do you think they're coming after us?" Inanna asks softly.

"Surely, yes," Peter replies, overhearing her question. "They won't let two pieces of future science get away so easily."

"Do you think one of their primary purposes in our creation was to enhance their defensive capability?" Inanna asks.

"Of course it was," Rajeev interjects. "I know they definitely planned to use me as an advanced weapon."

"Why would they need to do that?" Inanna asks. "I mean, they certainly don't seem to need to do that now, given what's happened."

"No, you're right they don't," Peter replies, "but they're already planning ahead. For the time when they'll emerge from their rabbit holes with all the others who are just like them around the world, and they'll want tactical and weapons superiority to them."

"No lessons learned. Perhaps your kind, Inanna and Rajeev, and others like you will be more peaceful than we are," I add.

My observation is followed by a long silence as we drive, each absorbed in our own thoughts. Finally, however, Rajeev speaks, as he turns to look out the window at the flat, dry countryside. "As I think about it myself and your kind, are not very different from each other despite the fact that you could be described as organic skin sacks with biological organs, and Inanna and I could be described as artificial skin sacks with biological organs and mechanical parts. I think the bigger question is whether there is an independent force inside all of us that's connected to something bigger."

"I don't think small differences like what we're made of really matter in the end," Inanna murmurs, "because despite what our biological or mechanical parts are, none of us wants to fight each other all the time. I believe we're all just really looking for a meaningful way of being together in the world."

There is a brief pause as we all consider these observations.

Peter's beliefs run no further than the science he holds to be empirical and therefore provable. He does believe quantum physics will provide many of the answers we seek and is willing to admit there are many things about ourselves and our Universe he doesn't understand.

I, on the other hand, because of my father Raphael, have access to something much bigger. As a scientist, I would define this characteristic by saying my pineal gland is very highly developed and I am therefore connected to a source that is infinitely smart, and that constantly downloads its knowledge into my brain. So far, I don't see any evidence I've passed this characteristic along to Sarah, but it's probably too early to tell.

We pull off the road in a small town to take a five-minute bathroom break. Clearly, the town has been deserted for quite a few years since the buildings are boarded up and the main street looks desolate. The early spring hot spell has brought an unusually warm breeze that ruffles the weeds sprouting in the cracks of the sidewalks and in the center of the main street. The usual cameras we would ordinarily have to worry about are not functional because this area has no value to our present government.

We see a large, abandoned supermarket at the end of the street and a pharmacy with a sign whose letters are still slightly visible. We go into the supermarket, wander down the aisles and find products that were popular at least fifteen or twenty years ago. There are rodents scuffling about everywhere, and there is an overwhelming dank smell of decaying cardboard and wood. The floor below is thick with the droppings of bats that visibly hang underneath the eaves.

"We need to be careful of rabid animals," Peter says, as he holds Sarah's hand tightly.

Because Inanna and Rajeev haven't ever been outside of the city, the desolation they see all around them appears to be shocking. I am drawn to the graffiti someone has written on the walls of the white evangelical church in the middle of town. The words read: *But the cowardly, the unbelieving, the vile, the murderers, the sexually immoral, those who practice magic arts, the idolaters and all liars—they will be consigned to the fiery lake of burning sulfur. This is the second death.*

"Weird words," Inanna says, pointing at it.

"Yes," Peter tells her, "*Book of Revelations*—many believe this is a book of prophecy that foretells the end of the world," he says, and continues reading, "*Since you have kept my command to endure patiently, I will*

41

also keep you from the hour of trial that is going to come on the whole world to test those who live on the Earth."

"It seems, despite this prophecy, that the plutocrats will after all, despite their wicked behavior, somehow miraculously escape this so-called test and hour of trial," Rajeev remarks with irony.

"Indeed," Peter replies smiling.

As I listen to them talk, I feel fortunate we're all simply still alive.

As we walk back to our van, we notice someone standing beside it. Rajeev and Inanna go on high alert, as do Peter and me. We don't look at each other as we walk over to the silent figure standing there.

"Hi folks," he says, waving in a friendly manner. "Don't see many people out and about these days," he adds.

He's wearing blue jeans that hang on his thin body like clothes on a line, and a sleeveless, green shirt. His face and arms are covered in blisters. He reaches over and shakes our hands. "Where you folks headin'?" We reluctantly do the same, hoping he is not infected with some kind of virus.

"St. Louis," I say quickly. "We're visiting friends there."

"Getting a whole lot warmer these days," he remarks, "hard on us, water bein' scarce and all that."

"Yes," Peter replies.

The man nods at Inanna and Rajeev.

"Them two with you?" he asks, looking as though he's instinctively aware on some level that they are different.

"Yes, colleagues from work," Peter says, "thought I'd take them out and show them the countryside. How're you all making out here?"

"Not much food, but we make do. Built us some underground tunnels, so when it gets too hot or them tornados come, we got somewhere safe to go," he says.

He turns around and calls, "you can come out now kids, it's safe. These folks ain't mean us no harm."

Two young boys step out of a nearby building and walk hesitantly over to the man. One looks to be about twelve and the other younger. The man draws them towards him and rests his hands on their shoulders, "You say hello now, and shake these good people's hands."

Both boys put out their hands like mechanical toys, and politely shake Peter's. I can tell by the way he holds them that they feel damp and sticky.

"Well," Peter says, "nice to meet you all," and, as he moves to unlock the van, the man and the two boys step back. After we all get in, Peter rolls down the window on the side next to where they're all still standing staring at us.

"Ain't seen one of those except on the TV," the man comments as he points a thumb at our vehicle.

"Yes," Peter agrees, "you won't find many of them outside of city limits."

"Should make it to St. Louis soon after dark, particularly in one of them," the man says.

"We're hoping," Peter says. "Oh," he adds, "if any other vehicles like this come around, I'd be obliged if you don't tell them you've seen us."

"Like that, is it?" the man asks without smiling. "I hate those goddam city rats anyway, takin' our resources and all," he pauses then adds, "just like you lot, I guess."

"Yes, like us, but not anymore," Peter says quietly.

"I guessed as much," the man says. Then he leans in and grasps Peter's shoulder. As he does so he brings the acrid smell of dirty skin and hair into the van with him.

"You stay safe no matter what it is you're up to, you hear?" he says, as he steps back.

We drive away in silence, and as we turn onto the main road heading towards St. Louis, I look back to see the two thin, blistered children grow smaller in our rearview mirror.

I realize, as I sit there silently and sadly, that they are part of the sacrificial offerings to climate change made by all our world leaders of countless human beings. They are examples of the ones they describe as "the takers", nameless, faceless people, who are seen as having no value and whom they refer to as "human disposables or collateral damage."

Chapter 8
Tom and Noemi

In preparation for the arrival of all their community members, like Sophie, Peter, and Sarah, Tom has been living at Ogallala with his wife, Noemi, and their two children, Seed and Rosie, for the last year, where he has been refining and expanding the community's technology hub. In 1998, Tom's own father had been the mastermind behind the development of one of the most successful search engines in the history of the Web. After implementing this cutting-edge technology, his father's company then became one of the primary producers of the first robotic cyborgs, the driverless car and the space elevators, which had been used to create settlements on the Moon. Tom, who has followed in his father's footsteps as a brilliant inventor, is now utilizing his own designs for solar powered turbines and low-cost heliostats as power sources for Ogallala.

As far back as 2014, Tom's father began investing in "cellular reprogramming," based on his personal interest in medical research. Tom has used the income from this profitable investment to set up a fully functioning lab in Ogallala, where Sophie and her colleagues will work to create new drugs to enhance human longevity. Her research will be based on a study of modified plant bacteria that have been found effective in attacking specific diseases related to aging.

It was more than fifty years ago that Tom's father's company began to use complicated algorithms to predict the future and so Tom knew he needed to build a survivalist, underground, community that would keep his family and friends safe. Tom was also convinced it was vital to protect the intellectual assets of his father's company, which he now owns, from an inevitable takeover by the Ruling Cabinet.

Although primarily designed as a living experiment by Sophie, Peter, Tom and Tom's wife, Noemi, to accommodate their close friends and relatives, Ogallala will also include a small number of colleagues who have been selected by them to fill in the gaps of their combined, overall knowledge. It has been decided by Tom, Noemi, Sophie, and Peter that one of the key focuses for these additional community members should be on individual creativity and hands-on problem solving. As a vital resource, everyone will have the use of a super data system Tom has developed, which he has dubbed 'Halle,' a feminist version of the fictional 'Hal,' conceived by film maker Stanley Kubrick in the historic film, *2001: A Space Odyssey*.

Tom's wife, Noemi, is an agronomist, a botanist and a key member of their team. She was brought up in Mexico in the eco-village of Huehecoyotl (Spanish for 'very old coyote'), an hour's drive south of Mexico City, located near the Sierra del Tepozteco Mountains.

Huehecoyotl was founded by Noemi's grandfather, Raul, a musician, who achieved a small amount of notoriety in his youth through his membership in *The Illuminated Elephants Traveling Gypsy Theater* that promoted a message of environmental harmony in street performances across Europe, Asia, and North America in the 1970's. Twenty years ago, when Noemi had still lived in Huehecoyotl, all the homes were already 'off the grid.' Residents collected all their water from a nearby waterfall and utilized only solar and wind power. Now, because of Tom's patronage, the surviving members, including Naomi's brother Jorge, have established a small, hidden, technologically advanced village located directly under the Sierra del Tepozteco Mountains.

Because she grew up in a community where care for the natural environment was paramount, Noemi decided her study of agronomy would include a concentration on the effects of genetic plant modification.

Since the mid-Twentieth Century, big corporations had consolidated the seed industry by focusing only on the profitable varieties that responded well to synthetic fertilizers. One hundred years ago, there were 497 varieties of lettuce in the world. Now, in 2060, due to corporate consolidation, there are just thirty-six forms of lettuce. Similarly, while 288 varieties of beets originally existed, seventeen currently exist; and, where once there were 307 varieties of sweet corn, now there are only twelve. Many of the seed varieties remaining have been genetically re-engineered and require much more water than the older forms. As a result, unlike the original seeds, which were more adaptable to a changing environment, the newer ones were less likely to survive drought-like conditions, causing a massive breakdown in the commercial food supply.

To preserve as many varieties of non-genetically modified species of plants as possible, many of which are over a hundred years old, Noemi has been creating a seed bank over the past twenty years. The thousands of varieties she has collected and catalogued to date, represent millions of years of natural biodiversity, and will, because of her work, now be preserved for future generations. In addition to other classifications, the seed bank is also categorized by region and identifies which seed varieties are better adapted to specific eco-systems.

Noemi's research and extensive writing also addresses optimal germination, ripening time, flavor, storage, and disease resistance. Her work strongly emphasizes the importance of developing adaptive, open-pollinated varieties of plants. Because the underground environment of Ogallala will include pollinating insects and birds, she will have the opportunity to grow some of the seed varieties from her collection that have adapted to uniquely different growing conditions. Noemi understands she will have to strictly separate the species so cross-pollination will not occur.

Noemi's pride and joy is her heirloom collection, which has been passed down from multiple generations of her own and other families. She has stored all these seeds in labeled, airtight containers. As a lover of roses of all types, she has also accumulated grafts of her favorite hybrid varieties. Whenever she thinks of her daughter, Rosie, she associates her with the deep, pink hybrid rose called 'Bendiciones,' which smells spicey and sweet, and is her absolute favorite.

Chapter 9
Sophie

It's mid-afternoon and our journey to Ogallala has brought us close to St. Louis. Driving along, we notice a strong rotation in the cloud base and feel a marked increase in the humidity level. Then suddenly as the barometric pressure drops, to our right, a tornado forms. As the power lines explode into sparks all around us smelling of burning rubber, we feel an intense wind shift.

Peter turns to me and says, "No safe option here. If we're caught out in the open and the tornado hits us, we'll be in the path of all kinds of flying debris."

Looking for a sturdy building to provide some shelter, I spot an old concrete, gas station ahead on our right and urge Peter to pull into the driveway. The few windows in the building are boarded up. After explaining to Inanna and Rajeev that we're taking shelter until the tornado passes, I ask them to grab the sleeping bags from the back of the van to use as covering to protect our faces.

As we drive into the garage, Peter asks Rajeev to help him shut the two rusty doors. Using a heavy iron rod and the strength he now has as a modified human being to secure the handles of the doors, Rajeev has them closed in a few minutes.

Waiting in the dark, we hear hail pounding on the roof, the loud, continuous roar of the tornado as it surrounds the building and reverberating 'thunks' as objects flying around outside hit the solid, concrete walls protecting us.

The main portion of the storm continues for a full hour before it moves on. Due to the ever-damaging effects of climate change, tornados like this one are now forming with greater frequency, density, and strength.

As we huddle inside the van and under the sleeping bags within the concrete garage, Rajeev says, "Climate change has certainly affected the buoyancy of the air, but the element of chance and natural variability come into play as well. More frequent tornado activity is an integral component of the pattern of stronger droughts, bigger heat waves and, in some places, heavier rainfall."

I kid him, saying, "Rajeev here we are huddling together in fear of our lives and you're giving us the facts."

47

He laughs out loud and says, "You're right Sophie your husband should have installed a 'note to self' in my brain, which reminds me to always approach serious subjects with humor first."

Peter grins at them both, and then becomes serious again as he suggests that, since multiple tornadoes now often happen on the same day and especially here in Tornado Alley, we should stay inside the garage for the night then head out again towards Topeka, Kansas, early tomorrow morning. We all agree this would be the best idea.

As we eat using flashlights to see our food and try and make ourselves comfortable in the van, Inanna reads to Sarah before we all finally drop off into an uneasy sleep. There is no doubt everyone is very concerned about being captured, so we intensely look forward to arriving safely at our destination in the very near future.

Chapter 10
Persephone

Worldship *Persephone* is on course for Mars, and given the power of her
EPPP system, she'll get there as scheduled in four weeks.

The crewmembers have settled in and begun to systematically
construct and maintain a living biological and chemical environment
inside and outside the ship. They are at work designing software
programs that will enable water, rocks, and soils to perform a variety of
functions falling into the category of what they call 'ecological
architectures.' Amazingly, just like in nature, these non-biological
materials are becoming capable of regeneration, never breaking down
or needing replacement.

Persephone's outer skin has also been ingeniously conceived. It is
embedded with 'nanotubes' that constantly monitor the condition of
her exterior surfaces and are programmed to react and repair any
damage made by penetrating objects such as space debris. The non-
metal surface of the spaceship means crew members inside the ship are
protected from Galactic Cosmic Radiation (GCR), solar flares, and
cosmic rays by this lattice-work system of featherweight, carbon
nanotubes, which have also been constructed to store hydrogen at high
density, one of the ship's primary fuel sources.

As an integral component of *Persephone's* holistic approach to
living, special labs have been created by the crew inside the ship for the
study of microbiological matter and to determine how microbiological
matter impacts human beings living in space. The biologists have
already noticed that organic matter within the spaceship is forming
completely different cellular patterns than those on Earth. To observe
these new patterns more closely, they are monitoring the 'personal ecosystems' of bacteria that exist within and around each individual
crewmember.

While scientists have known for many years that the human
body is made up of symbiotic bacteria and any substance which kills
the 'good' bacteria may also end up killing the body that hosts it, what
Persephone's biologists hope to learn by these activities, is how they can
prevent death should they encounter an unknown, 'bad' bacterium
during their travels. In a way, the biologists are behaving like 'artists' as

they 'mix' the right bacterial 'paints' on a palette appropriate for the changing environment they're creating within the spacecraft.

One of the bio-informed design experiments biologists are conducting involves cultivating plants, which through *bioluminescence*, provide low energy lighting systems throughout the ship. As part of this particular experiment, *Persephone's* living spaces are interwoven with **algae bioreactors, anaerobic digesters, bioluminescent light sources,** heat absorbing and emitting substances, and even *hygroscopic materials*, such as calcium chloride.

Since proper air circulation is critical on board to avoid unpleasant odors created by stagnant bacteria, **bliss bacteria** are being cultivated by the biologists to ward off potentially dangerous pathogens and to ensure the air on *Persephone* is fresh at all times.

And, to conserve resources as much as possible, a full 90% of wastewater used by the crew on board *Persephone* will be recovered through membrane-filtering techniques. Other waste products will also be recycled: the indigestible fiber in the crew's feces will be transformed into a material resembling adobe brick walls. These 'building blocks' can then be used for constructing housing on any new planets they discover that contain enough oxygen in the atmosphere to support human life.

***

Rachel, like all her fellow crewmembers, is building her own individual living environment inside *Persephone*. As an example of how living architecture is being used successfully throughout the interior of the spaceship, the two rooms she is creating have physiologies that allow them to process nutrients, filter water, and create cooling and heating systems. In addition, her dwelling, which has been constructed out of crystal rock, can remove all of Rachel's waste and transform it into soils that will grow plants and vegetables outside of her home.

Rachel has chosen white, blue, and purple as the color scheme. Consequently, her two rooms resemble the surfaces of Waterford vases joined together, inverted and like a human body, filled with thin, life-enabling, vein-like crystalline tubes that flow from ceiling to floor and from floor to ceiling. Rachel's bed, created with protocells, responds automatically to pressure, light and heat. Inflating and deflating in response to Rachel's movements, the bed provides a finely tuned support for her body while she sleeps.

Because the sound of water is important for her well-being in any living environment in which she resides, Rachel can activate the sound of falling rain throughout her space. Before she falls asleep, she loves to watch the flickering of diffused light caused by the activities of giant bioluminescent mushrooms that shines gently across the reflective walls and ceilings of her 'home.'

In addition to the bed, Rachel's covers are also made of protocells and regulate to her body temperature, as are numerous articles of clothing, including her space suit, shirts, pants, and underwear, which all automatically grow thinner as temperatures increase and thicker when temperatures drop. The clothing and shoes 'self-repair' as needed, to ensure a limitless life span in space. Because her shoes respond minutely to the pressure she puts upon them by changing shape to conform to her feet, they are very comfortable. All told, the protocells in her clothing and shoes are a much superior material to the oil-based plastic that was so destructive to the environment and used ubiquitously on Earth for many years.

Rachel is still amazed at the malleability of protocells, even though she knows that they were, in fact, the precursors to life on Earth, i.e., 'clues' that created a path for scientists to follow as they studied the transition from inorganic to organic life. Because they respond to their environment like plants in changeable and adaptable ways, it is clear they demonstrate a certain 'innate intelligence.'

The fact she has created this beautiful 'nest' for herself and doesn't have to share with anyone else, fills Rachel with serenity and joy. As the leader of this important expedition with primary responsibility for every aspect of the ship and crew, she needs a place to which she can escape for just a few hours, a place where she can play her tango music and dance with herself, as often and for as long as she likes without being observed. (This doesn't mean, of course, she wouldn't sometimes have liked her Argentinean lover to materialize and dance with her.)

In his living quarters across from Rachel, Yuri has built his home out of clay with a surface consisting of several strong, spherical shells, between which, to keep the clay pliable, water flows continuously like a stream. The spherical shells protect the structure from becoming saturated and wet. Like Rachel, he uses organic bioluminescence for lighting, as well as bed and bedding made from protocells.

Yuri's reddish-brown, domelike ceilings and clay floor tiles are painted in a variety of Mexican reds and greens. Windows strategically spaced look out onto the gardens situated around the ship that provide a pleasant place to walk and sit. In addition to enjoying his own living space, Yuri also admires his neighbor, Anna's, home, which like his, is constructed from red clay on the inside, and, like Gaudi's Casa Batlló, contains windows asymmetrically designed and bent inward as if reaching for each other like lovers.

From his windows, Yuri can see the many different types of clay, coral and crystal dwellings of fellow crew members that, from a distance, look as if they are part of a sophisticated art installation. Some of the surfaces of the dwellings, like his, are covered with a 'lattice work' of nanotubes that resemble natural bamboo and are used to recycle carbon dioxide within the interiors of the ship. The nanotubes grow in many different sizes, varieties and patterns: some fat, some thin, some very long and weight-bearing while still maintaining a tensile elasticity, and some covered with shining, black, **graphite** leaves that look like sugar decorations on a cake, intertwined among the winding structures.

Once nanotubes are 'harvested' by *Persephone's* scientists, they can be 'doped' with nitrogen and converted to batteries for storing lithium, becoming 'carbon peapods' to be turned into oscillators and rotational motors; and they can also be stacked on top of one another like plastic cups, so they become semiconductors. Most importantly, they can be used, if necessary, to replenish the nanotubes on *Persephone's* outer skin.

Yuri wants his home to be welcoming and open to any crewmember who wishes to join him in a game of chess or a drink of single-malt scotch. Although he also, like Rachel, doesn't want a permanent relationship with anyone, he does like to sometimes 'hook up' with Anna, his thirty-something, six-foot tall, Somalian neighbor, to first play chess and then have a sleepover.

Overall, *Persephone's* renewable exteriors and interiors allow Rachel, Yuri, and the rest of the crew to live in a self-sustainable environment that does not rely on any non-renewable infrastructure. They are happy to be leaving the outdated and wasteful technology of the past far behind.

***

As well as working on their assigned projects, the crewmembers are also adjusting to their new social lives. In some ways, their complete separation from friends and families on Earth has been a little more gradual since they will still be able to communicate for the short term by taped video-messages through the ship's communication systems. These video messages take up to twenty-two minutes to be delivered. Once they travel beyond Europa, though, they know and dread the fact it will become virtually impossible to maintain contact.

To facilitate this communication among crew members and their loved ones on Earth as well as provide on-going entertainment, *Persephone's* communication devices will continue operating continuously while the ship is within satellite range. Access to information networks as well as other comforts that crew members have brought with them from home, including DNA memory sticks containing their favorite music and video programs, will assist in their transition away from Earth.

Unlike Inanna and Rajeev whose very bodies contain information systems, the crewmembers on board *Persephone* must rely upon traditional methods, physically separate machines, for personal use and daily tasks. Worldship *Persephone* itself, however, is intuitively connected in the same way as Rajeev and Inanna are, to both its own organic and non-organic components.

In recognition of the vital service they are performing for the United States, all of the immediate families of *Persephone's* 200 crew members have been included as part of the elite Mount Weather community. Rachel's own mother, who is in her sixties, is among the lucky few.

Although she doesn't live in the luxury condominiums at the center of the city like Alistair, Rachel's mother has a nice apartment assigned to her on one of the canals, near the suburban shopping centers and other amenities. Even though it has been very difficult for her to let Rachel go, she takes comfort in the fact that she has a son, a daughter-in-law and a grandchild who are also now living in Weather City. Rachel's mother is very proud of her daughter, and understands the mission is of primary importance to the survival of "Species Human." Stoically, she has learned to accept that she, like the other family members with whom she shares so much, will never see her beloved child again.

Chapter 11
Alistair and Weather City

The evacuation to Weather City has been carefully orchestrated in stages. Unlike Alistair, some government officials have remained in Washington, D.C., and will only leave at the last minute as conditions disintegrate and it becomes increasingly impossible for them to live on the surface of the planet.

They remain above-ground in order to provide a semblance of normality to the populations who are still living in the cities and scattered around the rest of the country. All these inhabitants have been advised to construct underground shelters of some kind, where they must be prepared to live for many years. To assist them in building these shelters, the government has provided easy-to-use blueprints as well as some financial assistance from FEMA to qualifying individuals and communities,

When he has time, Alistair has been slowly exploring the city of which he is now part. Generally, he has been impressed by its orderliness, cleanliness, and expert ventilation system, which provides a constant stream of fresh air to the residents through the use of thousands of air ducts controlled by a complex set of algorithms that have been designed for the city by Tom, Peter's close friend. He also understands a similarly efficient, automated vacuum waste collection system removes garbage at high speeds through pneumatic tubes and directs it to recycling stations and composting plants. The compost created by the waste collection system is then delivered to the farms located around the underground city. Bio-gas digesters, in turn, use the methane produced by the compost and convert it into electricity and heat.

Recently, Alistair has visited several factories on the outskirts of the city that are powered by 'clean fuel,' meaning few pollutants are released into the outside air.

In researching how the dead will be disposed of in Weather City, Alistair has learned mortuaries will use **alkaline hydrolysis,** a 'cremation' process in which bodies are placed in a **resomator,** which is then filled with water and lye and heated to a very high temperature. As the alkaline hydrolysis breaks the body down into its chemical components, it produces a green-brown liquid containing amino acids, peptides, sugars, and salts. In addition to this liquid, soft, porous, white bones also remain intact and are subsequently ground in a **cremulator** into a fine, white 'dust.' The "dust" and left-over chemicals provide an excellent fertilizer for green spaces scattered around the city. Alistair is vaguely amused by the thought of this kind of 'immortality' that his body will continue to inhabit and fertilizes the grass on which millions of feet in the future may tread, including those of his grandchildren.

Although Alistair has made a slow adjustment to his privileged life, he still lives with constant feelings of 'survivor's guilt' that he hides well from Robyn and Styx. He frequently asks himself as he lies awake late at night, why he and his child and future grandchildren will survive, while his other family members may not. He rehashes in his mind why, given his senior position, he was not able to protect or save them. Because he is an atheist, Alistair finds that he cannot call on faith-based wisdom and answers to comfort himself during these dark moments but must rely upon his own internal strength.

Although he wants desperately to communicate with Peter again, Alistair, like everyone else, is closely monitored. So, to protect Peter and maintain the secrecy of his whereabouts, he has refrained from trying to make any contact with him whatsoever.

Because Alistair has been thoroughly briefed on the actions that Peter has taken to sabotage the systems that held vital information on the two trans-humans, he knows Peter is now considered an Enemy of the State and a dangerous fugitive. It is only just recently, though, he has learned how Sophie released a powerful, intelligent, self-aware virus before her departure, one that completely crippled many defense and weather re-engineering programs. She, too, is now wanted by the authorities as well.

Since his own research on climate change has led him to believe Earth's ozone layer will slowly readjust and calibrate itself in time, Alistair agrees with Sophie's actions and her opinion that the planet needs a chance to heal itself without help or interference from human agencies. Although the natural 'calibration' of Earth will probably not happen for a hundred years or so, he continues to hope his great grandchildren will once again be able to live safely on the surface of a newly rejuvenated planet.

In spite of his guilty conscience, Alistair feels supremely grateful to have the calming presence and support of his wife who is working just minutes from his own office. Robyn's top-secret, gene modification program has attracted the attention of a small handful of plutocrats who are now implementing inheritable gene modifications on their children, using **CRISPR technology**. During the first phase of the project, their proposed changes to human genetics will focus on increasing human resistance to disease, physical strength, and overall intelligence. The plutocrats then hope the second phase will incorporate the science and technology Peter had been developing. Because retrieving Inanna and Rajeev are clearly imperative to this plan, they are desperate to get them back.

One of the strangely amusing facts Robyn has told Alistair in confidence is that all these 'new age humans' will receive a permanent, distinguishing birth mark in the shape of a red serpent. The serpent image is modeled after the staff of Asclepius, the Greek demigod of medicine. Alistair, as an astrophysicist, is fully aware of the Greek myth in which Asclepius was able to restore the health of the sick and bring the dead back to life until Zeus turned him into a constellation for disrupting the natural order of the world. He has therefore told Robyn, "Using the symbol of a failed god as a permanent, genetic mark seems to me like an ironic and unfortunate choice on their part."

Styx, Alistair's twelve-year-old daughter, has begun attending a school located within walking distance of their condominium. She has met and quickly befriended a number of compatible girls. She has recently informed him, "I'm only a little sad to leave my old home on the surface." In reply, he has told her he understands since her memory of Earth unlike his is not one that includes its gorgeous green forests, sage-filled mountains, blue seas, and running streams.

Because she has only seen the terrible and ugly effect of increasing droughts, massive earthquakes, and destructive volcanic eruptions, he knows she will soon forget her life above ground and be very content to live in their well-ordered, weather-predictable, underground prison.

Chapter 12
Sophie

Once the full impact of the tornado has passed, we exit the shelter of the old, concrete garage and continue our journey towards Kansas. So far, we haven't seen any signs we're being followed. It's impossible to ignore the devastation from the tornado all around us as we travel down the highway and pass through St. Louis. Since tornados have been occurring more frequently and are greater in strength, most of the towns in "tornado alley" are no longer inhabited. Frequent tornadoes, combined with drought-like conditions in Texas and the Southwest, have forced surviving populations there to move North to the Great Lakes, Canada, and beyond as well.

Sadly, though, no matter where these survivors go, I know for certain they won't be safe. If they don't create adequate, long-term shelters, they'll soon die from exposure to solar radiation.

I sigh loudly as we are driving along, and Peter asks, "What's bothering you?"

"Just the mess we're in and how insane we were to implement climate engineering on top of everything else we did. How our little Earth, a perfectly and elegantly constructed biosphere, has been willfully destroyed by us."

He replies, "Glad we disabled the programs controlling the release of that weather changing muck into the atmosphere. We'll have to hope this will force them to leave things alone for a bit, and perhaps without humans living on her surface and screwing things up, Earth will have a shot at self-correction."

He reaches over and squeezes my leg.

"So far so good, at least we don't seem to have been stopped." I reply looking over at him gratefully.

"No," he says, smiling at me. "My hunch is Tom is successfully bargaining with them."

I think, however, Peter is lying about this to keep us all calm. I know 'them' and there is no way they'll let Inanna and Rajeev go no matter what Tom offers in return. I am sure they're pursuing us as fast as they can—right now.

Inanna and Rajeev sit silently in the back listening to the conversation, while Sarah lies limply across their laps, dozing.

As we move along towards Topeka, I allow my mind to wander and think once more about what our lives will be like when we actually make it to Ogallala. I know our genetic pool will be small, since we don't have access to the enormous banks of human sperm and eggs Weather City and even *Persephone* will have, and we'll have to guard against the weakening of the gene pool as relatives marry each other. We'll also need to adapt to the vagaries of living in a small in-grown community with its squabbles, feuds, and peculiarities, like many small societies have had to do in the past.

Perhaps when our descendants reemerge onto the Earth, they will be able to seek out other small communities like ours that will have survived and join forces with them. I have doubts the plutocratic form of government existing now will have changed much during these dark years, but I am hopeful perhaps their power and reach will have diminished so new kinds of societies can freely evolve. I am wondering, too, if, once we begin this 'new world' experiment, advanced intelligences like Rajeev and Inanna, who will most certainly still be alive, will come up with innovative ways for us to live together, and that they and others of their kind will, in essence, become humanity's biggest 'problem solvers.'

As I sit there beside Peter, I reflect on my mother, Mehr's, predictions about the future, and wonder if my father, Raphael, is near and will in some way protect us. Looking at Peter, I know how lucky I am to have found such a wonderful friend and companion.

Peter and I have always been revolutionaries; two swimmers fighting against the strong riptide of a society whose values were much in question. During the limited number of years we have been alive, science and technology has advanced beyond both of our wildest dreams, but we are very wary of its gross potential for flagrant misuse. Human beings have not yet adopted a universal set of ethical values that will anchor us all in our own humanity and in our spiritual as well as our material wellbeing.

My mother brought me up to believe in a universe that was based on an elegant scientific design: a universe perfectly combining the sacred and profound formulas that led to its creation. I have always known instinctively humans should never tamper with its design injudiciously.

I have been a firm believer in what Peter and other scientists have been investigating as part of their work to improve human genomes and human capabilities because, like my mother, I do think our bodies, or whatever other external shape we may ultimately have, are merely hosts for indestructible forms of energy. I am convinced everything in our universe is made up of this energy, and it is this energy that is the building block of all matter. In fact, the same energy fills bodies, machines, stones, animals, trees, flowers, and mountains, and flows and changes form constantly. This energy can neither be created nor destroyed by us, no matter what new forms of so-called 'life' we end up making, because it comes from the place where all things begin. I call this place, "that which is."

Sometimes, because I believe we live primarily in an '*electrical universe,*' and, because parts of us are also galaxies and stars and magnetic fields; twisted filaments of pink, yellow, coral, blue, and green that one day we will burst out of our bodies, and finally connect to everything which exists beyond us, including what is out there in deepest, impenetrable space.

***

We arrive in Topeka around midday. We still don't see any evidence of human settlements and pass very few other vehicles on the road, some of which are DARPA vans like ours. Knowing this route will eventually bring us to the town of North Platte then finally to Ogallala, we use US 24 West to take us across Kansas and up towards Kearney, Nebraska. Seeing what was once the Platte River, we experience first-hand the effects of the region's life-killing drought.

I turn towards Inanna, Rajeev, and Sarah and tell them, "We're taking the same route that the long-horned cattle drives followed from Texas in 1875. The animals would arrive from the Western Trail covered in dust, sometimes stampeding, snorting, and bellowing loudly in protest against the long, hot journey they had just completed. Stock hands hustled the cattle into yards where they waited, penned closely together, to be shipped East in railroad cars from Ogallala. The drive was very difficult for the cowboys. Besides traveling over really wild, inhospitable territory, they had to manage large and extremely headstrong herds."

"What did they look like?" asked Sarah.

"Well, they were like cows with very big horns," I reply.

"Look at the land now—desert," Peter chips in. "Hard to believe that any farming of any kind took place here now, isn't it?" Waving his hands at the parched, dry dirt visible through the windows of the van.

"It was only thirty years ago," I tell the three in the back, "because of the severe droughts, that Ogallala, the town nearest to where we will be living, under Lake McConaughy, closed down its cattle industry. After that, people left in droves. This part of the country is now deserted and virtually uninhabited.

"Even just forty years ago, Lake McConaughy was 22 miles long, 4 miles wide and 142 feet deep from shore to shore, stretching like a small interior ocean," I continue. "It's hard to believe that at the beginning of the Twenty First Century, the lake, which is completely dry now, covered 35,700 acres with 105 miles of shoreline and sandy beaches. Lake McConaughy was created in 1941 when engineers built the Kingsley Dam in the North Platte River to trap water for irrigation and hydroelectric power. The dam is still there today, a towering monument of steel and concrete that serves no useful purpose. Someday, when people emerge onto the planet's surface again, they will wonder as they gaze at Kingsley, why it was built in the first place."

"What does Ogallala mean?" asked Sarah.

"It's a Dakota Sioux Indian word, 'Oglala,' which means 'scatter one's own.'" I reply.

While we chat, we travel rapidly towards Ash Hollow Caves and Highway 26 that will take us north out of the town of Ogallala and bring us along the south side of the Lake. I think it's ironic we're so close to the Oregon Trail and the last time we were here to work at the site, we found the fossilized marks of wagon wheels near the entrance to the Caves. In our own way, we'll be living like those Nineteenth Century pioneers as we explore new territory in a new land.

Luckily, subterranean lakes below the Ash Hollow Caves were never discovered by the Nebraskan State Park system or the farmers who lived in the area. The entrance leading to the massive limestone caves and lakes, was extremely well hidden behind a very high rock wall for centuries. It is only because of the deep springs beneath the Aquifer, which is like an enormous underground sponge extending thousands of feet below the Earth's surface that the lakes have retained, and continuously replenished, their water levels, even in this terrible drought. Unfortunately, the state of California, which is now mostly underwater, also experienced a life-killing drought, and even though weather modification programs brought back some rain in the form of massive storms, its underground Aquifers were never replenished in the same way.

It was Tom who ultimately found the lakes through the mapping program his father's company had developed in the early Twenty-First Century. He never disclosed their existence to anyone and has used his fortune over the last fifteen years to slowly build our postmodern, survivalist community.

We reach Kearney by mid-afternoon and expect to arrive in North Platte soon. From there, it should take us another hour to get to Ash Hollow. We're tired of travelling and ready to be out of the car so we can stretch our legs and move around freely.

Chapter 13
Persephone

During the first few days of their journey, Rachel and Yuri and the rest of the senior crew members meet regularly to review how effectively the many systems of the spacecraft are operating. They generally gather in the cafeteria, because the large, numerous windows overlook a pleasant quadrangle, giving it a light, airy feeling. The cafeteria has been constructed out of coral and, as such, resembles a grayish, purple reef.

Since the senior crew members have been handpicked for their emotional stability and general equanimity as well as their superior scientific skills, meetings proceed smoothly without many interruptions. This had not been the case in the DARPA department where Rachel had previously worked. There, many of the scientists felt compelled to express their views and contradict each other constantly to impress their bosses. They argued long and hard about the merits of their own research versus that of other scientists.

Also, in contrast to DARPA, all of *Persephone's* multi-racial, multi-cultural crew members are generalists who are skilled across a variety of scientific fields; several are also writers, painters, musicians, and poets, and, once they've finished discussing technical and administrative matters, one of them often shares a painting, a piece of music or a poem.

Overall, the crew members of *Persephone* have committed themselves to balancing their scientific research and work within the context of a humane system of values and beliefs. They are all adept at critical thinking and are dedicating themselves to a lifestyle being developed within *Persephone* that promotes the concept of an essential unity binding all living and inorganic matter together.

Since Rachel also believes in this 'tissue of connectivity,' she is convinced that, if her crew members are open and sensitive to it, they will all surely learn to live together within their shared environment respectfully, supportively, and harmoniously.

In addition, Rachel's personal philosophy includes active imagination and the 'collective unconscious,' a process that enables an individual to be consciously 'open' to 'information' constantly flowing throughout the universe. Acknowledging their similar brain and body structure allows for common memories and creative images and ideas,

Rachel hopes all her crew will exercise this collective imagination as they confront the inevitable problems that will occur in the future.

Rachel has discussed her ideas about connective energy and collective consciousness with Yuri, who is mostly in agreement. While he's fairly intuitive in his intellectual and personal life, unlike her, his pragmatism generally triumphs over anything else. As a result, he ends up spending most of his free time weighing the relative merits of single malt scotches, playing chess, eating food, and engaging in sex rather than in deep, philosophical thought. Sometimes Yuri thinks conversations on Eastern philosophy he has with Rachel are what he would refer to as "crazy," but he's willing to entertain them because he respects her deeply and wants to be as supportive as he can.

Yuri's scientific acumen, however, even if he doesn't acknowledge it, is fully engaged with his active imagination, and he is one of the most creative engineers they have on board. In fact, because of his intuitive brilliance in engineering, once they've advanced beyond Earth, he will lead *Persephone* and her crew of physicists and engineers as they explore the full capabilities of their catalytic "'warm' nuclear fusion ion drive."

Yuri has often thought that if Earth's scientists and engineers had been able to duplicate a warm fusion system earlier in the Twenty-First Century and then found a way of cleanly disposing of any waste it generated, they would have been able to prevent the effects of large-scale climate change.

***

This morning, at their meeting in the cafeteria, the crew is discussing the approaching reconnoiter with the Mars base. Rachel explains to the crew that Yuri will remain on board, while she and a small group of scientists land the transport on Mars, where they will stay for a day and a night.

"As you know, it's a virtual military base," she explains, "despite the presence of non-com personnel."

"Our orders specify that we are to pick up fifty of their engineers and scientists and take them with us to Europa. We'll leave them there, together with a transport, so they can eventually return to Mars. For the engineers and scientists to continue the work that's been started on Europa by robotic cyborgs, the base there has already been fully equipped with all the supplies they will need, so we won't be taking on extra cargo."

DARPA has planned that the Mars military crew, which Rachel and her colleagues are to deliver to Europa, will live there for five to ten years in order to test Europa's ability to successfully support human life in the long-term.

As the staff meeting progresses, one of Persephone's crew members facilitates a discussion with the group on the feasibility of terraforming Venus.

"Interesting to think that it might have been easier to terraform Venus than Mars and Europa, because of the higher gravity on that planet, which is close to ninety-one percent of Earth's," she says. "They would have had to figure out a way first, though, to reverse the greenhouse effect that basically broiled the planet alive like a lobster years ago. We could, I suppose, have used heat-loving microorganisms to remove the CO_2, making it more hospitable to Earth-like life." Her comments and observations spark an animated discussion amongst the crew as lunch is served.

For their meal, some will have hamburgers and some chicken. Since no animals are carried aboard Persephone, they are actually eating protocells that have been biofabricated. Having been made from the same cells, the 'faux' food has all the characteristics of beef and chicken, including taste.

As they sit around relaxing and enjoying their meals, one of the astronauts brings out a piece of leather to show the group.

"Feel this," he says, "this is what we're also growing in the lab from beef cells. I can make you anything from it once you place your orders: pants, shirts, furniture, you name it."

The leather he passes around is opaque and very nearly transparent.

"I can make it soft, breathable, durable, elastic and patterned, abracadabra bio- fabrication," he says, laughing.

A few scientists put in their orders. Rachel wants a pair of pants and gets a lot of back talk from everyone about what their design should entail. Yuri, on the other hand, would like leather covers for some bar stools in his house.

This group of young, star sailors are all in good spirits as they eat their lunch together continuing their animated discussion. They are looking forward with enthusiasm to the next chapter of their space odyssey. They don't dwell for long on the dangerous problems Earth is currently facing; rather, they look towards the future and the many possibilities it may hold.

Chapter 14
Alistair

Alistair has been trying covertly to determine what has happened to Sophie and Peter by combing through several password-protected databases, but unfortunately, he has not been successful. Because he does not have easy access to other top-secret files or databases, he has been restricted in his search to information pertaining only to the space program. To get around this problem, he has considered going directly to General Myers, one of his superiors. If he takes this route, he will tell Myers he is making inquiries about his colleagues in order to assist in the capture of the trans-humans.

Alistair knows he can easily make a case to the General based on his own 'need-to-know status.' He can emphasize to the General that the trans-humans will be extremely important to him as he continues to develop the space program, and he can also tell him that he had been an integral part of the previous discussions at DARPA on how Rajeev and Inanna would be used. In the end, however, and after careful thought, Alistair decides he will not inquire about Sophie and Peter immediately; rather he will wait a week or two to avoid raising any suspicion.

Meanwhile, he is in daily contact with Rachel and *Persephone* and, so, feels confident they will, as previously planned, be on Mars within thirty days of leaving Earth. Once they arrive, he will ask Rachel for her impressions *ex-officio* on how successful she thinks his staff has been in accomplishing ***par terraforming*** there.

Privately, rather than her visit to Mars he is most anxious for Rachel to arrive safely on Europa, a blue-tinged planet whose geological activity he has often observed through satellite images, as its warm interior liquid erupts onto its icy surface in large feather-like plumes. Knowing Europa was named by an Italian astronomer in 1610 after a daughter of the King of Tyre, Alistair has always thought of the planet as a beautiful woman. Recently, cyborgs have found the existence of oxygen on Europa, which means it can sustain living organisms.

The cyborgs building underwater habitats for future settlers on Europa have been using ***sterilized cryobots*** to melt through the planet's ice surface. In addition, they've launched a series of ***hydrobots,*** which have recorded a great deal of scientific data and fed it back to

Mars and Earth. So far, the hydrobots have found sea life that look like varieties of fish, tubeworms, clams, crustaceans, and mussels, as well as many other unfamiliar aquatic life forms. The living organisms appear to feed on a species of **chemosynthetic** bacteria that clearly does not need sunlight to survive.

As a result of these observations, Alistair believes Europa may ultimately be best suited primarily to sustain aquatic lifeforms rather than human ones. He is firmly of the opinion that any future human colonies will need to be small so as not to fundamentally disturb native species. Reflecting on the enormous damage done to Earth and the number of species that humans have eliminated through their thoughtless activities, he has little confidence that human-galaxy-wide colonization will leave a 'light footprint.'

As he goes about his daily work, Alistair regrets he himself will not be able to explore all the strange and unknown worlds as part of *Persephone's* crew in the years ahead. If it had not been for Robyn and Styx, he would have liked to be part of this mission, but he does recognize he would most likely have been disqualified due to his age.

Alistair has come to realize almost immediately that he hates living and working underground. Even though this Earth-like biosphere is green and beautiful, he feels claustrophobic and yearns to live on the surface of the planet. In some ways, he is sure his psyche has been irreparably damaged by this forced separation from where he has been designed and was meant to live, and what he cared for and most deeply loved.

Every day now, Alistair hopes this constant low-grade depression he is suffering will dissipate. Despite closeness to his wife and child, he realizes he has no interest in continuing to live like he is now, and he often daydreams of being set free, of floating away peacefully and weightlessly, like a small palpable entity amongst the stars and galaxies he also loves.

Chapter 15
Sophie

The van shudders to a halt as we arrive outside of North Platte, just eighty miles from Ash Hollow. Peter, Rajeev and Inanna immediately jump out and examine the engine carefully, after which Rajeev tells us, "looks like the heat exchanger is broken and not warming the stored air anymore. Also, when the tornado came along, the outside air became cooler and moister. That humidity was transferred to the compressed air, which has iced up and stopped the engine. We'll need access to a compressor to dehydrate it."

"So basically, we're without a vehicle until we can tow it to Ash Hollow where they've got several of those compressors," Peter says. "We're going to have to start walking. If we can average fifteen miles a day, it'll only take us four or five days to get there."

To provision our journey sufficiently, we unpack the van and take sleeping bags, food and water, leaving everything else inside. Peter then locks the van, and we push it into an abandoned shed in order to hide it there. Peter informs us, "Once we get to Ogallala, we'll return with another vehicle and tow it back." Peter can't risk contacting Tom for help because he is sure the government will track any satellite transmissions immediately. After I had received the earlier text from Alistair, we immediately turned off our communicators and hadn't turned them on again.

Since it will be dark soon, we travel only a short distance from where we left the van before deciding to stop for the night. It is not cold enough to need a fire. In the morning, we will hike up the depleted, sandy, riverbed of the North Platte towards Lake McConaughy.

As we settle down for the night, I explain to Inanna and Rajeev, "The water table under North Platte is now bone dry like a mummified body. Water that used to come rushing down so abundantly all the way from the Colorado Rockies and generously fed this river and its wetlands, has now completely disappeared."

I give them a further bit of geography, explaining that at one time the Platte River flowed like a giant python to the Missouri River then onwards to the mighty Mississippi, its larger sister, before finally making its way down to the Gulf of Mexico. Now they can see for themselves the Platte is just this dusty, sandy passageway, a sad reminder of the water that once graced its contours like the generous, flowing scarf of a beautiful woman. Sadly, extensive amounts of this water were drained off, even before the droughts of 2030 and 2040, to irrigate the corn, soybeans, wheat, hay, sugar beets, and potatoes used to feed the rest of the country, and eventually just the ones who could afford to buy them.

The next day we head out again, and after walking fifteen more miles, we spend the night under an overhanging riverbank, lying huddled together close to each other in our sleeping bags. Sarah sleeps with me; Peter lies on my right side, Rajeev on my left and Inanna next to Peter. I don't sleep well because I'm worried the longer the trip to Ash Hollow takes, the more likely it is we will be stopped. According to our pre-arranged plans, we should have been there by now and I know Tom and Noemi will already be worried. Every noise in the night startles me, and at one point I think I hear a lone coyote howling somewhere out there. I wonder how many are still alive, given the scarcity of water and food.

As I fall in and out of a light sleep, my dream that night is strange: I suddenly find myself part of a mule train carrying furs south to trade for supplies. I'm confused and can't tell whether I'm a man or woman. I look out at swaying backs of the mules in front of me. I hear and am grateful for the river still running strongly beside the trail we are following. Eventually, Sarah stirs in my arms, wakes me, forcing me to return to the dark, starless, waterless night.

***

In the morning, we rise well before dawn, drink some of our bottled water, and quickly eat protein bars. We are hoping we'll do better than the fifteen miles we were able to travel the day before. Sarah walks beside me for a bit, but Rajeev soon picks her up like a small weightless sack and carries her effortlessly on his broad shoulders. Inanna and Rajeev have decided they will take turns carrying her so we can make better time; unlike us, they seem indefatigable as they rely on their bionic legs and arms.

At midday, we stop for a break and stay close to the banks of the dry riverbed, hoping to remain undetected from any government drones. We are resting now, sitting with our backs against the sand and compacted mud, when we hear a sound above us. Peter motions for everyone to be quiet, and none of us moves, hardly daring to breathe.

"It sounds as if it's hooves," I whisper.

He nods and puts a finger to his lips as the echo of hooves gets closer. Once the heavy thudding reaches the edge of the bank, whatever animal it is, abruptly rears off to the right. We wait a few minutes until it is quiet again then scramble up the sandy sides of the bank, like wary crabs, to peer over the top, leaving Sarah crouched below curled into a small, protected ball. Not far away, we catch a glimpse of a lone girl riding bareback on a horse, her long red hair flying out behind her, as she gallops swiftly away across the dusty plain.

"Wow," says Inanna, "beautiful."

Silently, we watch as the girl disappears into the distance. We then slide back down to the bottom of the bank, dusting ourselves off as we stand and pick up our things.

"I wonder where she comes from." I say to Peter.

"Well, it's possible that a few people decided to stay here, though how they live with so little water is a mystery," he replies.

"Perhaps they catch rainwater," Rajeev says. "Though unpredictable, there are still enough summer storms to fill a few tanks or maybe they have found a way to access the parts of the aquifer that still contain water."

We walk on silently in the midday heat. Sarah dozes, her head resting against Rajeev's neck, her arms loosely wrapped around his shoulders. As we move steadily along, we pass acres of dried wetlands with few signs of any bird life. The absolute silence of the vast prairie is eerie; the sky is white and hot above us, and every now and then dust devils carrying dried brush chase behind us, creating clouds of sand and sediment as they pass. Since we're not drinking much to conserve our water supply, we suffer from a continual and nagging thirst.

As night approaches, we come to an inlet caused by a break in the riverbank. A few scruffy trees, their leaves dull and covered with sand, invade the small sandy space like the hair on the side of an old man's head. We walk into this pathetic group of trees and find a spot that looks soft and comfortable to lay down our sleeping bags. While we're sitting around, taking off our boots and socks and rubbing our feet, we hear a sound in the trees to our left. Rajeev puts his fingers to his lips as he reaches into his backpack for one of the laser weapons he has brought with us from the car. He motions for us to follow as he moves for cover, stealthily like a Native American scout, behind the thin, water-starved trunks.

A young girl, the same one we had seen riding the horse earlier on in the day, steps out into the small clearing where our things lie scattered, and looks around. A few minutes later, she is joined by a woman carrying a small boy who is about three years old. The child is quiet and holds onto his mother like a baby chimpanzee with his legs gripped tightly around her waist and his arms wrapped around her neck.

The girl appears to be carrying a basket covered with a cloth. She sets it down on the ground amongst our things then all three of them wait expectantly for us to emerge. Rajeev comes out first, motioning for us to follow. He steps forward and carefully lays his weapon down on the ground as he holds out both his hands in greeting. The mother comes forward, touches them briefly, and says, "Pleased to meet you. My name is Mary, and this is my daughter, Caro, and my son, Stefan. We've brought you some food—thought you'd appreciate it. My daughter saw you walking down the riverbed, heading our way."

"You live near here?" I ask.

"Yes," she says, waving a hand behind her and pointing to the West. "About a quarter of a mile that way."

"Same direction we're heading," I reply.

"Where're you going?" she asks.

We're silent for a moment then Peter jumps in and says, "Up beyond Lake McConaughy."

The woman looks intently at them and in particular at Rajeev and Inanna, but she doesn't say anything more.

Instead, she bends down, opens her basket and takes out some canned beans, and tomatoes then unwraps a small square of very white goat cheese.

As the little boy looks up at me from where Mary has placed him gently on the ground, his eyes like large dark holes, I lean over and squeeze her shoulder.

"How are you really making out?" I ask gently.

She's silent for a bit then says, "Okay. Getting hotter and hotter though, more storms, more dust. We got water in our well though," she adds, "don't know how - most of the others, they run dry now."

"You live here with your daughter and son?" I ask, still looking at her carefully.

"Yes, Ma'am I do, since my husband…." She is silent.

"I'm sorry," I say, as I squeeze her shoulder again.

Her daughter, who looks to be about twelve and has been watching us intently, says in a soft high voice, "They killed my Daddy."

Peter, Rajeev, Sarah and Inanna have been silently watching me as I speak to the woman. Now, Rajeev steps forward and puts his arms around the young girl and pulls her towards him in a brief embrace. He doesn't understand that it's unusual for a man as large as him to reach out and touch a child he doesn't know. Particularly a girl child.

When the woman sees him do this, she moves towards them protectively, but, looking calmly at her, I say with a smile, "It's alright, Mary, as long as you don't seriously piss him off, this man is one of the gentlest you'll ever meet."

She relaxes, turns towards me and utters, "Some men and women, they come to see what they can find. Hungry wolves they are. Reminds me of the few coyotes that somehow managed to survive, all skin and bones in their brown fur," and she pauses. "The others too."

"We were in the cellar hiding when they came. My husband had his gun, went out to stop them from taking our food. When the gun misfired, they jumped on him and knifed him up real good, nothing to be done," she adds quietly and sadly raising her hands slightly, "they ended up killing him."

Inanna is standing by, holding Sarah's hand while she also listens to the conversation. Unlike Rajeev, it's still hard for me to read what she is feeling at any given moment. Looking over at her now I wonder briefly how she will act at Ash Hollow. Will she be a loner, or will she participate willingly and become an integral part of our newly formed community?

Peter sits down and gently draws Sarah, who is like a soft, limp bundle onto his lap. Rajeev and Inanna then squat down on the ground where they're standing. Mary kneels and opens the canned food she had previously laid out in front of her basket, which she then spoons onto plates and passes around to the group. The tomatoes release a strong odor of summer and sweetness, it makes my eyes briefly well with tears because of the memories they evoke.

She cuts the cheese into slices and offers it as well. This simple food tastes delicious to me after eating only protein bars for several days. She has a jar of fresh water, which she also shares with us. We pass it around carefully to one another, each taking small sips. This water, unlike the recycled, over-chlorinated city water we've been used to drinking our whole lives, smells of hope and tastes of gritty stones, gravel, and soil.

"Cheers," Peter says, raising the glass bottle to his lips, taking a

72

long swig.

Once we've eaten, the woman packs up her basket.

"I'd better be heading home now. Good luck, folks, with your journey!"

Rajeev nods over at Peter and gets up off the ground, firmly declaring he will go back with them to make sure they arrive safely.

"No need," the woman says, shaking her head, but he insists, and taking the little boy onto his shoulders, begins to walk. Stefan rests his chin gratefully on top of Rajeev's head, and like a small, tired puppy, he will surely be asleep very soon.

As Peter and I get up and embrace the woman and her daughter before they head out, I softly and gratefully kiss the soft, warm cheek of the small, healthy boy. Once they are out of sight and only the flicker of the light that Mary had suddenly produced can be seen in the distance, I turn to Peter. Before I can speak, though, he puts up the palm of his hand to stop me. "No, absolutely, not. We'll talk to the others and if they say yes, we'll come back and get them when we pick up the van."

Inanna as usual remains silent throughout this exchange. I wonder again what she's thinking as I look over at her, and unexpectedly she nods back at me to show she understands where I'm coming from.

"You have too soft a heart, Sophie," she proclaims. Then she adds, "That's a good thing. I lost my heart when they killed my father and mother. No more crying, Inanna, I told myself, it doesn't do any good, human beings will never change. I would hear the other girls I lived with whose parents had also been killed in the bombing raids crying under their covers at night, and I would pinch myself hard on the arms until I had bruises. I would concentrate on the physical pain rather than the one burning me from the inside. In the morning, the blue marks on my skin reminded me to stay strong, to never care about anyone or anything the way I had once loved them."

"You're brave and very smart," I tell Inanna, "and when you meet other brave, smart people—men or women who makes you feel comfortable—you'll find your feelings again." I walk over and give her a hug. She kisses me softly and says, "You mean like you, Sophie?"

After running wildly back like a cheetah on the African Plains, joyfully experiencing the full bionic capabilities of his legs for the first time,

73

Rajeev returns to our campsite much sooner than we had expected.

As a result of our meeting with Mary, Stefan, and Caro, I spend most of the night awake as I worry what life will be like for those small pockets of human beings like them, who've casually been left outside on the surface, left to fend for themselves.

***

As usual, to maximize the daylight hours, we leave well before dawn the next morning. So far, we've covered fifty long, hot miles with another thirty-five more to go before we reach Ash Hollow. As a break from the monotonous walking along the dry, riverbed, we are relieved to reach the tip of Lake McConaughy stretching out in front of us like a long index finger. We realize with a great sense of relief that if we travel along the shorter, Southern shore, we should be at Ash Hollow by the following afternoon. The air around us smells like hot rocks and burning sand.

As we had suspected, the Lake, too, is completely dry; where it once undulated so magnificently in the sunlight and wind, there is only a vast, cracked, mudflat, across which a dry, hot breeze now blows. It's a scabrous reminder of what we've all destroyed. Fossil fuel was the drug we couldn't give up because it made us feel so good, and like most drug addicts, we didn't care about the damage it was doing to our other body, Earth, the one we needed to live on.

Despite the welcome break in our monotonous walk, the sight of the dried-up lake deeply depresses us, and we remain silent as we trudge along its bank. We pass the smaller Lake Ogallala on our right, and then we finally see Kingsley Dam with its outlet tower and morning glory spillway. The tower really is huge, reaching up like a concrete skyscraper about 185 feet into the air.

"A very unique water release and control flood system in its day," Peter tells us as we pass. I look across the massive passageway above me and can see the wooden gates, which resemble a row of rotting teeth.

Peter continues, "It's got a twenty-foot, steel-reinforced, concrete tube that runs underground to the power plant on the other side. Forty years ago, when all the gates were open, it released a mountain of water, 7,000 cubic feet per second at over 420 gallons a minute."

As if we were taking a permanent snapshot for posterity, before we move on again, we pause on Ogallala Beach to imagine a picture in our minds one last time of what the lake must have looked like. At that moment, I am acutely aware of the sharp rocks poking into my feet through the thin soles of my shoes. Nothing stirs around us except for a brittle wind rattling around on the stones and swooshing across the mud. The faint cry of a lone bird can be heard far off among the low, sand hills opposite us, which shimmer in the heat, sending up bursts of air that look like wavering glass.

We make it to Eagle Canyon Campground by that evening and are delighted to find abandoned wooden cabins nestled among the sand hills. Since they will provide some shelter from the unrelenting prairie wind that has bothered us all day, we decide we'll stay there for the night.

As we lay out our sleeping bags on the floor of one of the larger cabins, Rajeev says, "I've been thinking about what could correct the damage we saw today as we walked along, and it's unlikely it can be done fast. In the last one hundred or so years we've cancelled out the next ice age, and it's the ice ages that produced our rivers, lakes, and northern landscapes. Even though the next ice age isn't projected for 50,000 years or so, the carbon dioxide we've all emitted already will take more than 100,000 years to go away."

"Well," Peter says, "All I can say, Rajeev, in answer to that is, yes, it's a tragedy." Here he pauses and continues, "but you never know, perhaps evolution and adaptation of the species, as evidenced through you and Inanna, will enable us to survive on a far less hospitable planet than was originally designed for us."

Chapter 16
The Group

Peter, Sophie, Inanna, and Rajeev continue to talk quietly as they lay atop their sleeping bags in the wooden cabin, sheltered from the harsh elements outside. They finally fall asleep as the wind dies down to a soft moan. What they don't know, or even suspect, is that for the last few days a team of six SEALs has been following them silently and relentlessly and has also found its way to the Campground.

To avoid detection, the team landed its helicopter just outside of North Platte, beyond where the travelers would have been able to hear its approach. Since the SEALs know the group left the city with a supply of weapons, they have been careful in developing a plan to apprehend them.

As the six black shadows silently surround the cabin, two slip inside. Peter jerks awake just as one SEAL grabs him; the other grips Rajeev's arms, shoves them behind his back and handcuffs him. Once they are both secure, the first SEAL shouts out to his companions, "Main targets secure, no weapons in sight."

This is a signal for the remaining four SEALs to burst through the door and take hold of Sophie and Inanna. Fortunately, though, Inanna had awakened just as Peter and Rajeev were being handcuffed and had leapt out the window and had run at bionic speed towards the lake. Two of the SEALs had rapidly pursued her, but she had been so fast they had lost sight of her as she projected herself forward, like a compact, black, panther, into the dark void of the night. After searching for her, the two SEALs had given up and rejoined the group.

Now, the team leader radios his pilot and superiors at Mount Weather. "Three targets in custody; one female cyborg escaped. Will wait until it's light and find her."

He then handcuffs Sophie and Peter together, back-to-back, and allows Sarah, who is crying like a small, injured kitten, to lie on her mother's lap, where she sobs herself to sleep. Sophie and Peter don't communicate with each other so as not to inadvertently give away any of their plans. Like them, Rajeev is silent, too; all they can see of him are the whites of his eyes, staring at them across the dark cabin. They don't have to wait long, however, before daylight begins to break and they are roughly pulled to their feet and taken outside, with Sarah clinging firmly to her mother like a limpet to a rock.

"We need water," Peter says loudly.

Their captors give them each a drink. Sarah is allowed her own small bottle of water to carry with her. Two of the SEALs have already searched for Inanna, but they come back empty-handed. Any tracks she might have left behind initially were quickly blown away in the night by the unrelenting wind.

"Okay," the leader says, "let's get going. We'll have the pilot land the helicopter on top of the dam, and we'll meet him there."

They set out in a single file; one of the SEALs carrying Sarah on his back. He tries to reassure her that her mother is coming with them, and everything will be all right. Out of the corner of his eye, Peter can see that Rajeev has easily broken apart his handcuffs, so both his hands are now free.

He also observes Rajeev scanning the surrounding countryside for Inanna, whom he can tell by Rajeev's facial expression he has sensed is nearby. Peter surmises they will be communicating electronically with each other on how best to coordinate an attack.

Meanwhile Peter who has moved closer to Rajeev finally manages to catch his attention as he is communicating with Inanna. Rajeev nods his head imperceptibly at Peter towards the path they are following. As Peter picks up Rajeev's message, he tenses his muscles and prepares himself mentally for Inanna's approach, linking his fingers with Sophie's and pressing them to give her some warning to be ready for action.

One minute they are all walking quietly beside the lake then Rajeev suddenly leaps forward and breaks the necks of the two SEALs in front of him. At nearly the same time, he has ripped Sarah from the other SEAL's back and smashed open the man's chest. Meanwhile, Inanna has attacked the two SEALs in front of Sophie and Peter and broken both their legs and arms. What they haven't accounted for is that there is a sixth SEAL who is still walking a distance ahead.

After hearing the commotion made by the attack, the sixth SEAL turns back and begins firing his weapon at Peter, Sophie, and Inanna. One of the bullets inadvertently hits Peter in the chest, and another has entered Sophie's head. In a flash, Rajeev sees what is happening and has begun to run in the opposite direction holding Sarah against his chest, and zig zags wildly to avoid being struck by a bullet as he races to the edge of the lake. Traveling at over one hundred miles an hour on his bionic legs, Rajeev easily escapes without being wounded.

As he runs away, Inanna on the other hand quickly drops to her knees, as if in prayer, to help Sophie and Peter, but soon realizes they are already dead. Almost immediately she's up and running herself at top speed to avoid being captured. A bullet however has penetrated her thigh, and she is losing quite a lot of blood, causing her to become disoriented, and instead of travelling along the South side of the lake after Rajeev, she runs towards the Colorado border.

Once she's gone, and the last remaining SEAL acknowledges that three of his companions and two of his targets are dead, and two additional SEALs are badly injured, he radios the helicopter pilot. Giving him the exact coordinates of his position and instructing the pilot to land on the lakebed close to them.

As soon as the helicopter lands, the SEAL and pilot load all the dead bodies into the craft, throwing them aboard like sacks of rice. They also place the two injured men, who are moaning in pain, on the floor of the 'copter and administer shots of morphine. With everyone secured inside, the helicopter takes off in a cloud of dust, rapidly heading back to Mount Weather with its cargo.

In the meantime, Inanna, is miles away. Because of her leg wound and blood loss, she has finally been forced to stop and look for shelter. She is lucky enough to find a deserted farmhouse, climbs up the stairs and throws herself onto the dusty mattress left there by one of its past inhabitants. Knowing her skin and body parts have been created from protocells and her laser wound will, therefore, close and heal itself, she lies down to wait. As she rests quietly on the filthy mattress trying to sleep, she feels the pressure of tears forcing themselves from under her eyelids, and she pinches her arms tightly to induce pain. It is only through physical pain that she can stop the tears, brought on by the knowledge that Peter and Sophie, her two best friends, are dead. Finally, however, she is able to regain her balance as she electro magnetically readjusts herself to feel calm and peaceful.

Chapter 17
Sophie

As the bullet enters her head, Sophie has the strange sensation of physically leaving her body. She is then able to gaze down at Rajeev and Sarah, who are rushing like a tornado through the woods towards Ash Hollow. She is also able to observe Inanna, kneeling by her side and holding her briefly in her arms. She cannot see Peter, but somehow knows he is grievously wounded.

Sophie feels tremendous sadness at 'leaving' her daughter in this way, but she trusts Rajeev will take good care of her. Soon, she sees Inanna get up from the ground and run. Sophie realizes with satisfaction that, despite her wounds, Inanna is still able to move faster than a non-engineered human. She travels at eighty miles an hour, twenty miles faster than a cheetah. Sophie, however, sees sadly that Inanna is becoming disoriented and is running away from Ash Hollow, instead of towards it.

As Sophie continues to float above her body, gazing quite calmly at the landscape below and at Peter, she gradually becomes aware of a silent figure waiting beside her. Turning to see, she realizes immediately it must be her father, Raphael.

Raphael is exactly as her mother had described him—tall, fluid, sexually ambiguous, and full of a strange amber light. He smiles then embraces her, surrounding her with warmth and comfort. He asks silently if she is ready to leave, and despite the fear she feels at saying goodbye to everything she has known and loved, Sophie nods her head. She asks him if he knows where her mother, Mehr, is, and when he doesn't reply, she asks again, more urgently, if he will be taking her to meet Mehr. Rather than reply to her question, Raphael asks Sophie once more if she is ready to leave.

Reluctantly, Sophie gazes one last time at all she has consciously known on Earth—her husband, Peter, her child, Sarah, and many of her friends, who, miraculously, she can now see in front of her. In that moment, she realizes that time and place have ceased to have meaning for her. At last, however, she understands the "why". As she fully comprehends this "why," Sophie can completely release the ties to her current life, turn to her father and follow him along the generous trail of light he is leaving behind him.

Somehow Sophie knows Raphael will lead her out of her material reality on Earth to a 'place' she will not recognize or comprehend.

Chapter 18
Rajeev

Running at one hundred miles an hour across the stones that line the banks of Lake McConaughy and away from the SEALs, Rajeev is trying to absorb the jumble of thoughts coursing through his mind. He has registered clearly that Sophie and Peter have been shot, though he doesn't know whether they are dead or not. He also knows Inanna has been injured because he had seen fleetingly that she was bleeding.

Computing all this information in nanoseconds, Rajeev concludes that it is his primary job to get Sarah to safety because that is what her parents would have wanted first and foremost. He, therefore, activates his own internal GPS to guide them immediately where they need to go.

They arrive at Ash Hollow within twenty minutes of leaving Eagle Canyon. Using his enhanced hearing and sight, he makes completely sure he hasn't been followed before he enters the cave. Once inside, he decides to wait for a short interval of time. Taking Sarah onto his lap to distract her, Rajeev recounts a story he remembers from his childhood.

"Anjaneya was the little monkey son of the beautiful Anjana and the incarnation of the Great Heavenly Lord Shiva," he tells her, as he strokes her hair. "When Anjana leaves her son to return to heaven, her home, she tells him that if Anjaneya gets hungry, he must eat the sun," and as Rajeev says this, he gently bites Sarah's fingers causing her to laugh and pull them away. "So, Anjaneya flies up to the sun and scares the sun, telling him he wants to eat him all up."

"And then what happens?" Sarah whispers.

"So, there's a big fight amongst all the gods, the ones who want to protect Anjaneya, and the ones who want to protect the sun. To end the 'war,' the wind god, Vayu, leaves the Earth and there's no air left in the world for anyone to breathe anymore."

"Does he come back?" Sarah asks, horrified.

"Well, he does," Rajeev says, "because all the gods decide to forgive Anjaneya for trying to eat up the sun, and they make him the great warrior, Hanuman."

After he's finished telling her the story, Sarah looks at him like a frightened colt with her big eyes, and asks, "But Rajeev, even though

I liked your story very much, I still want to know where my Mom and Dad are?"

"They'll be coming along soon, I know it," Rajeev says, as he hugs her closely against him, desperately wanting to believe this as well. Rajeev is struggling enough with trying to absorb their loss himself without having to face a five-year-old child and tell her she'll never see her parents again. By avoiding telling her the truth, Rajeev is counting on the fact there are more qualified people in the Ash Hollow community who can do a better job at this than he can.

Rajeev is also anxious to see if he can contact Inanna, but not wanting either of them to be tracked by any DARPA devices, he decides to wait and see whether she turns up on her own. Since she can also program her own internal GPS to guide her to the cave, Rajeev assumes Inanna will follow him to Ash Hollow. He is certain when she arrives, she'll bring more detailed news of Peter and Sophie.

After an hour has passed, Rajeev picks up Sarah and moves towards the center of the large cave. As he walks across its dry, dusty interior, he hopes the people on the other side of the wall will recognize her and let them both in.

Noticing evidence of a dry riverbed, Rajeev concludes the cave must have contained a flowing spring at one point. As he scans the cave's history on his internal databases, he learns that at least four distinct cultures inhabited it in the past, including a prehistoric people. Not so long ago, the cave was an Apache base camp, used for hunting and food gathering.

Locating the electronic mechanisms that operate the doors at the back of the cave, Rajeev wonders whether he should break the security code and just let himself and Sarah in. However, when he spots the surveillance cameras installed around the cave, Rajeev decides instead to announce their arrival by waving at the cameras vigorously and pointing just as vigorously at Sarah.

In a matter of minutes, a microphone crackles loudly to his left and Rajeev hears a disembodied voice asking, "What has happened to Sophie and Peter?"

Rajeev quickly replies, "Sophie and Peter have been wounded and captured by a team of SEALs sent from DARPA to take them back to Mount Weather."

After a brief silence, the voice on the other end asks, "Are you Rajeev?"

Rajeev responds, "Yes, and as far as I know I haven't been followed."

Hearing no reply, Rajeev informs the disembodied voice, "the helicopter will most likely have already returned to Mount Weather with the injured and dead."

After a few moments, the voice requests, "please step back from the wall."

As he watches, the simulated rock wall slides open noiselessly, like a well-oiled spring, and two massive lead doors behind it slowly unlock and swing widely apart. Rajeev picks up Sarah and moves once again to the front of the cave. Through the hidden entrance in the rock wall, he can now plainly see a substantial metal staircase descending into the lighted space below. After he and Sarah have stood silently watching all of these intricate maneuvers, they are told they may enter.

Rajeev walks slowly and carefully through the open doors then down the stairs into the interior of the well-lit caves. Once he has descended about 500 feet, he sees a long metal bridge that connects to another set of metal stairs in the distance. He proceeds down the final set of stairs carrying Sarah on his left side and gripping the railing with his right hand. Rajeev's eyes rapidly adjust to the artificial light, which is quite adequate for him to see where he is going. As he reaches the bottom of the stairs, he is greeted by a small group of people, including a man who must surely be Tom, and his wife. When Tom reaches out and tries to take Sarah from Rajeev's arms, she clings tightly to Rajeev's neck like a tenacious spider to its web. Keeping Sarah securely against him with his left hand, Rajeev holds his right hand out to Tom and says, "Good to meet you, Tom."

"Welcome," Tom replies, as he returns the handshake and hugs Sarah's back.

"Let's get you some food and settle you both in. Then you'll have to tell us about your journey."

Rosie and Seed, Tom's two children, are among the group that has welcomed Rajeev and Sarah to the caves. Rosie, who is eight, goes up to Sarah and tugs at her leg. "I've got something to show you, Rah,' she says. "You're going to really like it."

Rajeev whispers to Sarah that perhaps she should go and find out what Rosie is talking about, and then, when she finds out what it is, come back and tell him, "Even though Rosie might say it's a secret," he adds mischievously, smiling at her.

Once she hears Rajeev's gentle tone and looks down and sees Rosie's toothy grin, Sarah slowly unhooks her arms from around Rajeev's neck and drops down onto her feet. She takes Rosie's hand and allows herself to be led away, with six-year-old Seed, as usual, traipsing stoically behind his determined sister.

Once they're out of sight, Tom turns to Rajeev and asks urgently, "Are they dead?"

"I don't know," Rajeev replies honestly. "I saw Sophie get struck in the head then Peter in the chest. I can conclude Sophie is most certainly dead, and as for Peter, I don't know. If he's alive, they'll take him back to Mount Weather and keep him there until he recovers sufficiently to be questioned. They are most interested in retrieving Inanna and myself," he adds, "since they were training us to develop, and perhaps even be, the next generation of information technology and of weaponry."

"And Inanna?" Tom asks him.

"Don't know," Rajeev says. "I haven't contacted her because I can't risk their satellites picking up my transmission. She will be thinking the same way. Perhaps I'll try tomorrow if she doesn't show up, but I would still be taking a chance that they will find us."

"Hopefully, one way or another then, we'll see her soon," Tom replies. "Now we need to get you fed, show you where you're going to be living, and give you a tour of our community."

As he continues to speak, Tom leads Rajeev to a small rowboat moored nearby. They both get in. Traveling deeper into the caves, Rajeev sees several large, glass, dome-shaped structures covering the underground lakes. Constructed to let in natural light, they are similar to the biospheres he knows exist on the surface of Mars and on the moon. Rajeev also observes shutters on the domes that can be opened to let in the outside air, as well as heat shields that can be lowered to protect the domes when it is too hot outside.

As they continue to traverse the lake, Tom speaks. "You probably already know there's still sufficient oxygen on the surface for us to breath even though we've broken down the ozone layer above, meaning we can still open up the shutters in the glass roofs."

"Quite," Rajeev responds calmly, as his mind whirls crazily like a pinwheel in the wind. Most of all, he wonders and worries about what has happened to Sophie and Peter and especially to Inanna.

Chapter 19
Inanna

Inanna wakes up to the sound of voices. As she slowly becomes aware of her surroundings, she realizes her wounds have not yet fully healed. She tries to get up, but the pain is so intense that she passes out.

When she comes 'to' again, Inanna senses she is not alone in the room; in fact, there are two heavily bearded men staring down at her. This time, when she attempts to stand, one of them pushes her back down roughly and tells her she needs to lie still because she is bleeding. After Inanna asks for some water, one of the men goes downstairs and comes back with a metal canteen that he puts to her lips, letting her drink for as long as she wants.

Once they have left the room, she lies there listening while they carry on a conversation with other men who are waiting downstairs. Arguing among themselves, their voices increase in volume. "Can't come … just leave her … you're right, she'll slow us down … she'll die if we leave her here … not our problem."

She passes out again, comes back to her senses as night is falling and sees the shadow of one of the men moving across the window. He's tall and comes over to sit on the bed next to her. He puts a water canteen into her hands, saying, "Water. Drink when you need, after we leave." As he passes the canteen to her, she notices his hands are rough and the skin of his palms feels like sandpaper. They are not like Peter's hands, which are soft and pliable.

"We have to move on, hunting for what we can find. Scarce these days," he stares at her intently and continues speaking. "Not seen wounds like those before. Look like burns, skin all black," he touches her leg where she's been wounded. "Don't know weapons that cause wounds like these. Where they come from?" he asks her curiously.

She gazes back at him and, sensing he probably doesn't like or support the current government, says, "Government after me, gone away now."

He spits on the floor and grinds it away with the heel of his boot.

"Bastards, left us out here to die."

She doesn't answer, just looks back at him.

"What you got, pretty one, that they want?" he suddenly asks softly, leaning forward and touching her cheek with his fingers, which are surprisingly pliant despite their roughness.

"Was the people I was with," she says quickly, immediately picking up on his dangerous feelings and intentions towards her, which are coming to her electro-magnetically through his fingers.

"I'd take you with us," he says, caressing her neck, "but them," he points his finger downstairs, "they don't want a wounded woman slowing us down. Now of course if you'd been okay, I'd have taken you with us anyway, but don't know if you'd have liked it much—hard going for a woman," he says smiling, caressing her neck again. As he does so, she feels her whole body contract away from his touch.

He bends down and kisses her, his stinking breath invading her mouth like a foul pesticide. She turns her head away.

"Not so fast, girlie," he says grabbing her cheeks, holding her face up against his, and squeezing it hard.

While he keeps his hands on her leg trying to kiss her again, one of his friends calls and he lets her face go, roughly. Abruptly rising from the bed and looking down at her, he says loudly, "you'll be dead anyway soon. Those wounds will fester and get infected. Not so desperate I need to screw a future corpse," he says as he turns away. "Got a wife back there," and he jerks his finger in some direction she can't see because it's already too dark.

After he leaves the room, she hears the men loudly exiting the house as they head out to hunt for whatever they can find that is left to eat on the dry, dust bowl of a prairie spreading around them for miles and miles.

She lies there without moving for what seems like hours, wondering what she'll do next and whether Rajeev made it safely to Ash Hollow Caves. She refuses to think about Sophie and Peter. She can't imagine why the brutish, bearded man left water for her when it was so scarce, but grudgingly concludes that human beings, despite their flaws, are sometimes capable of acts of kindness. She is comforted by the fact that in a few days, her wounds should close without any threat of infection. Although this knowledge doesn't help her deal with her present dilemma, she forces herself to concentrate on a plan to join Rajeev and Sarah at Ash Hollow as soon as she is stronger.

***

It's about three in the morning, the quietest time of night, and Hototo silently approaches the house. Nothing stirs, not even the dry wind, not even a piece of brush scoring the mud, like a witch scratching her broomstick on the tops of the trees. Hototo has come up from Deep Creek in the Flat Tops Wilderness area to hunt for whatever he can find still alive. He uses a bow and arrow in the old-fashioned way and moves as silently and quickly as a cloud slipping across the face of the moon. His movements are fluid like water as he checks the downstairs windows, peering into each one before scaling a drainpipe to reach the second-floor balcony.

Hototo is tall and thin and wears his black hair tied into a ponytail that reaches down into the small of his back. He pauses to flick his hair away from his shoulders to make sure it doesn't impede his pathway, as he carefully steps over the railing onto the balcony. Before he does so, he tests the floorboards to make sure they will sufficiently hold his weight. Once he's stepped onto the uneven surface, he gingerly inches past several boards that look particularly suspect then, so he can see more clearly inside, wipes the dust from the outside of the windowpanes with his sleeve. In addition to his naturally sharp vision, Hototo has also trained himself to see well in the dark for night hunting.

He's surprised to see the figure of a woman lying on a filthy mattress in the center of the room. He notices quite clearly that there is a wound on her leg. Standing quietly watching her, he wonders if he should reveal his presence to her. Since he needs to get the food he has found back home quickly, he can't really afford to be involved in anything that will slow him down significantly or redirect his attention from this important task; his community is waiting hungrily for meat.

He continues to watch her patiently from his position outside the window of her room for several minutes while she stirs and reaches for a canteen of water, drinking shakily from it. Once he is sure she has passed out and is soundly asleep again, he silently moves along the balcony to an open window in the next-door room, and eases his thin, snake-like, almost boneless body onto the floor. Without making any sound whatsoever, he creeps along a narrow corridor and through the door of her room until he reaches the bed. Inanna is still sleeping soundly there with her arm flung over her face and eyes.

With the rope he has been carrying, Hototo swiftly binds Inanna's hands and feet together. Awake and alert once more, she struggles to escape his grasp, but in her weakened state, she can't do anything but curse, which she does loudly and vociferously. Not responding to her, Hototo lifts Inanna and slings her over one of his shoulders as if she is a deer or a coyote he has just shot. Then he walks carefully down the stairs and out the door with her, travelling at a fast speed for several miles until he reaches his campsite.

Once there, Hototo drops Inanna onto a soft piece of fur that once belonged to a starving bear he had killed several years ago, and swiftly unties her arms and legs. Unbound, she hits him across the face weakly, after which Hototo steps back away out of her reach and quietly utters, "do that again and I'll keep your hands tied."

Hototo then gives Inanna some water to drink, looks carefully at her wounds and moves towards her with the intention to wash them, but she stops him, saying sharply, "Don't touch them," and again, more urgently, "don't touch them; my skin isn't like yours, it's self-healing."

Hototo tries to absorb what Inanna has just said and looks at her with an expression she can't read. Rising from his knees, he takes a piece of smoked meat, which he cuts into small pieces as if for a baby and stabs a piece with the edge of his hunting knife, using it like a fork. Looking down at her seriously he reaches forward and offers it to her asking, "You eat?"

She laughs and taking it from him says, "Sure I eat, and I piss, and I shit too."

Hototo doesn't smile but, unlike the brutish, bearded man in the cabin, his eyes are warm as they look straight back at her. In fact, she sees that the skin at the corners of his eyes is significantly lined from many years of laughter.

"I've got to move on tomorrow; I'm heading back down to where I live with what I've caught so far."

As he talks, she notices a dead coyote and a couple of foxes and rabbits hanging on a pole nearby. Since Hototo has already smoked them, the animal bodies look dry, brittle, and cadaverous. I wonder what they smell and taste like she thinks as she observes them swaying in the slight wind.

"Where do you live?" Inanna asks.

"Down to Deep Creek, in the caves there. We've set up a community so when the heat gets worse, we'll be somewhere sheltered."

"What will you do for food when you can't hunt?"

"We'll hunt as long as we can and gather what we can."

"How many are you?" she asks.

"About 200, more or less."

After this exchange they are both silent as Inanna dozes on and off. Once dawn begins to break however and since the early mornings are chilly, Hototo builds a fire and sits quietly by it for a while staring intently into the glowing embers as the flames burn down. Finally, he gets up and walks towards two sorry-looking, scraggly, birch trees. After cutting the trunks of the trees into two, long poles, Hototo picks up Inanna, moves her onto the bare dirt and lashes the bearskin onto the poles, creating a hammock of sorts.

"Got to keep moving," he says. "I'll take you with me; can't leave you here."

"Yes, you can, if you also leave me with food and water," Inanna replies. "In about a week, I'll heal and then I need to head North."

Hototo is silent for a bit then shakes his head adamantly. "I'm not leaving you here. It'll take us four weeks to get to my home. I'll make a bargain with you; as soon as you heal properly, you can head North again as soon as you like."

Inanna thinks about his proposition for several minutes and finally nods her head in agreement. Ultimately, she knows she needs water and food while she is healing. Although they will be traveling a great distance away from her own intended destination, she's really not at all concerned about the detour. Once she has healed, Inanna knows full well her bionic legs can carry her to Ash Hollow in a day by running at one hundred miles per hour.

They head out just after daybreak, making their way across the Pawnee National Grassland into the Roosevelt Forest.

Laying on the bearskin that Hototo drags along behind him with his other belongings, Inanna knows she normally possesses five times his strength and is frustrated by her current inability to move on her own. In less than a week, though, she figures she should be strong enough to start heading back to Ash Hollow Caves.

"What's your name?" she abruptly calls out to Hototo as he trudges along, suddenly realizing he hasn't told her.

"Hototo," he replies, glancing back. What kind of name is that, she wonders, as she bumps along behind him, like an animal in a sack. She searches her databases as she lies there to see if she can find out what the derivation of his name might be.

She realizes as she scans her data that while she and Rajeev have been programmed for satellite communication between each other, she cannot risk communicating with him in case her transmission is picked up. It had been Peter's ongoing intention to enable **quantum teleportation** of information between them so they could ultimately communicate privately over long distances without using satellites, but Peter had not yet figured out how to do this yet.

What Inanna does already possess, however, is **parabolic hearing** and **network sonar sensors** that allow her to map out their journey's visual field. She is also able to monitor her cardio flow and internal **whole body navigational grid**, to determine whether she is healing well and ensure her solar protected skin is renewing its **tone-textured changeability**.

As she lies there looking up at the grey sky caused by the effects of the chemtrail spraying, she maps out the course in her head that Hototo is taking and sees he is probably heading towards Dotsero in the Rocky Mountains. Suddenly however with the aid of her parabolic hearing she recognizes the distant sounds of people ahead of them, and she recognizes the voice of the man who made advances to her in the house the day before.

"There are bad people about five miles ahead of us," she warns Hototo. "I think they're the men that were in the house with me last night."

He glances back at her briefly and asks, "How do you know that?"

She doesn't answer immediately, but finally says, "Perhaps I'm dreaming them."

Her answer appears to satisfy him as he turns back to follow the path he is taking. Because of his heavy load, he rests frequently to drink from his water jar and lift the poles off of his blistered shoulders, which have given them the appearance of a bad sunburn.

After they stop in the late afternoon and make camp, they eat dried meat of some kind and a handful of roots Hototo pulls from the ground. Although he doesn't tell her what they are when he hands them to her, she finds they seem to give her some energy. She holds one out to him and says, "What are these?"

"Wild ginseng root."

Because Hototo doesn't seem to enjoy idle chat and Inanna is just as happy not to have to explain herself, they don't converse much that night. Hototo deliberately doesn't question her anymore about her wounds and why they appear to be healing on their own.

When she looks at her leg now, Inanna can see clearly that the two, deep burns are almost closed, and the protocells from which her skin is made are in the process of reconstructing it and removing any trace of scars. In fact, she is sure that by tomorrow she'll be able to walk without any difficulty; admittedly, not as fast as she normally would, but she will be able to keep pace easily with Hototo. As she lies on the ground, she decides she'll travel with him for a few more days until she feels completely healed.

When Inanna wakes up the next day just before the sun rises, before he is awake, she stands and tests her legs, bending and stretching her body. As she spreads her arms and legs wide with her back to Hototo, she is unaware he's been watching her carefully from his position beside the ashes of the previous night's fire. Eventually after a few minutes, he asks, "sure you should be doing that?"

She turns and smiles over at him. "I'm sure."

Hototo gets up and bends down on one knee in front of her leg, taking it gently in both his hands. She is surprised at how soft his palms are, given the fact that, like the other man who touched her leg, he hunts and traps and fishes for a living. He moves her knee up and down then to the side, and finally traces with his forefinger the faintest scar where the laser had entered her skin. He can see the wounds have closed completely and will leave no marks. Finally, he holds her leg up to the light and places his palm on the skin of her inner thigh, which he feels carefully while he bends his head to look closely at the texture of her skin. As he lets her leg drop and looks up at her quizzically, he grunts, "Don't know another woman with skin that feels or looks like yours," he says.

"And how does it feel?" she asks, looking down at him where he is still kneeling on the ground.

"Different," he says quietly, looking up at her, "just different."

Hototo gets up after this exchange and walks over to the two poles, wordlessly lifts them up and unties the bearskin on which she's been sleeping. He bundles up the skin then folds and re-ties it with string. He picks up the bags of meat, tosses her a few pieces, gives her his water flask from which she drinks, grabs his bow and arrows and flings them over his shoulder. He's already carrying his hunting knife, which is attached securely to a strap at the top of his trousers.

91

Inanna walks over to where he's getting ready to leave and reaches over, taking the bearskin from him and putting it on her own shoulders. As she adjusts the weight to make it more comfortable to carry, he watches her carefully for a minute, then he shrugs and turns around and starts to move ahead of her through the trees. From time to time, she checks their course internally on her data bases, and thinks either he has a good memory or an innately good sense of direction, for he is taking them exactly where he has told her he wants to go without using a compass.

Chapter 20
Alistair

On the fourth day after Sophie and Peter have left Washington, D.C., Alistair is called into the offices of the secret police. General Carter is there as well as two senior members of the force, who invite him to be seated. After a brief silence, during which everyone stares at the desk in front of them, General Carter leans across and asks, "have you heard from Sophie and Peter yet?"

Alistair looks up at him and says unequivocally, "no, I'm not in touch with them. I told you I consider both to be traitors. We needed those trans-humans they took to complete our deep space programs."

"Not just that, Alistair," the General replies quickly. "As you already know by now, they also caused irreparable damage to our weather modification program and some of our important defense programs."

There is a thoughtful silence as one of the two senior police officers taps his pencil repeatedly on the table and stares at Alistair intently. While Alistair meets the officer's gaze, he is calmed by the repetitive sound the pencil makes and to distract himself further, tries to insert a particular beat into its disparate rhythm.

Finally, after what seems like a long time, the General moves away from his desk, leans back in his chair, as if he was a well-fed gorilla resting after a meal, and folds his hands over his extensive belly. As he watches him do so, the tall, slender Alistair wonders idly whether gravity will come into play and the General will fall onto his back like an obsolete, imploding building.

While the silence extends, Alistair hears the clock on the wall behind the desk ticking loudly and feels blood rushing to his head. Because his ears are blocked, he wonders whether he'll be able to hear anything when they finally do speak to him. He feels as if he will pass out at any minute.

Finally, after what seems like hours, the General unclasps his hands and leans forward. "We've got them," he says. "We caught them in Nebraska. Unfortunately, Sophie was killed as well as three of our men. The two trans-humans escaped, and we don't know where they are, since our electronic surveillance was effectively blocked, and we were unable to track them by satellite or on radar. However, we are continuing to search the area around Ash Hollow. Tom has let us know categorically that they never made it to the Ogallala settlement. Rajeev dropped Sarah off at the entrance then left. Our thoughts are that they could be anywhere in the country given the speed at which they move. It will take us a few weeks or even months to locate them."

As the General talks, Alistair feels a lump form in his throat the size of a small golf ball. He sternly wills himself to remain outwardly calm about Sophie's death, and to show an appropriate degree of concern about his three fallen comrades and the escape of Inanna and Rajeev.

"Sorry to hear it, Sir," he says as his airways finally clear.

"And Peter?" he asks the General.

"We have Peter," the General responds. "He's in a maximum-security ward and still unconscious. We need you, as one of his colleagues and friends, to talk to him so he has some reason to live. It's essential we access the information he carries regarding the creation of the trans-humans."

"I'd be happy to do that, Sir," Alistair replies, and then adds for emphasis, "glad to be of service to my country, Sir."

Alistair has barely had a chance to absorb this information before the two secret police officers get up from the table and motion for him to follow them. They ride an elevator down two floors. Alistair is then taken through two metal security doors into a room in which there is a single hospital bed. He sees Peter lying there attached to a heart monitor, which beeps steadily, indicating he's still alive. A chair is placed next to Peter's bed and the two officers motion for Alistair to sit in it. They order Alistair to take Peter's hand, so Peter knows someone is there. Alistair does as he is told, lowering himself heavily into the chair next to his friend who has a major chest wound and doesn't look at all well.

"When he was hit in the chest, one of his lungs deflated. He's also experienced damage to his tracheo-bronchial system, his esophagus, diaphragm, thoracic blood vessels and thoracic duct. However, the heart and the mediastinal structures appear to be intact," one of the officers says. "With the right care, we're hopeful he'll eventually recover."

While the officer is speaking, Alistair gazes down at his friend with tremendous compassion, wishing both he and Sophie had made it safely to Ogallala.

94

He talks to Peter gently while sitting there under the watchful eyes of the police officers, telling him his daughter, Sarah, is safe. The officers suggest he leave after he's spoken to Peter intermittently for a couple of hours, but that he should tell Peter he will be back the next day.

That night after Styx had gone to bed, Alistair and Robyn talk quietly in the bathroom with the shower turned on.

"Do you think he'll recover?" Robyn asks.

"I'm not sure; his wounds are pretty bad. He might not want too either."

"I feel terrible about Sophie. What do you think they've done with her body?" Robyn asks.

"Probably disposed of it already. I can't show too much interest in her."

"No news of your brother or my sister, I suppose?"

"No news is always a good sign, and, in this case, I suspect their departure has gone undetected," Alistair replies seriously. "If they happen to catch them, however, then our asses will be in a sling. I'm sure you know that."

Robyn nods then reaches out to hug him.

"I hope they make it," she says. "Selfish as that may sound, in light of what's happened to Sophie and Peter."

"Me too," he says, burying his face into her fragrant hair, holding onto her tightly, as if she's a life vest that has been thrown to him as he drowns.

Chapter 21
Rajeev

Rajeev has been at the Ogallala Aquifer settlement for a few weeks, orienting himself to life there and taking care of Sarah. No one has yet told Sarah her mother is dead, and her father is most likely as well. Noemi and Tom are still maintaining the lie that Sophie and Peter will be joining them soon.

Finally, Rajeev takes Tom and Noemi aside and suggests they tell Sarah what has really happened. Agreeing immediately, Tom and Noemi sit down with Rajeev to discuss how to present this information to her.

Since Sarah has not been exposed to any particular religious teachings, Tom, Noemi, and Rajeev settle upon what they consider to be the best way to frame her parents' death. Using elements of natural science and mythology, as well as the concept of *Karma* that Rajeev proposes, Tom and Noemi decide to tell Sarah that Peter and Sophie have in effect gone back to being 'stars'.

Rajeev adds he will show Sarah a picture of the endless knot, which according to his Hindu religion, symbolizes continuous life. Emphasizing that Sarah and Peter were very good human beings whose work has helped the Earth and the many people on it.

While they are chatting, Rajeev broaches the subject of retrieving the broken-down, abandoned van. He tells Tom and Noemi about their encounter with the family on the trail. "When we were walking, we met three people—a woman, a twelve-year-old girl and a small boy. I would very much like to bring them here. Peter had agreed that, once we arrived, he would ask you himself whether this would be possible."

Tom considers the request for a few moments then responds, "We follow an Ubuntu society here, as you know, Rajeev, and have a governing body to which we elect members every year. Since I can't make this decision unilaterally, I'll put your request to them today and see what they have to say."

Rajeev nods his head. "If they're left out there, there's no way they'll be able to make it. If it helps, I would agree to take care of them, make them part of my family with Inanna and Sarah."

Tom looks at him for a minute. "Are you saying you plan on marrying Inanna?"

Rajeev is silent for a moment then answers, "I don't know if she'll marry me and I haven't thought that far ahead. I mean, I'll be like an uncle, a father, a brother, something of that kind to the family. I haven't thought about marriage for myself, not like Inanna. She wants to create a child," he pauses then continues thoughtfully, "But now as I reflect more carefully about what she means, I believe she wants to do this on her own without a male partner. She has a powerful will and is learning rapidly to control her own internal body functions, including the formation of an embryo. *I want to create a new kind of human being, one that is strong like me'* she has often told me, whenever we talk about it."

Tom looks surprised. Noemi smiles, "Oh, so she wants to bud. She wants to create a clone, develop a tiny, individual Inanna, or even perhaps two daughter cells which she'll produce inside one of her own cells," she informs them.

"Sounds challenging," Tom replies, laughing.

Rajeev computes the information Noemi has shared with them quickly then says, "You're talking about asexual reproduction?"

"Yes,' Noemi replies.

As Rajeev thinks about Inanna, he feels a great torrent of sadness spread over him. He notices two tears have forced their way out of his eyes and are trickling unimpeded down his cheeks and onto his chin. Without any regret at having shown his emotions so openly, Rajeev wipes the tears away.

When Tom see Rajeev's tears, he gets up and embraces him, "my dear young man, you must consider us your family now," he tells him softly.

On hearing these words, Noemi also rises and holds them both within the wide grasp of her two broad arms, the arms of a six-foot-two woman who lifts very heavy objects in the process of completing her daily work.

Later that day, Tom informs Rajeev that all the members who currently live in their community have agreed to accept the woman and her two children. He does not mention, however, that their main consideration when they made this decision was Rajeev's mental health, and how it might affect his behavior in the future if they had refused.

Tom and Rajeev decide later that evening that Rajeev will scope out the disabled van on foot early the next morning. He will do this to ensure the area is cleared of SEALs. Tom wants Rajeev to use his electronic equipment, laser eyes, supersonic hearing, and running speed for surveillance and help the group avoid detection when they go to retrieve the van. Tom also suggests that Rajeev stop at the woman's house on his way, to make absolutely sure she and her family do indeed want to live at the Ogallala settlement.

***

Once Rajeev leaves the caves the next day, he runs smoothly at almost top speed across the prairie and around the side of Lake McConaughy. He stops briefly by the Eagle Canyon cabins to check them out. During his inspection, he finds electronic surveillance equipment that had been placed there recently, showing evidence the government is still actively searching in the area.

It doesn't take much time to quickly locate and wipe it clean to make sure he's not been visually recorded. Once he's satisfied everything is clear and there are no SEALs currently in the vicinity, he travels along the dry, sandy, riverbed, hugging its banks tightly to avoid anyone seeing him. Even with electronic equipment or the unvarnished human eye, tracking him would be difficult since he's travelling so fast. For him however this is merely a pleasant jog; in an emergency he can raise his speed to 120 mph without much effort.

Reaching Mary's house, Rajeev slows down to a walk, like a car braking hard. He opens the garden gate and calls out that it's Rajeev, the man who took them home from the riverbank a few days ago.

Noting an eerie silence surrounding the house, Rajeev wonders if Mary and her children are still there. After a few minutes, however, she finally comes to the door. She holds the little boy, Stefan, on her hip, and smiles broadly delighted to see him again. Struggling to get out of his mother's arms, Stefan runs towards Rajeev once he is let loose, and grabs tightly onto his legs. Rajeev eventually manages to unlock the little boy's fingers gripping his calves like a crab's pincers, lift him high over his head and then turn him upside down. He swings Stefan wildly from side to side while the boy laughs loudly and tries ineffectively to grab hold of Rajeev's ankles as he flies past them. Finally, Rajeev sets him down gently on the ground and bends down to wipe some dirt off the child's face with the corner of his shirt.

By this time, Caro has come to the door and looks at Rajeev with her wide, violet- blue eyes as she says, "where'd you come from?"

98

"Oh, just passing and thought I'd stop by for a coffee," he replies.

"Smart ass," she says smiling shyly.

He walks over and takes her hand in his and shakes it formally.

"Nice to see you again too," he says.

After this brief exchange, they go inside the house and all sit together at the kitchen table and Mary informs him, "no coffee, but I have a little prairie bush tea?"

"Perfect," says Rajeev. "In my home in India, we used bush tea to cure colds—and it worked."

As she boils the water and crumbles some dry leaves into it, Rajeev asks Mary whether she's seen anyone else come by within the past day or two. After pausing a moment, she says she has not, but a few days before this one they had heard several helicopters land and take off over by the Lake.

After he hears about this, Rajeev doesn't waste time or beat around the bush, and asks Mary if she and the kids would like to come to live with him in an underground settlement of families, just like them, near Lake McConaughy at Ash Hollow.

The information about the settlement doesn't seem to surprise Mary. She tells Rajeev her husband and she had observed the comings and goings at Ash Hollow for many years after the Park was closed. They'd also seen helicopters land there regularly. They'd both concluded the government was responsible for the activity and so, kept away, since neither trusted anything the government did or said anymore.

Mary then becomes silent as she sits there and considers Rajeev's offer. Her daughter eventually comes over to rest on her lap and threads her arms around her neck.

"I want to go, Mom," she tells her. "You know we don't stand a chance out here on our own, and it's only a matter of time before," she pauses, "one or all of us gets sick or are killed."

After Caro has finished speaking, her mother looks over at Rajeev as she informs him, "we've got a few neighbors, folks that left the towns and cities and came to live around here where they knew they could dig wells. We make up a community of sorts. They'll be wondering where we've gone."

"You absolutely cannot tell them or even say goodbye," Rajeev says fiercely, and then adds, "we have something the government wants, and they're not going to give up until they find it."

"That wouldn't be you, would it?" Caro asks, looking over at him curiously. "I saw you running out there today from the upstairs windows. I also tracked you and the others when you stopped to rest for the night at those cabins." She pauses before she adds "I heard the helicopters landing as I was riding Buddy back home once it got dark."

Rajeev doesn't answer, but instead, gets up and takes her hand.

"You have to trust me, Caro. Nothing these days is simple; nothing is easy to understand. If you come with me, I promise I'll explain it all to you."

While Rajeev is speaking to her daughter, Mary looks up at him and puts her hand on his arm in a gesture of friendship. Observing Mary closely for the first time, Rajeev estimates she is about forty years old, older than he had originally thought, and there are many fine, worry lines etched around her blue eyes. Now, as he turns and looks down at Caro, he realizes that she, too, may be older as well. However, from skin cells left on his arm and hands, his internal databases soon do their magic and send him a message that Mary is, in fact, thirty-nine years old and Caro is thirteen and a half.

"Okay," Mary eventually says. "We'll come with you, but we have to take the horse and the goat."

"Hadn't thought about that," Rajeev replies. "There aren't any animals where we're going, and I'll have to ask Tom if you can bring them."

Caro and Mary regard him silently. Rajeev can tell they've become hesitant about accompanying him without his assurances they can take their animals with them. Thinking quickly, Rajeev says he doesn't perceive any problem with that. He knows however as he speaks that the goat will be an easy sell to Tom since it will eat just about anything and might actually be a source of entertainment for the kids as a communal pet. However, he is pretty sure the horse will turn out to be problematic since it will need to be fed and stabled.

"Okay, don't worry, I'll take care of it," he says quickly. "I'm going to leave now so I can check out the condition of the van we left outside of North Platte. If it's still there and if it's still salvageable, I'll return later with my friend, Tom, to pick it up." Here he pauses before he adds, looking down at her, "And I'll be back to get you as well."

While Rajeev is speaking, he reaches out instinctively and lays his hand comfortingly on Mary's shoulder. He asks her to start packing up their things immediately, so they'll be ready to leave as soon as he returns.

"What about all the canned and dried goods we've stockpiled—should we take those with us?" Mary asks.

"I'll have to ask Tom's wife, Noemi," he says, "and perhaps she'll come back here with me so she can check them out."

"How many are there with you at the settlement?" Mary asks.

"About 200 of us —Caro and Stefan will have a nice group of kids to play with."

"I'm not a kid," Caro says under her breath.

"And by the way Caro you need to know something about me," Rajeev tells her smiling, "besides running very fast, I have supersonic hearing and anything you say, or even think, I'll know about."

She sticks her tongue out at him. He laughs, saying, "as your new family member I feel you deserve this." He buries his fist gently in her head, in response to which she punches his arm, then immediately recoils as she realizes how hard and inflexible the muscles are.

Shortly after having had this exchange with Mary and Caro, Rajeev leaves the house to return to the van, The family watches him leave through the side windows, and after he has turned and waved goodbye at them from the gate, he immediately seems to disappear from their sight, as if he's a piece of paper caught up in a violent wind.

A short while later he approaches the shed by the abandoned farmhouse where they had left the van, and he sees with relief it's still there. Although he has no doubt the SEALs will return to the site, he's surprised they didn't find it already. If they had, they could have searched it for clues that might lead to information about his and Inanna's whereabouts.

Rajeev opens the doors and mentally tallies what is inside—a sleeping bag, some food and water, and all their suitcases. As Rajeev catches sight of one of Sophie's sweaters, he feels a pain in his chest, causing him to stop for a moment to catch his breath.

Continuing with his search, Rajeev finds the remaining laser weapons Peter had brought with him. They had deliberately not taken any other electronic equipment except Peter and Sophie's communication devices. Rajeev assumes these were probably in their pockets when they were shot. However, when Rajeev searches the van's glove compartment, he discovers both devices and immediately puts them into his coat. Breathing a sigh of relief, Rajeev is grateful they had not gotten into the hands of the government, since the person who had sent Sophie a message just as they were beginning their journey, would surely have been implicated in their escape once it was discovered.

Rajeev easily makes it back to the Caves just after midday. Once back there, Rajeev locates Tom and gives him the communication devices and all the laser guns, including two he had found at the campground. Then, he informs Tom that Mary, Caro, and Stefan have agreed to join the Ash Hollow community. As he turns to go to locate Sarah, who is being cared for by Noemi, Seed and Rosie, he says casually, "Oh, two more residents are coming with them—a goat and a horse."

Tom immediately places a hand on Rajeev's arm to detain him and says, "you probably don't know, but we have a no-animal policy here."

"Well, animals have good bacteria and prevent children from getting asthma when they get older," Rajeev says quickly, looking away.

Tom replies with resignation, "Okay, I'll ask the others what they think. The goat is no problem, but the horse—where in god's name are we going to put it?"

"I've already thought of that," Rajeev says. "It can live alongside the cars and vans, and I can create some kind of vegetarian protocell food for it. Inanna has the formulas. They're the same ones they're using on *Persephone*."

"And what if something has happened to Inanna?" Tom asks.

"Well, I'll try to figure something out, and if not, we'll have to get rid of it— later on."

Tom is silent, then says, "Okay, I'll make your case saying that it'll be good for the kids and that they'll love them. Also, I'll remind them that we needn't fear reproduction, and so their stay with us will be limited."

"Well as an added benefit, I could work on cloning both of them—oh and creating protocell goat and horse meat for us too. Yummy!" Rajeev says smiling back at Tom.

Tom slaps him on the shoulder and replies, "It's good to have you here, Rajeev. I wish I could still muster your optimism and humor. I do know, however, that I can't wait to see what your amazing mind will produce in the future."

102

Chapter 22
Retrieval

Later that day, Rajeev, Tom and Noemi head out in one of the settlement vans. Noticing an unknown car parked on the side of the road as they exit the park, Tom stops the van. He walks over and points a laser gun at the front window. Not seeing anyone inside, Tom turns to go back towards the van, when a voice directly behind him asks, "are you Tom?"

As he turns around, Tom swings the gun towards the sound of the voice and sees a tall, black man step out from behind some large, grey boulders at the side of the road.

"Yes," Tom says.

The man stops a few yards in front of Tom and signals for three other people to step forward from behind the boulders.

"I'm - well - I'm Neil, the brother of one of Peter's colleagues at work. My brother, Alistair, worked with both Peter and Sophie at DARPA. He's still with DARPA now but the government just evacuated him to Weather City with some other scientists. He's running the *Persephone* mission."

He holds out a letter to Tom and says, "Peter gave Alistair this letter inviting us to come to Ash Hollow and join your community."

Tom reaches for the letter as Rajeev and Noemi get out of the van to join them. Before reading it, he turns to Rajeev and asks, "did you know anything about this deal of Peter's?"

"Not exactly. But I do know Alistair and Robyn were colleagues of Peter and Sophie. I also suspect it might have been Alistair who messaged Sophie at great risk to himself, warning her we were being followed. Alistair's in the U.S. Military—a two-star general. I was working with his boss, General Carter, among a host of others, on creating the next generation of weapons."

Tom reads the letter out loud. *"Neil, because Alistair and Robyn have been such good colleagues of ours, and because we know how heavily it weighs on them to leave you without a chance for survival during the uncertain days ahead, I want to encourage you to head to Ash Hollow Park in Nebraska. Wait outside the park until you see people emerging, which they will do from time to time. Please approach them and ask to speak with me. I cannot guarantee you will be accepted into this community, but I will do my very best to persuade them to take you in.*

Sophie and I will consider you to be a part of our family when and if that happens. I assure you your best chance to survive lies in joining one or another of the independent underground communities currently forming in the United States and around the world."

Tom looks carefully at the group standing silently in front of him waiting for his response. After a few seconds, he lays down his gun, steps forward, and holds his hand out to shake Neil's hand.

"Since I can see this is what Sophie and Peter wanted, I'll make a strong case to the Council to take you in. In fact, it will help us having someone like your brother Alistair as a contact inside Mount Weather. In good time, I'll reach out to him. I imagine Peter intended him to be a private source of information to me. I'm going to have to ask you to wait for a few more hours until we come back from retrieving a van that has broken down. Hopefully you have enough food and water to be comfortable?"

"We do," Neil replies, and embraces his wife, then introduces her, his sister-in-law, and Julienne his eight-year-old son to the others.

After saying their temporary farewells, Rajeev, Noemi, and Tom leave. Once they've reclaimed the disabled van, they stop at Mary's house, as planned, to transport the family back to the settlement. Instead of traveling with the others, Caro rides Buddy all the way back to Ash Hollow, arriving sometime after dark. While Rajeev feels somewhat uncertain about Caro going to the caves on her own, he is reassured by the fact she has been roaming alone and safely all over the prairie since she was very young.

After loading the goat and some canned goods into the back of the van where the goat creates quite a ruckus, Tom, Noemi, Rajeev, Mary, and Stefan eventually leave the farmhouse. In the end, Mary is forced to ride with the goat to keep her calm, while Stefan sits uneasily in the front, on Noemi's lap.

Tom has decided Buddy will temporarily be housed with the cars and other vehicles as Rajeev had proposed. After that, Caro will be allowed to ride the horse outside for as long as she can. When this is no longer possible, a decision will have to be made as to what to do with him. They'll be able to easily create a nice habitat for the goat on one of the floating parks, so she will come to the caves below immediately. Creamie is a sweet-tempered animal and will be an excellent community pet.

Privately, Rajeev has already decided that once Inanna arrives and he's had a chance to study the advanced protocell technology being used on *Persephone*, they will work together in creating some goat meat protocells, using muscle tissue harvested painlessly from Creamie and a protein that will produce tissue growth. Taking these harvested *'satellite cells,'* they will first check them for genetic stability, place them in a warm broth of synthetic nutrients then apply a jolt of electricity so the cells contract spontaneously. Finally, they'll make synthetic fat and grow the meat on biodegradable scaffolding, feeding it nutrients through artificial nanotube veins.

Rajeev knows once the process in the bioreactor has begun, he will be ensuring the settlement will be able to continue goat meat production indefinitely. Since they will need to use a natural preservative like cochineal to protect the growing meat from yeast and fungus, Rajeev will have to consult with Noemi about locating a source for the preservative. As a result of the goat meat protocell-producing process, Creamie will provide a unique legacy to the settlement and, in a sense, 'live forever.' Rajeev assumes that eventually they'll try to duplicate the same process with some of Buddy's muscle tissue.

Although Rajeev knows the settlement was originally planning to use plant-based protocells only, he believes he'll be able to persuade them to try meat-based protocells. As an added advantage, the meat-based protocell technology is the same process they will need to use in the future to regenerate human organs.

Rajeev has learned from Sophie that during the early years of the Twenty-First Century, human beings slaughtered the equivalent of 1600 mammals and birds every second for food consumption—a number that didn't even include fish or crustaceans. In addition, animal livestock occupied approximately 30% of the Earth's usable surface, compared with only 4% devoted annually to crop growth. Sophie also explained to Rajeev that meat production has created a large percentage of the world's global CO_2 and methane gas emissions. In fact, half of the impact of global climate change attributed to human activities has been correlated to meat consumption.

Because the movement for ethically reared, free-range animals has become large enough for corporations to invest in its production, it became common in developed countries for meat to be grown artificially. As a result, Rajeev has been able to eat and enjoy beef again for the past few years because it hasn't involved the killing of cows.

During the early development phase of artificial meat

production, the global meat industry viciously fought against the creation of protocell meat by lobbying to remove the subsidies that would have supported research and development at an affordable cost. This stonewalling practice was very similar to the way the gas and oil industry tried to deter, for as long as possible, the development of alternative energy sources.

As he anticipates eating Creamie's protocell meat sometime soon, Rajeev acknowledges that "cooked meat hunger," or the craving for red meat, has been a basic component of the human diet since the cavemen roamed the Earth. In fact, this 'addiction' is the contributing factor to the development of very large brains in human beings and has made it so difficult for the vegetarian movement to gain overall acceptance. Now, with the development of protocell meat, Rajeev is convinced that even vegetarians at Ash Hollow can eat the product without violating their core beliefs.

Chapter 23
Inanna and Hototo

Inanna and Hototo are making their way across Colorado towards Steamboat Springs. They will eventually climb up into the Rockies then descend into Hototo's Deep Creek settlement. Since Inanna is almost fully recovered and they both keep themselves well hydrated, they can cover twenty-five miles per day by running at a semi-jog.

On their first day out together, and as Inanna had predicted, they reach and pass the hunters, one of whom had given her the unwanted kiss a few days before. Inanna confesses to Hototo that she really wants to stop and place the tip of her knife on the throat of this man. In fact, she would love to place it in such a way that it brushes menacingly, yet gently, against the soft skin covering his carotid artery. However, she also remembers he had left her a canteen of water and that almost cancels her desire to teach him a painful and humiliating lesson. As they slip by the men, giving them a wide berth, Inanna is amazed at how silently and quickly Hototo, an unaltered human, can move. She imagines for a minute what he would be like if given the same bionic advantages she has.

That first night, they make camp well after dark. They don't converse much, nor build a fire in case the hunters are nearby. On the second night, though, they stop just beyond Fort Collins, near Rocky Mountain State Park, picking a comfortable spot where they can safely light a fire and remain for several hours. Because they will cross the mountains in the morning and head diagonally down the Rockies towards Dotsero through extremely difficult and steep terrain, Hototo knows they will need to rest well.

As they sit by the fire enjoying its light and heat, Hototo turns to Inanna and tells her, "It'll take me at least another four or five days to reach Deep Creek. Now that your wounds have healed this would be a logical point in our journey for you to head back to meet your friends. You can go up that way," he says pointing North, "passing through Cheyenne, Wyoming and on into Nebraska." He pauses and then assures her, "I'll give you a supply of water in the extra canteen and some dried meat for your trip back as well as some wild ginseng root, which you can chew to boost your energy."

But later that evening, as they lie near each other on the bearskin beside the fire, Inanna makes an alternative suggestion.

"I'd like to come with you to Deep Creek and see what kind of settlement you have going on there."

"Why?" Hototo asks, rolling over onto his side and staring at her intensely. "I thought you wanted to get back to your people as soon as possible."

"I do," she says. "But I have a feeling, an intuition perhaps, there might be a way for our two peoples to work together."

"How is that?" Hototo asks.

Inanna is silent for a minute, wondering if she can trust him with her secret. Ultimately, she decides it's too soon. She really doesn't know enough about him yet or about his settlement, so she won't answer his question. Finally, he is the one to break the extended silence that has unnaturally fallen between them.

"How come you can walk so fast?"

"I'm a marathon runner," Inanna tells him. He looks at her quizzically but accepts her explanation for the time being.

"How come YOU walk so fast?" she asks in return.

For the first time that day, Hototo smiles at her. He sits up, cross-legged, and throws another stick onto the fire.

"I'm a Hopi, we're natural born runners. It's in our genes, you might say."

She stares into the flames, mesmerized by the heat and flickering colors, as humans have always been from the beginning of time.

"I guess your name is Hopi too?"

"Yes, it means, 'Warrior Spirit Who Sings.'"

Inanna looks over at him. "How about a song, then, Warrior Spirit?"

"You wouldn't want to hear it," Hototo admits, still smiling. "And your name, what kind of name is that? Inanna? Never heard of it before."

She pauses before she answers to drink from the canteen in front of her, then pushes her long black hair away from her face. As she does so, she realizes suddenly they look alike in some strange ways: their hair is the same color; both are tall and thin and muscled. Her skin, however, is a light caramel, while his has a much darker pigment to it.

"My name has a story too," Inanna says. "My mother was Jewish, and my father was an Arab. I'm named after the Sumerian goddess of love, fertility, and warfare."

"So, fertility love goddess, what brings you to the plains of Nebraska?" Hototo inquires jokingly, as he scans her face intently.

"There is a settlement like yours in some caves up by Ash Hollow. I was heading there when our party was attacked. I ran away, but became disoriented and wandered into Colorado, where you found me in the abandoned house."

Since that part of her story sounds authentic to him, he nods.

"So where did you come from when you started your journey here?" he asks.

She pauses, before answering. "From the capital, from Washington, D.C."

He is silent for a long time as the fire crackles and the starless night wraps its long delicate ribbons around them both.

"I first came up here to Colorado from Texas," he finally announces. "A cousin and I, well, we were hunting and came across the Deep Creek wilderness. Hadn't been touched for years, had no value, you see, to anyone. We realized, because of warnings coming from your hometown that we had to find somewhere underground to live for a bit. Over the last fifteen years or so, we've been setting it up, using a helicopter to bring in all the stuff, bit by bit. We've got about 200 people living there now—lots of our Hopi relatives from Hotevilla and some others too—quite a mixture."

"I suppose you've got water?" Inanna asks.

"Yep. Some nice, deep wells inside those caverns. We Hopi," he adds, "have been using dry farming methods for thousands of years. We know our soils, we know our science, and we know what is required for deep-root planting. Since farming has always been the focus of our culture, we've devoted the last fifteen years to developing a successful method of growing plants in caves. Not just how to grow but also how to store our crops, how to save our seeds and how to prevent mildew. We're already growing blue corn, squash, beans, chilies, wild onion, lettuce, tomatoes, carrots, and melons. We grow cactus, juniper, and wild berries too."

Hototo pauses, leans forward and pokes the fire with a stick, causing the sparks to fly around them like summer fireflies.

Inanna's thoughts race as she listens to Hototo. She knows the advanced protocell technology she carries within her databases will help these people greatly— IF she is willing to share it with them.

Finally, she asks, "And cross pollination, how do you deal with that?"

Grinning, he responds, "Well, normally during the day, it's the bees and insects that pollinate plants, isn't it? But we - well, we've got bats. They come out at night, and they're drawn to all the flowers. Our bats visit up to thirty flowers over the course of one single night, flying from flower to flower and feeding on their pollen."

"So, you're a farmer and a hunter?" Inanna asks.

"Me?" he replied, pointing at himself, laughing. "No, Ms. Love Goddess, I'm an engineer. I'm the one that runs the lines, fixes the turbos we use, etc., etc. There are others in our group far more skilled at farming than I am."

"Okay I get it," Inanna says, thinking to herself. *He's going to LOVE nano tubes and growing them with CO_2.*

As their conversation dwindles, becoming a trickling stream, and the fire dies down, Hototo and Inanna settle at separate ends of the bearskin and drift off to sleep. Being predatory by nature, they are acutely aware of every crack and rustle the trees and Earth make around them, even in their sleep, which for both, is sporadic and filled with uneasy dreams.

In the morning, they break camp quickly and head out, climbing up a steep mountain path taking them into the Rockies and closer to their destination. Inanna follows Hototo carefully, never letting him know that for her, this is an easy walk and if she were not with him, she'd be travelling three times as fast.

***

After an arduous hike over and through the Rockies, they arrive at Deep Creek late on the fifth day of their trek. Deep Creek is located at the bottom of a 2,500-foot, narrow canyon, which reduces considerably in width as it extends into the distance. Its geological features include limestone formations as well as dolomite and sandstone cliffs. Checking her internal database, Inanna learns that Deep Creek has always served as a protected area and the surrounding states of Nebraska, Kansas, and Oklahoma have never been successful in securing permission to divert its water for farming and cattle ranching.

Because there is still a sufficient level of water in the creek, the vegetation on its banks is flourishing and includes spruce, Douglas firs, cottonwoods, and sagebrush. Inanna asks Hototo whether the creek still contains fish. He nods and clarifies there are some trout, but they are much scarcer than in previous years.

In answer to Inanna's next question, Hototo adds that a handful of deer, elk, black bear, mountain lion, bobcat, big horn sheep, and bald eagles still come down to the creek to drink. As they walk deeper into the canyon, Hototo points to a peregrine falcon nest in the cliffs above. "Lot of birds still, too," Hototo says, looking around at a few. "Flycatchers, swallows, wrens, warblers, and also butterflies."

Inanna is amazed a place such as this still exists on a planet that is rapidly becoming a burnt, dried-up desert.

As they jog at a steady pace along its banks, Hototo describes how the fifteen-mile-long creek originates just below Deep Lake then plunges 7,200 feet from the White River Plateau into the dry Colorado riverbed.

Over forty caves have formed in the canyon because of the rapid water flow through the limestone cliffs. These are the caves in which his group of settlers are living and in which they've created their farms.

Arriving at the settlement, Inanna and Hototo climb up into the caves. Inanna immediately observes that the housing consists of closely-knit 'apartments,' two or three stories high, carved into the limestone walls. Ladders avail accessibility to the uppermost levels

Hototo is greeted warmly by a group of men and women at the entrance of the largest cave. He then introduces Inanna.

"A friend I met along the way," he tells them simply.

As Inanna shakes hands with each person, simultaneously logging his or her name into her databases, she realizes suddenly that she doesn't know whether Hototo is married or has a family. She wonders which of these women is his wife, and could he be the father of any of the children who suddenly appear around them?

Food and water are offered to Hototo and Inanna immediately. Carved into the walls of the caves are a series of shallow limestone 'bowls' that serve as comfortable 'bathtubs.' A geo-thermal spring flows within the caves, providing an endless supply of hot water to the community, so the women prepare a warm bath for Inanna who is grateful for the opportunity to wash after so many days on the road.

She does, in fact, have to wash her nanoskin occasionally to maintain its intelligent sensors and sun protective qualities, but has to be careful not to immerse herself in the water for too long so she doesn't disrupt the electrical flow of information to her brain.

After the bath, Inanna puts on a clean pair of cloth pants and a shirt, which have been brought to her by a tall woman with long, blond hair. The woman leads her over to the exterior of a three-story 'home.' She motions for Inanna to climb up the ladder to the dwelling. Inanna easily ascends the steep rungs and follows the woman onto the roof of the structure. Using a second ladder, they descend into the intimate interior of the house, containing small, open windows that face outwards towards the main cave. There appears to be a ceremonial altar in one corner of the apartment as well as brightly colored paintings and a variety of pottery placed in many of the wall niches.

Hototo is already sitting at a table near one of the windows. As they enter, he turns towards Inanna and asks, "You doing okay, love goddess?"

Inanna feels surprisingly embarrassed when she hears this but in the spirit of the moment smiles back at Hototo. He addresses the blond woman. "Running joke, Alice, that's what her name means in Sumerian is it?" he jabs Inanna, a smirk on his face. Inanna doesn't reply but instead gazes back at both of them taking their measure. She is unable to determine whether Alice and Hototo are a 'pair,' and realizes it would be impolite to ask.

Instead, she says awkwardly, "Don't think I'm being rude, Hototo, but I can't stay long and need to leave tomorrow. My folks will be worried about me and will want to know that I'm all right."

"I figured as much," he replies.

"I've been thinking about all of this—you know what you've made here—and I think our communities have much to share with each other."

He doesn't reply immediately, but eventually asks, "Is yours really like ours here?" and then laughs. "Well, now that's a stupid question, isn't it?" His question hangs uncomfortably in the air.

Inanna thinks carefully about her response. She finally decides she will tell Hototo everything about herself, so he knows there could be real risks in associating with her. She realizes this place has captured her heart. It seems somehow so familiar to her because it reminds her of the manmade cave at Galgala near her home in the Jordan Valley in

Israel. Inanna loved visiting Galgala as a little girl with her father before he was killed.

Looking over at Alice, who now stands silently watching them, Inanna sits down in front of Hototo as Alice instinctively leaves them so they can be alone together, climbing swiftly up the ladder onto the roof.

"It's a long story."

"I've got time," he says smiling. He reaches across the table and takes her hand, turning it over and examining the skin very carefully.

"What and who are you?" he asks quietly. "It's safe to tell me now."

She pulls her hand away to protect herself from the warmth of his fingers and the excess data she is receiving about him from his skin cells.

"Simply put, I'm half human and half machine," she says.

He looks at her intently then asks, "How so?"

"I'm what's referred to as a trans-human. When I was seventeen, I volunteered for an experiment that would turn me into the next iteration of what we, as humans, might become—might need to become—that is, if our species was in danger of going extinct. I have chips inside my brain. I have bionic arms and legs and super vision and hearing. I consciously control my inner body and organs. I also control how I feel, so if I don't want to be sad, I'm not, so if I …" Her voice trails off.

He cocks his head and raises an eyebrow.

"And your self-healing skin?" he asks.

"All part of the same package."

"And Inanna, what and who were you before—before they changed you?" he asks with gentle curiously.

"An Arab Israeli who spent her childhood in refugee camps."

He whistles through his teeth as he expels air out of his mouth slowly.

"Jeez," he says. "I'm trying hard to figure out how I got me an Arab/Israeli girl in the middle of Colorado who is some kind of superhuman."

She laughs and leans over to him.

"And I can't hold your hand for too long either because all your biological and psychological data feeds through my fingers into my brain."

113

He pulls his hand away abruptly, kicks back into his chair and starts to laugh.

"Holy mother. I can tell you're a dangerous woman. That's why I tied you up when I first caught you—I knew you were a strange one."

Then he remarks more seriously, "Who are you working for in D.C., and were they the people who were chasing you and tried to kill you?"

"For DARPA," she replies. "I was part of a secret experiment that the United States Government has been conducting on creating trans-humans. My colleague, Rajeev, and I were the first successful prototypes for the project. There had been failures before us, not pretty ones, but somehow my maker Peter, who was brought into the project very recently, figured out a way to meld our neurological and biological parts seamlessly together with our machine parts. Peter, and his wife Sophie, were taking us secretly and without the government's knowledge, to a settlement their friends had built under Ash Hollow Cave on the Ogallala Aquifer. We had almost made it there when the SEALs caught up to us and killed Peter and Sophie. Rajeev escaped with their daughter, Sarah. I need to let him know that I'm still alive," she says all in one breath.

He leans over but does not take her hand again. "I'm sorry to hear that they were killed," he says simply.

"Yes," she replies softly. "They were really good people, by figuring out the right way to make us trans-humans, Peter stopped a great deal of suffering by others as they were experimented on."

"Do you want me to go with you to find your friends at Ash Hollow?" he suddenly asks.

She smiles and brushes his hand in acknowledgement of his concern for her.

"No disrespect to you, but I will get there in about five hours without you."

He silently appraises her then grins lopsidedly.

"Were you laughing at me and what a slow poke I was all the way here?"

She doesn't smile back but looks at him seriously.

"It would have taken me some time to recover from my wounds and when my water ran out and without food, who knows, I might have died without your help. Anyway, I'm very glad we met. I've decided once I spend a few days at Ash Hollow, I'll return here with some things you will want to have. I may even bring Rajeev, my fellow trans-human. We'll set up a communications system between our two camps. Members of our two communities can visit each other regularly until we can't travel outside anymore without protective clothing. Of course, Rajeev and I won't need anything special to cover our skin because it has been created to protect us naturally from the sun."

Hototo asks, "The wounds you have—I've not seen those before. Were they caused by some kind of high-tech weapon the government's developed?"

"Yes," Inanna replies. "The injuries were accidental, though. The SEALs were meant to bring Rajeev and me in alive, because as you can imagine, we're considered high value assets. I believe, however, that when they come back to Ash Hollow looking for us and don't succeed, they will never think of searching for us here. Your settlement could provide us with a very good hiding place. There is some risk for your community, however, and you need to consider that."

Hototo is silent for a minute then responds, "I will have to ask the Matriarchs, but I'll persuade them to accept the risk. When will you leave?"

"Tomorrow, just after daybreak. I'll need some water and lunch, of course, since I get very hungry." Inanna picks up his hand and mimics biting down on it.

Hototo quickly pulls his hand out of her grasp. He then describes the heating and lighting systems he has devised in the caves. Impressed with the sophistication of the design, Inanna asks how he intends to block UV rays from entering them during daylight hours. Hototo explains how he has developed light-penetrating UV resistant blinds to hang at various entrances and exits. Hototo and his friend, who as a dentist uses titanium for dental implants, have engineered a translucent, liquid titanium coating on the cover slips of the blinds.

While the soft glow of Hototo's solar lights provides them with a gentle ambience similar to moonlight falling across their faces, Inanna explains how, through protocell technology, he and his colleagues would be able to engineer living buildings. Hototo grasps the scientific principles of protocells very quickly and becomes quite animated as they discuss the various ways in which this advanced technology could be interfaced within the Deep Creek community.

At some point during the evening, Alice joins them with dinner. A Norwegian agronomist, Alice has brought heirloom seeds with her to Deep Creek from the Svalbard Global Seed Vault on the Norwegian island of Spitsbergen, in the remote Arctic Svalbard archipelago.

Because Inanna has not heard of this place, she asks Alice to explain about it in great detail in order to permanently record all the information into her databases.

"It's a global seed vault," Alice tells her, "which preserves duplicates of seed samples from the world's crop collections. The thick rock ensures the seeds remain cool, even if power is lost."

"An ultimate insurance policy for the world's food supply," says Hototo. "Humanity's final back-up plan, if you like." He pauses and continues, "Or, let's say not everyone's—it's a back-up plan for the ones that govern."

"The seed bank has the capacity to store 4.5 million varieties of crops," Alice continues. "Each variety originally contained an average of 500 seeds—so a maximum of 2.5 billion seeds have been stored in the Vault.

"These seeds originated from almost every country in the world. They range from unique varieties of African and Asian food staples such as maize, rice, wheat, cowpea, and sorghum, to European and South American varieties of eggplant, lettuce, barley, and potato. In fact, the Vault holds the most diverse collection of food crop seeds in the world," Alice says. "The vault only accepted seeds that originated in the country of the depositor. Countries owned and controlled access to their own seeds. Secured by the Black Box System, the vault administrators only allowed the original depositor to withdraw and open the boxes," Alice continues.

"So how did you get them?" Inanna asks, curious.

"Well, about twenty-five years ago we, that is a group of us, realized it was the governments or corporations who owned the seeds, and we figured it was important for more people to have access to them, so we found a way to break in and steal some of them."

"How do you store the seeds here? It's too warm."

Alice and Hototo smile, and answer in chorus, "The deep caves have the right temperature. We store them there."

"And how did you two meet?" Inanna asks, with hesitation.

They both start to answer together then Alice takes over, "My brother, a geological engineer with much experience in drilling for oil and gas in the North Sea, came to work on the oil rigs with Hototo in the Texas Gulf. I visited him fifteen years ago, just when they were beginning to set things up in Deep Creek. Now I'm here with my brother and his wife and some of our European friends who survived the virus outbreaks in Europe, after the permafrost melted and released them."

Shyly, Inanna asks, "Are you two married?"

Hototo laughs, as he takes Alice's hand. "Don't you know we're—that is, the Hopi are—we're matrilineal? Alice has yet to ask me for my hand in marriage. But seriously, though, we—the younger ones in the community—don't marry because we realize it may become necessary for us to, well, 'cross-pollinate' with others to keep ourselves going."

"Oh, I understand," Inanna replies. "Sound thinking. Sophie and Peter's friend, Rachel, who leads the crew of the spaceship *Persephone*, has a plan for the survival of our species devised along similar lines."

Alice asks with great surprise, "You know the leader of that mission?"

"Yes, and I have all the details of its super technology and science stored inside my internal databases." Alice looks at her as she tells them this not quite knowing what to say.

While Inanna is speaking, Hototo touches Alice's arm lightly and motions he will explain everything about Inanna in detail, but later. Inanna has said she needs to rest, since she'll be leaving early in the morning.

Nodding to Inanna, Alice gets up to show her a small bedroom in the back of their house where she can sleep.

After Alice has left the room, Inanna lies down on the single, narrow bed, and begins to ponder how she might help this community. She quickly calculates that a bio dome similar to the ones at Ash Hollow might be created over the narrower portions of Deep Creek—one that will allow its vegetation to survive aboveground. She figures if they are lucky, they will have a few years to obtain materials they need to build the bio dome, perhaps ten to fifteen years before both communities will have to go into lock-down mode. Also, if she and Rajeev use protocells as an integral part of its construction, Inanna thinks they can artificially extend the cliffs by initiating a set of chemical interactions into their eco-system.

After laying there, synthesizing the biology, math, and chemistry necessary to implement all her elaborate plans, Inanna finally falls asleep. Before she does, though, she allows herself to feel excited for a moment about seeing Rajeev and Sarah again, while carefully blocking from her mind any thoughts, memories, or feelings she may have regarding Peter and Sophie.

***

Setting off for Ash Hollow just after daybreak, Inanna climbs down from the caves onto the Creek bed and starts running at top speed along its side. With her computerized brain, vision, and hearing feeding information to her legs, she negotiates the rocky terrain easily and without mishap.

From atop the caves, having watched her leave until she disappeared from sight, Hototo returns to his house, sits down in front of his computer and adjusts the 3-D screen so he can monitor her progress. Inanna has programmed the computer so Hototo can easily follow and communicate with her as she travels. Watching her hologram, Hototo soon realizes he's able to see and hear everything she can, as if he is actually looking and listening through her eyes and ears. Despite this intimate connection to her, she hasn't allowed him any access to her main databases or biological systems. She's also been forced to utilize a low-frequency radio signal for communication with him rather than satellite connections so the folks at Weather City can't track her movements.

By knocking loudly on his bedroom door early that morning, Inanna had gotten him out of bed where he was sleeping soundly next to Alice. When he emerged several minutes later, she'd told him they needed to create a hidden radio antenna for sending and receiving transmissions outside the caves. He'd easily built the transceiver, which he linked by cable to his computer. Inanna had then created the equivalent of her own radio and TV station, tuning it to the parts of her brain to which she would allow him access to her journey, including sounds, pictures, some digital data, measurement values and navigational positions. Before she left, she'd instructed Hototo to immediately destroy everything containing information on her if he should receive any visitors from the government.

As Hototo follows Inanna's journey now, he is amazed at her sure-footedness and speed. After only two hours, she's already traversed the Rockies and is heading across Colorado towards Nebraska. She then crosses the Nebraska border and arrives at Ash Hollow after a total of only four-and-a-half-hours.

118

As she approaches the Caves, Inanna tries to contact Rajeev by way of a simple, radio transmission. A few minutes later, she receives a message from him.

"Is that really you, Inanna?" he communicates to her.

"It is, Rajeev, and I'm about half an hour away—see you soon."

After his contact with Inanna, Rajeev runs to inform Tom that Inanna is on her way. Because they are both excited and eager to see her, Rajeev and Tom immediately leave to wait at the entrance of the park. Wanting to surprise Sarah, they do not tell her the news.

As they wait impatiently by the gate, they catch a glimpse of Inanna running towards them. Tom thinks she looks like one of the beautiful, agile gazelles he had seen many years before when he observed them fleeing from a marauding lion in Kruger National Park. As she approaches, Inanna slows down to a trot then stops. Rajeev steps forward with arms outstretched for a welcoming hug. Tom shakes her hand from behind Rajeev's neck while she drapes it there.

Eventually, Rajeev steps back and, noting Inanna's old-fashioned clothes, smiles widely. "I want to hear every detail about what happened to you, but it can wait," he says.

"No, it can't," Tom interrupts him.

Before returning to the Caves, Inanna confirms to Hototo that she has arrived safely at Ash Hollow and that she will be in touch again soon, waving at him before turning off her transmission. As Rajeev watches her do this, he raises an eyebrow but knows she will explain it all to him later.

At the Caves, Inanna greets Noemi, Seed, Rosie, and a tearful Sarah, who grabs her and won't let go. After spending a good hour with Sarah, she goes into Tom's study, promising Sarah she will be back soon.

Inanna describes her journey in detail to Tom and Rajeev—where she's been, how long it took her to get there, and about Hototo and the Deep Creek settlement. Tom whistles through his teeth. "Sounds like quite a place they've built there. Noemi is going to love the Norwegian seed bank theft."

"Yup," Inanna says smiling. "And she's going to love seeing what they're doing around farming. It's amazing."

Turning to Rajeev, she adds, "And with protocell technology—guaranteeing their survival will be a piece of cake."

Rajeev smiles. "Stop showing off about Rachel's research and information, pretending like you're the expert."

"Okay," she replies, holding up her hands. "Credit given where credit is due. I agree."

"By the way, have you heard from Rach?" Rajeev asks.

"No, it wasn't safe. I turned her off. However, with the radio transmission system at Deep Creek and a similar one we can build here, I think we're good to go, at least here on Earth, from the privacy angle."

Tom listens to their technical banter then interjects, "So Inanna, what's the plan? I take it you want to form some sort of community collaboration, a kind of unofficial merger of our two camps?"

"Yes," she says. "They would serve as a great extension for us until we go into lock down and even after that. Most importantly they could add substantially to our gene pool. Prevent it from getting too small and ingrown. Anyway, we've got more than a few years to figure out how we would handle in-person meetings since we don't have underground maglev technology, and there will be few roads we can safely travel on to reach them."

"We'll cross that bridge when we come to it," Tom says thoughtfully. "So, what's the next step?"

"Some of us go back there and meet with them," Inanna answers.

As Tom listens to them, he realizes how happy he is they still seem so innocent—that they have not, like him, become corrupted by cynicism, and still remain optimistic about finding potential solutions to any future problems they might encounter. Clearly, they do not live, like he does, with a constant sense of unease about what will happen to this settlement in the future, a dread he feels is tightly curled up inside him like a poisonous snake. It is a feeling that governs the underlying rhythm of his life and will not go away, like a popular tune stuck forever in his head.

"Okay," he says now, interrupting their conversation and looking at them seriously. "I've made an executive decision. Tell them, Inanna, when you re-establish communications, that we'll be going back with you to visit soon."

Tom then swings around in his chair and begins mapping a route to Deep Creek. He asks Inanna how long it will take them to get there. She estimates they should be able to reach the settlement in a couple of days by car or van. He swings his chair back around and asks, "Who do you think should go, Inanna?"

"I think Rajeev, myself, Noemi, and you should make the first trip. Then Hototo and Alice and some others from their camp should come back here."

Tom nods his head, agreeing with her. "Tell them we'll be there in a few weeks–after I return from D.C.," he says emphatically.

Chapter 24
Tom

Since his family became one of the most powerful and well-recognized in the world, Tom has been untouchable by the Ruling Cabinet and can do as he pleases when it comes to his own underground community. The family's invaluable scientific research that took place over the last fifty or so years is now stored by Tom in highly encrypted, hidden databases. This research as well as his access to billions of dollars' worth of capital, provide Tom, an only child, with unquestionable leverage within the Ruling Cabinet.

To communicate directly with the Ruling Cabinet, Tom travels to Weather City from time to time. While it is still possible to do so, he attends meetings in person with the members of the Cabinet and others who are actively participating in the country's economy and government.

Tom has negotiated over the years with the Ruling Cabinet to allow his community to live undisturbed at Ash Hollow under his leadership, if he provides the Cabinet with limited access to the advanced technology his family has controlled for decades. In return, the Ruling Cabinet has agreed to abide fully by the laws that protect private property and refrain from taking his capital and technology by force. Although they could, easily descend upon Ash Hollow, they understand that illegally confiscating private property of wealthy individuals would expose their own significant holdings to similar action. They also understand Tom would not hesitate in sabotaging and destroying the most highly advanced technology Weather City currently uses to keep its residents alive.

At the last minute, after Peter and Sophie had already left Washington, D.C., and informed him they were bringing Inanna and Rajeev to Ash Hollow, Tom struck an additional, hasty bargain with the Cabinet. He had agreed, in return for their safe passage, to share all the information Peter was bringing on the trans-human project. Of course, Peter and Sophie had no idea about the extent of the deal he had been obliged to make to keep them safe. While they knew Tom was clearly still in touch with the Cabinet for business purposes, Peter and Sophie were unaware of the depth of his quid pro quo relationship. Even his wife, Noemi, remained unaware of the extent of Tom's involvement and secret agreements. She does know he needs to go back from time to time to meetings that involve his business interests. It is very possible if she knew what a pragmatic, self-preservationist her husband really was, Noemi would lose a lot of respect for him.

Tom felt okay about providing information on the trans-human project to the Ruling Cabinet so long as he profits from its technology for his own purposes. As a successful entrepreneur, he believes strongly in his inherent right to earn as much as he can off his own hard work. However, knowing the gross inequities of trickle-down economics, Tom has always supported the idea that it is his responsibility as a very rich man to ensure even the poorest people in the world have access to the basic resources necessary for survival. His insistence that everyone deserves a decent life is opposite to the attitude of many other families with whom he now sits on the Ruling Cabinet. They, in contrast, have always favored eugenics of a sort, wealth entitlement, and social Darwinism. In fact, the Weather City community was designed to be the physical embodiment of the Ruling Cabinet's sense of entitlement. Tom is one of the few 'freethinkers' among them.

***

After Inanna and Rajeev have left his office at Ash Hollow, Tom contacts Weather City and informs them he will be attending the next meeting of the Ruling Cabinet. During the same phone call, Tom officially learns Sophie and Peter have been killed in the recent efforts by the government to capture the group of travelers alive. He is also told this was a decision made by the highest levels of government, despite the agreement they had made previously with Tom for Sophie and Peter's safe passage to Ash Hollow. Tom's contact stresses he will be fully briefed on the whole situation by the Cabinet at the upcoming meeting. When Tom is asked once again if he knows where the trans-humans are currently located, Tom repeats he believes Inanna was killed and Rajeev, having delivered Sarah to the mouth of the Caves, has run off somewhere. Tom does not reveal, not even by the slightest change in his tone of voice, that he was already fully aware they had killed Sophie and Peter or that he is furious with them for double-crossing him. In fact, because of the government's actions, he is now fully resolved not to give them a "damn thing from that moment forward." Of course, he does not yet understand how complicated things have become—he doesn't know, for example, that Sophie had sabotaged the government's weather modification systems and some of its most secretive research.

Once he's sent his message confirming attendance at the meeting, Tom kicks back in his chair and furiously runs over in his mind the potential usefulness of the Deep Creek settlement. One of its major advantages is that, as far as he is aware, it's completely unknown to the government. Under these circumstances, Tom thinks that, not only will it be an invaluable fallback should their own community fail, but it will also be an excellent long-term hiding place for the trans-humans. He knows there's a good deal of money to be had from the technology used to create them and he now intends to be the one to make it.

***

Tom leaves the next day by helicopter for Weather City, after confirming with Inanna and Rajeev he will be back in a couple of days. Upon arrival, he meets almost immediately with the Ruling Cabinet. It is at this meeting he learns once again of Sophie and Peter's death and, for the first time, of Sophie's treasonous sabotage of the weather-modification system and many of the sensitive defense programs. While his first inner reaction is to condemn Sophie as a damn fool to have jeopardized the entire Ash Hollow community, he also recognizes, when he thinks about the consequences of her actions, that she is actually a national hero.

A new idea is introduced during the meeting. The military is requesting authorization to use a powerful virus to swiftly kill any people left outside the underground cities rather than wait for them to die gradually from radiation poisoning or starvation; the justification being it would provide them with a kinder, faster death. With Tom passionately speaking against the ghastly proposal, it is ultimately voted down by the Cabinet. Even without Tom's pleas, though, it turns out few of the 'leaders' have the stomach for this kind of overt mass eugenics; they prefer the subtler, longer-lived kind.

Also, during the meeting, the James family, one of the Cabinet's most powerful and outspoken clans, introduces their experimental work involving CRISPR technology and genetic modification, in which Robyn, Alistair's wife, is currently engaged. At this point in the conversation, Tom informs the group the trans-humans have been created to prove it is possible for human beings to live longer, healthier lives, adding angrily, "The desire to pursue and ultimately kill Sophie and Peter overrode more common-sense solutions that might ultimately have resulted in the return of the trans-humans to Weather

124

City. Now, it seems, through your dammed incompetence, we've completely lost track of the two of them."

Beecher James responds, "Despite this grave loss, I can assure you Tom that our research will continue to explore the possibilities of the human genome and find out how we can prolong human life by many hundreds of years. I know we will ultimately be successful."

Now, as Tom, sits and listens to his colleague Beecher talk about genetic enhancement, he is inclined to agree with him that if enough time and money are invested in the process it will be highly successful. Since achieving a substantial increase to the human life span is also one of his foremost goals, Tom recommits privately to his own research and understanding of how Peter created Inanna and Rajeev. During his most altruistic moments, Tom is even able to envision a time when anti-aging technology could be made available at no cost to all of Earth's remaining inhabitants. Realistically, however, he knows in his heart that the idea of including the masses in this plan would be completely antithetical to the rigid, exclusionary, ideology of the Ruling Cabinet.

Chapter 25
Beecher

Beecher James is among the elite group of twenty families who make up the Ruling Cabinet and whose personal holdings exceed 250 billion dollars.

Apart from Tom's family based in Ash Hollow, all the wealthiest 'club members,' live near all the underground cities scattered around the United States in separate, luxurious compounds that are always guarded.

This handful of families continue to maintain control over most of the sources of energy, production, and goods and, consequently, over daily issues of governance. While the residents of the network of underground cities over which they govern receive all material supplies they need to survive, these citizens have little say in the decision-making that determines every aspect of their lives and futures, including: the number of children they can have; where they live; how much they work and where; and their privacy.

In his heart Beecher knows the current societal structure is, in fact, not very different from the so called 'freedom' people experienced before the disaster, when the middle classes automatically believed the myth that because they had a bit of free time and could buy a few luxury goods, they were, like Beecher's contemporaries, in full control of their own financial and personal futures.

Beecher is not a spiritual or religious man. He is a pure pragmatist who believes in finding ways to prolong and enhance his and his family's lives. He supports the notion that the money and privileges they have amassed over time were rightfully earned by whatever means required and they must, therefore, do everything in their power to keep these riches.

Privately, amongst his friends and family members he discusses a new world order in which he puts forward the theory that the human beings currently remaining on Earth will gradually evolve into a permanent subclass, as he and a few others become a genetically engineered race of super beings.

Beecher has a son, Jared, who in utero received some genetic engineering using a bacterially derived protein that removes a targeted gene and replaces or repairs it with a new and improved molecule. Jared will now pass these altered genes to any future children he might father. The genetic modifications have enhanced his intellect and his physical capabilities.

At seven, Jared attends a school with a group of children whose parents are also members of the Ruling Cabinet, and who like him are being groomed to govern in a future society. In addition to learning the usual academic subjects, they are all mastering interpersonal and intrapersonal leadership skills. Because of his enhanced intelligence, Jared has little difficulty with mathematics, physics, chemistry, and language. He is not being educated with any particular religious or philosophical ideology in mind; rather, he is being directed to endorse an ideology that supports his own family's survival at all costs.

These elite children of which Jared, Beecher's son is one, are currently happy little things who have not yet fully realized what their destiny is. Entirely innocent and free of worry, they enjoy their friends, swimming, soccer, ice-cream, and old movies involving space heroes such as *Star Wars*.

None of the children born to this elite group of plutocrats, including young Jared, are being exposed to the Socratic notion that truth, beauty, and justice have objective content or that a moral life will bring them happiness. Rather, they are learning how to maintain dominance and power within their specific gene pool and become accustomed to the idea they have inherited dominium through natural selection.

Since they are being groomed to run a teleocratic government, one directing the finances, education, religion, health care, media, family life, arts, and sports of its citizens based solely on outcomes they prescribe, they are being taught that they must suppress all subversive activities that might endanger those outcomes.

In a few years, they will surely become recalcitrant teenagers and then mature adults who will eagerly assume the mantle of leadership for which they are being indoctrinated and carefully groomed.

Chapter 26
Tom and Alistair

While he is in Weather City, Tom contacts Alistair and suggests they meet outdoors by one of the canals so they can talk privately. At this point, Tom is still unaware Peter is, in fact, alive; some members of the government have decided it best he not be told for now. However, after Tom relates the information to Alistair that his relatives, including his brother, Neil, have arrived at Ash Hollow safely and are now part of their settlement, Alistair informs Tom about Peter. That he is unconscious and on life support in one of the top-secret military hospitals, under the new DARPA building.

"Can we get him out?" Tom asks urgently. Tom immediately realizes that if Peter regains consciousness, he will be forced to share his critical knowledge of trans-human technology. The government would then own what Tom has already decided he will keep exclusively for himself.

"Very difficult," Alistair tells him. "They have him under a twenty-four-hour watch."

As they talk further, Alistair begins to realize how very deeply connected Tom is to the Ruling Cabinet, and, as such, he should, perhaps, not have trusted him with this sensitive information. Alistair for his part begins to suspect that Tom has known all along that they intended to come after Peter and Sophie and capture the two trans-humans.

Tom however surmises from the expression on Alistair's face what he's thinking. "No, I didn't know they'd come after Peter and Sophie and try to kill them. Nor did I know Sophie and Peter would put themselves at such great risk and sabotage the whole damn system. I did have a deal, though, with the Ruling Cabinet that I'd work with Peter and the trans-humans and then share all the research he was bringing with him. You know—the high tech, laser weapons Rajeev was developing and the source of Inanna's unique capabilities. And no, Peter didn't know I had made those deals; he was a purist, an ideologue."

From the beginning, ever since we were in college together, Tom thinks, *Peter wanted to save the world. I, on the other hand, wanted to create a buffer between the world and me, by making as much money as I could.*

After defending himself to Alistair, Tom remains silent as they continue to walk along the riverbank, their hands behind their backs, heads down. While doing so Tom recognizes that the smell of chemically cleansed air circulating in Weather City is quite different to the much more organic air they breathe at Ash Hollow. He prefers the latter.

Speaking pensively in a very low voice, he breaks their silence by saying, "If we can't spring Peter, I'll have to buy him out... "I'll tell them I've got Rajeev and Inanna and that I know Peter is alive. I'll say I need Peter to help me work with the trans-humans. I mean, my company controls the technology for our space elevators to the moon settlements; we've got the patents for the biosphere technology, the protocell technology, in fact, you name it, and my company owns it. They won't be able to say no."

"What is it you really care about, Tom?" Alistair asks curiously after Tom has crudely listed off all his assets. Then he stops abruptly to face him as he says, "I mean, since you say you aren't an idealist and you've just told me you already own half the world. What is it that you want but don't yet have?"

Tom smiles strangely as he looks back at him and then replies thoughtfully, "Pretty simple. I want to live a long time and those trans-humans may hold the ticket. Peter figured out they could live for over 300 years, and that, my friend, is what I really want. That is what Peter and those two can give me that nobody else can."

"The only kind of immortality I'm interested in these days," Alistair says as he turns away, "is one that takes place outside of this elaborate prison we're all trapped in. One that takes place under a real sky."

As he continues to walk along silently with his head down, Alistair thinks bitterly, *damn you, and the whole lot of you who are so sure you can manipulate and control our lives with your money and your advanced technologies.*

Chapter 27
Rachel

Four weeks after take-off and exactly on schedule, *Persephone* is nearing Mars. Because deceleration in space is extremely difficult to achieve, the spaceship has been travelling at lower speeds in preparation for its arrival.

Beyond using each planet's gravitational pull to reduce the spaceship's speed, the crew will raise its solar sails, which are thinner than a human hair, as they move into lower orbit, and tilt those sails so the light from the Sun acts like a decelerant rather than an accelerant. The sails will serve as an additional source of power for *Persephone*, if necessary, during its eventual travels towards Proxima Centauri.

The launch window of the Mars trip was carefully planned to ensure an arrival date when Mars and Earth would be properly aligned. Once in orbit around Mars, Rachel and a few crew members are scheduled to leave the mother ship via a small, light craft to visit the colony of 10,000-plus individuals established there.

Like Weather City and similar outposts on the Moon, the atmosphere of the Mars Colony is comprised of elements from the Earth's own biosphere, which are enclosed within large pressure domes. The domes are clearly visible now as Rachel and her companions approach the planet's surface.

The settlers on Mars have worked to convert the planet's carbon dioxide into carbon monoxide by using solar-powered electricity. The carbon monoxide is then converted into liquid fuel, hydrogen gas and synthetic petroleum. The CO2, so prevalent on Mars, is also supporting the colony's extensive plant life, which the settlers are growing in the biospheres, providing an ongoing source of food. In addition, the Mars scientists have succeeded in making synthetic *soil ecosystems*. The 'farmers' on Mars have discovered the use of **hydroponics** is not enough to enable plant growth. Because hydroponics doesn't allow organic matter to decompose, they have created and introduced chemical worms for soil decomposition, using protocell technology like that on Persephone.

Mars colonizers have also been expanding their **par terraforming** by designing robots that are building additional, habitable, pressurized domes on top of craters, and by sealing off caves and caverns that will eventually contain parks, forests, and lakes. Equipment specially modified for the task will be used to distribute the carbon, nitrogen, and water among the structures that are necessary to create a habitable atmosphere.

Another long-term goal the settlers have adopted is to thicken the atmosphere of Mars and increase its temperature by gradually releasing large quantities of nitrogen and oxygen over a period of hundreds of years.

Geneticists on Mars are also studying types of microorganisms that could be used in the future to alter the muscles and skeletons of children born off-planet, so they are better able to adapt to the effects of long-term weightlessness. With investments from families like the James's, Mars scientists have begun to understand the processes necessary to develop genetic adaptations that would enable human beings to tolerate the constant bombardment by cosmic rays and extremes of heat and cold on Mars, and to function on low levels of oxygen or the absence of oxygen altogether. They are even at the point where they can conceive of creating a completely new species of human being; one that would be able to live outside pressurized domes on the surface of any planet.

As soon as Rachel arrives at Mars Central, she is escorted to meet Colonel Jeffries, the military leader of the Colony. Because all settlers on Mars are considered members of the military, military law prevails on the planet, as it does on the Moon and on other smaller, outlying asteroid mining settlements in space. Knowing this, Rachel understands she was fortunate in her ability to form a crew composed primarily of civilians. She is also grateful for the latitude Alistair and other government officials provided while she was selecting her highly individualized team of scientists and the genetic material they would carry with them to colonize Planet b.

Rachel's tour of the facilities on Mars is provided by Jeffries and, besides including a tour of the Orion Spar Defensive Space Fleet (OSDSF), whose function is to protect Earth's solar system, she is also given a walk-through of an impressive factory producing radiation-shielding materials. These plastic-looking 'Martian bricks,' are made from the sand-like **regolith** that covers the Martian surface and are overlaid with a polymer made on-site from carbon dioxide and water. She soon learns other factories are creating protocell shelters suitable for building outposts on Mars that, like those on *Persephone*, are self-sensing, durable, and self-healing. Thoroughly impressed with the orderliness and efficiency of the colony, Rachel concludes it has been built to last and could potentially serve as an emergency outpost for humanity, if necessary.

After her extensive tour with Jeffries, Rachel spends a pleasant evening with her host and his senior staff, enjoying a splendid dinner served with a selection of wines that, in her opinion, seemed to have badly survived the journey to Mars. Contrary to her assumption of its origins, though, Rachel soon learns the wine was produced from locally grown grapes and she is one of the first to taste it. As the evening progresses, Jeffries enthusiastically proposes toasts to Rachel's forthcoming journey, wishes her well, presenting her with several bottles of wine as a symbol of friendship. Sitting there sipping, she can clearly imagine Yuri whispering into her ear, "Only you Americans would drink shit like this and call it passable."

She smiles because he would be right in his assessment; it isn't really very good at all; *but no doubt,* she thinks, *it'll get better as they improve their techniques.*

Chapter 28
Inanna

Inanna has continued her communication with Deep Creek. She and Hototo speak to each other frequently and make detailed plans for a return trip there, as well as for a visit from Hototo and others to the Ash Hollow settlement. They decide Hototo's first visit to Ash Hollow will take place within the next few months.

Inanna and Tom will not allow Sarah to accompany them to Deep Creek, even though it will be difficult for her to be left behind so soon after being reunited with Inanna.

Having finalized their plan, and with Tom safely back from his meeting at Weather City, Tom, Rajeev, Inanna, and Noemi immediately set off from Ash Hollow the morning after Tom's arrival. They leave early, using the DARPA van to camouflage their identities. Since the city is still partially inhabited and hosts one of the larger underground cities the government has built, they deliberately skirt around Denver. Traveling by way of a series of deserted highways, they reach the entrance to Deep Creek in the evening. Once they arrive in Dotsero, they leave the van in an abandoned lot near the town. Parked behind some large boulders and covered in tree branches, it is well hidden from potential thieves.

Hototo meets the group of four at the lot and guides them to a narrow pathway leading alongside the riverbed to the Deep Creek cave entrance. As they hike on the compacted dirt, the group from Ash Hollow is impressed with the magnificent setting and the actual existence of a natural source of water around them. At the end of the secret, winding path, Tom, Rajeev, Inanna, and Noemi are finally able to make their way up a rocky slope and into the caves. They are immediately overwhelmed by what they see. Noemi, in particular, cannot believe the ingenuity of the growing systems being used as well as the enormous variety of seeds the community has been able to cultivate, all of which are apparently thriving in an environment that has little soil or light.

The settlers have prepared a communal meal for the Ash Hollow visitors that includes blue corn bread mixed with the burnt ash of juniper berries growing on the local mountain slopes. The bread is served with a vegetable stew consisting of squash, tomatoes, pinto and hominy beans, and wild greens. With good nature and humor, Hototo shows them how to mop up the delicious gravy from the stew with the crisp, smoky-grey corn bread.

Inanna, Tom, Rajeev, and Noemi will sleep in a pueblo house set aside for their use during their stay. They are also offered baths in the stone hot springs located further inside the caves. After dinner, they sit with a group of residents and share stories about their separate settlements and how they came to be. Hototo offers to take them deeper into the caves the next morning, where the temperatures are naturally controlled, to show them where the community is efficiently storing an abundance of seeds and dried food.

While the others chat, Inanna takes Rajeev to see the limestone rock on the exterior of the caves. She explains her idea to introduce the same protocell technology Rachel is using on *Persephone*, to train the rocks to grow in such a way that the community will eventually be able to enclose large portions of Deep Creek within a biosphere. By creating a self-regulating system of this sort, Deep Creek will be protected from solar and cosmic radiation.

"We should be able to stimulate the limestone to grow in the way we want," she says. "Like a plant grows. We can train it to form around the base of a series of treated glass domes sealing off the Creek bed, allowing the natural vegetation to continue to grow underneath, in the same way it's functioning now."

"Where will you get the glass and titanium domes?" Rajeev asks.

"I'll ask Tom to help us purchase similar ones to those we're using at Ash Hollow."

"Not a bad idea, Inanna," Rajeev says, "and it will probably work."

***

The next morning, they go deep into the caves to explore a series of extraordinary spaces that maintain a consistently cool temperature and dry atmosphere. Massive, carved 'waterfalls' of limestone fall for thousands of feet from ceilings stretching high above them that are covered in stalagmites. Around the edges of the mile-long cave, are a series of smaller caves that serve as perfect long-term storage spaces for food and seeds. Pathways carved into the rocks extend all the way down to the large expanse of dark brown earth at the floor of the cave. Solar lights cast ghostly white and gold shadows around them as they move more deeply into the depths of the underground passages. It is a silent and beautiful space, Tom thinks, as he looks around appreciatively—like the inside of a cathedral but without any of its obvious religious symbolism.

As the group walks amongst the huge monolithic structures talking quietly to one another, Inanna mentions her idea of a biosphere at Deep Creek to Tom. Since he's very interested in how it might be constructed, she explains that if he were to provide a few large, glass and titanium domes, she can put the chemical technology in place to start the process of design-based, natural architecture.

"We'd have to bring the domes in, piece by piece, using a helicopter, and then assemble them on site," he says, adding, "It's all certainly possible."

Tom has been very impressed with this Deep Creek settlement and confirms to himself that it can indeed serve as a viable alternative to their own, should there be a massive systems failure at Ash Hollow. IF they can keep Deep Creek hidden from the government, as it is now, he can with the help of Inanna and Rajeev, also develop technologies here that his business can use in the future. What's more, he can hide Peter here, should they succeed in removing him from Weather City. All in all, Tom is feeling a level of engagement and excitement he hasn't experienced in many months.

He's also pleased to see that Noemi and Alice have bonded well and are able to share a wealth of information about the seeds they have culled, stolen, and saved. Noemi has invited Alice to come back to their settlement to have a tour of her own growing techniques, graftings, and heirloom seeds. By the end of the day, they have both agreed to exchange some of their precious seeds and grafts.

Later that evening, Tom, Inanna, and Rajeev discuss with Hototo their ideas around protocell technology. He agrees to bring it up for discussion with the Matriarchs. Tom offers to bring the van back within a few weeks so that he can take a small party to Ash Hollow for a reciprocal visit and further discussion.

During the evening, Hototo asks, "I assume that under the proposed bio-dome, we will be able to keep a variety of surviving stray animals that are natural to this environment?"

"Of course," Inanna replies. "However, it'll be a little like a diorama in a museum—the animals will be 'just for show;' not being in pairs, unlike in Noah's ark, they'll eventually die off—so we'll also teach you how to preserve their DNA."

Inanna asks Hototo if she can use his computer to connect with *Persephone*. Once she and Rajeev are settled in front of Hototo's machine, they create a hidden software program that can interface with Rachel's personal computer. She then types her coded message to Rachel while Rajeev watches intently.

"Checking in from Planet Earth. How's everything going out there in space, Commander?"

After twenty minutes have elapsed, Inanna receives a reply.

"Inanna, is that you?"

"Yes," Inanna responds immediately, "and Rajeev is sitting right next to me."

"How is everybody? Did you make it safely to Ash Hollow?"

Inanna pauses then explains, "I'm sorry to have to tell you this, Rach. We were followed and Peter and Sophie were killed, but Rajeev, Sarah and I did make it to Ash Hollow."

There are long pauses in their conversation because of the time it takes for data to travel in space. Eventually, though, Rachel replies, "Damn them."

"Yes," Inanna concurs. "Damn them twice."

Inanna continues, "I may need your help soon."

"No problem," Rachel replies. "But you'll have to ask your questions before we go further into deep space."

"Where are you now?" Inanna asks.

"We've left Mars and are on our way to Europa. So far, all is going well."

"I'll communicate from here in the future, Rach, so if you need to contact me or Rajeev, leave a message on this secure network and our friends will make sure I get it."

"Okay."

There is a poignant silence when both of them stop typing. Drawn together in mutual sadness by the tragedy that has overtaken two of their closest friends, they are reluctant to say goodbye.

"Take care of yourselves," Rachel finally types.

"Same," Inanna sends before quickly signing off.

Hototo has been sitting near Inanna as she communicates with Rachel and once the conversation is over, he gets up and lets his hand briefly brush her shoulder. He remembers from their earlier experience that he can't touch her for too long. Responding with her human

136

capacities, Inanna grasps Hototo's hand firmly and holds it against her cheek. They stay like that for several minutes before she lets go. She then says, "I should tell the others as soon as possible that we've been in contact with Rachel."

That night as they all bunk down, Inanna asks Rajeev if she can sleep next to him. Despite her trans-human ability to control emotions, she still feels profoundly alone in the world at this moment and knows he is the only other individual right now who can really understand her. They lie next to each other on the narrow bed, holding hands and staring apprehensively into the dark—the first beings of their kind, not quite knowing yet what lies in store for them in the future.

The next morning, the group from Ash Hollow makes their preparations to leave Deep Creek. As they are saying goodbye to Hototo in the parking lot at Dotsero, he informs them, "I've spoken to the Matriarchs. They've agreed in theory to the creation of a biosphere. However, they'd like Inanna to come back soon and explain more about it."

"I'll come back on foot in a few days," Inanna says. "And then we can start the project. I figure we've got a few years left to complete it. Tom will provide us with two bio domes once the chemical and structural designs are complete. Rajeev will also help as we begin construction."

"Protocell technology is working well on *Persephone*," Inanna adds. "It's been tested now for over twenty-five years elsewhere. We will start by placing non-living chemicals in the limestone cliffs. Gradually, the chemicals will encourage a build-up of mineral growth, which we can then program to form around the base of the exterior of the bio domes as they span the canyon. These limestone foundations will effectively close the structure off from the outside environment on all sides, while allowing oxygen to pass laterally across interior spaces through shutter-like gaps. Of course, we will have to remove any interior build-up of carbon dioxide by venting, but also by using the carbon dioxide to grow nanotubes—just like they're doing on *Persephone*."

While she talks, Rajeev nods his head to demonstrate he agrees with what she is saying.

Tom smiles amiably as he listens to Inanna talk. Hototo stands next to her, watching her intently. As she finishes speaking, Hototo says, "From a structural point of view, what you are describing seems to make sense. However, once we close off the caves and create an artificial living environment around them, we'll have to ensure that if there's a failure in this new environment, we can still retreat back to our original living conditions and be able to survive as we are doing now."

"Of course," Inanna replies. "Major failure would mean we had not sufficiently protected ourselves from UV rays during the daylight hours. If that is the case, then we'd have to revert back to the system of artificial blinds you created for the cave entrances. Not a bad system, but it's restrictive, because too little natural light penetrates them.

After they've finished this discussion as they all stand outside of the van in the parking lot, Tom, Noemi, Rajeev, and Inanna finally get into it for the return trip. Before doing so, however, Inanna hugs Hototo and assures him she will be back in a few days. She waves vigorously to him through the back window, her hand like a flag in a strong wind, as she watches him recede into the distance. In preparation for her return to Deep Creek, it's been agreed Inanna will draft chemical and structural designs of the proposed domes to share with the Matriarchs.

Feeling a tingling in his arms and legs while the van moves forward at 100 mph along the virtually deserted roads, Tom's enthusiasm surges. He places a hand on Noemi's knee and squeezes hard.

Because he's about to double-cross his colleagues in the Cabinet, Tom is filled with a great sense of anticipation and pleasure. He has also always enjoyed playing both sides of the fence. For this reason, he is looking forward to rescuing Peter, bringing him back to Deep Creek and hiding him there indefinitely. As he looks over at his wife and then in the rearview mirror at Rajeev and Inanna, Tom is acutely aware that he has not yet told any of them that Peter is still alive and being held captive at Weather City. *Soon...* he thinks to himself as he smiles over at his wife who is surging over the huge potholes like a bat out of hell.

Chapter 29
Rachel

Persephone, along with the fifty Mars scientists now on board, is well on her way to Europa. When the ship arrives, the crew members will deploy one of their self-sufficient transportation modules to the surface of the planet. The module can hold a significant amount of cargo and up to one hundred passengers. Like this one, all of *Persephone's* transportation modules are fueled by liquid hydrogen and rely on electrical power for flight control and other functional operations. This particular vehicle will be left on Europa permanently so the new settlers can go back and forth to Mars.

As *Persephone* approaches the planet, Rachel directs the ship into a slow orbit around Jupiter's moon, switches to **electronic propulsion** then releases a series of calibrated sails that will decrease her speed sufficiently to maintain orbit. Powered by a process like the kind that has been employed for hundreds of years by sailors who manually manipulated mainsails and jibs to slow down or accelerate the speed of their ships, *Persephone*, is in fact, quite literally 'sailing' around Jupiter's moon.

Once *Persephone* is safely in orbit, the transport module is launched, carrying Rachel and a small number of crewmembers down onto an enclosed underwater landing pad. Like those entering a submarine from spaces containing dissimilar, internal air pressure, they go through a series of decompression chambers before they arrive inside the actual space station. Yuri, meanwhile, will remain on *Persephone* while Rachel is on Europa; he will switch places with her in a few days to ferry additional crew members to the planet. Their responsibility will be to carefully inspect all aspects of the facility.

The first group landing on Europa from *Persephone* is able to observe immediately that the underwater space station has been constructed around an Earthquake-proof, elongated spiral structure. With a diameter of 500 meters, it will house future inhabitants within multiple levels of well-designed, residential zones, very similar to the multi-story apartment buildings in Weather City. The bottom floors of the structure will be reserved for scientists who will continue to explore the planet and maintain the city's energy sources.

Rachel studies a factory that has been built on the lower floors and designed to turn carbon dioxide into methane using micro-organisms found on the planet itself. She observes the power generators, located along the sides of the underground structure, that will create thermal energy from the ocean's changing temperatures and desalinators, large silver cylinders located on the inside of the structure that will supply fresh water for the city's residents from a process incorporating hydraulic pressure.

Impressed with the work the cyborgs have already accomplished on the space station, Rachel spends two days in the ground floor lab examining life forms the cyborgs have been collecting from the planet. Inevitably, though, she discovers the construction of the station has led to some contamination of the surrounding environment from the building materials used, but she's also happy to see the cyborgs have been scrupulous about containing whatever has occurred within a tightly designated area.

Rachel carefully examines the material gathered pertaining to the large whale-like inhabitants that have been spotted swimming in the waters of Europa. Because she is fascinated by these creatures, she regrets only glimpsing one or two of them briefly as their massive ghost-like shapes float gently by the large, reflective, glass windows of the space station. The scientists and engineers now arriving from Mars will have the opportunity to observe these magnificent, whale-like species in depth, as well as put the final touches on this amazingly inventive, underwater city.

During the first night she is on Europa, Rachel's dreams are very lucid. In them, she carries on conversations with these sentient, whale-like beings. It is through her intuitive grasp of trinary language that she can understand what they are saying and learn the history of their race through a series of beautiful songs they sing to her. When the songs end, one of the whale-like beings communicates with her telepathically.

"We are a people totally devoted to the well-being of our kind. Even though we like you compete for resources, our social rules prohibit violence.

"We use a personal, 'ultra-sound' system to see inside the bodies of others so we know what they've eaten, whether they wish to mate, whether they have young inside them or if they are sick. Because our associative cortexes process information at lightning speed and can connect with other beings, we are able to see life through each other's eyes. In this way, we become part of a single whole, part of one sensory loop that brings us into tune with each other and our planetary environment.

"We have been observing and smelling you since you first arrived yesterday. We see that you manipulate objects with your hands, like octopi, and we sense you are singularly obsessed with abstract ideas. We also know that, unlike you, we feel things three dimensionally in ways you cannot yet understand."

Rachel listens carefully to what this strange creature is communicating to her. She asks, "How do we smell?"

The creature replies, "Like fungi, acid rain, waterless deserts, and much like organic waste."

"You will need to find a way to specifically teach us about you," Rachel replies. "Since we have not yet developed intuitive, non-verbal communication."

Still supposedly in her dreams, she finds herself somehow outside the city's glass walls, floating next to this large being. While she rests quietly there, as secure as though suspended in her mother's womb, the creature shows her, by transmitting the information brainwave to brainwave, its enormous ***paralimbic lobe*** that allows it to successfully bridge emotional and cognitive thinking. At the same time as she sees the being's specialized organ, she also feels the accelerated beating of the creature's heart, its softly breathing diaphragm and the strength of its enormous musculature that carries it swiftly through its watery environment.

Later, when she awakens from the dream, Rachel remembers vividly what she had seen and felt as if it had been real. Making sure to accurately record the unusual encounter in her captain's log, she also promises herself she will relate the dream to Yuri and the crew. Because the experience of conversing in another dimension with the strange creature had been so profoundly humbling and moving, she hopes incoming settlers will find a way to communicate effectively with them like she has and live peaceably with these highly intelligent beings.

Rachel now wonders once again, as she tries to return to sleep, if the planets circling Proxima Centauri will have inhabitants like Europa. She imagines what they will be like and whether they will be welcoming to her small band of intergalactic travelers, a group of refugees from a faraway planet called Earth who are on a peaceful mission designed to save the *hominin clade* from extinction.

141

Chapter 30
Alistair

Alistair has been waiting patiently for some solid communication on Europa from Rachel. Now that it has finally arrived, he reads it several times, carefully.

REPORT TO GENERAL ALISTAIR TRIMMINGHAM FROM CAPTAIN RACHEL CHEN

DATED SEPTEMBER 2060

I am confirming our retrieval of fifty astronauts from the planet Mars who we have taken to the planet Europa for colonization. As you know, Europa is a water-based planet, on which mechanized robots have built a habitable underwater city. Their work has been conducted over many years in preparation for the eventual arrival of 5,000 human inhabitants. The underground city is now five years away from completion.

I wish to go on record to state that the beings currently inhabiting Europa, are a species of large, highly intelligent mammals. It is my strong belief these mammals supersede human beings in their intelligence, and we can learn a great deal from them.

Because they communicate using 'empathic telepathy,' an instant form of thought and feeling transference without the sounds of linguistics or speaking, we will have to adapt our own standard methods of communication by using our right brain functions much more fully. I have always believed 'empathic telepathy' is natural to living beings and something which we on Earth have lost the capacity to employ—a sixth sense, if you like.

While I was on Europa, these beings allowed me to see inside their minds and bodies so I would 'know' them in the fullest sense of the word. That is, so I would understand how they sound, smell, see, hear, think, feel, move, etc. I experienced a kind of natural communion with them and was able to fully comprehend them, including their thoughts, ideas, and their entire history as a species.

I truly believe we can re-learn how to communicate telepathically with each other from them. Such communication would, of course, require us to develop unused parts of our brains and modify our DNA to some degree. Human beings have evolved over the centuries to be left-brain dominant, a condition which has caused us to become desensitized.

I rely on you to persuade our colleagues they must not think less of these beings because they do not operate in the same way we do.

Alistair is not at all surprised to read Rachel's report, and, in fact, feels extremely gratified to learn that the inhabitants of Europa may be a species of very advanced beings. If anything, her report gives him hope, because he has never thought of humans, despite their ability to manipulate objects with their hands, as being at the top of a Universe-wide evolutionary chain.

After studying her communication, Alistair initially decides to write a detailed memo to his superiors, strongly advising them to ensure minimal disruption is inflicted on the planet in future. He will also implore them to consider the worthy goal of focusing on communicating effectively with these fascinating life forms to advance human learning, rather than searching for more and more of Europa's natural resources to exploit.

Alistair feels a sense of personal satisfaction in being the one who lobbied hard in favor of enlisting a non-military crew for *Persephone*. The fact that Rachel has been able to communicate with the Europans so well, and without bias based on a desire for control, confirms his belief that non-military scientists hold out the strongest hope for the mission's success.

At home that night, Alistair tells Robyn and Styx about his communication from Rachel, and how optimistic he is for the success of their mission.

"Dad, they won't be able to communicate with us once they get very far outside our galaxy, will they?" Styx asks.

"I'm not sure; they'll try, but it will take a very long time for messages to reach us—maybe as long as four or five years. In space, there are so many obstacles radio frequencies must pass through, including interstellar gases, UV radiation from the sun, and even asteroid fields."

"Well, even if it takes many years, we may still hear from them and then we'll know for sure they got there," says Styx, innocently.

Alistair puts his hand on her head and strokes her hair. "We sure will," he says, smiling.

After Styx has gone to bed, Alistair and Robyn talk quietly in the bathroom about Peter's condition. Alistair tells her Tom is planning to remove Peter, who is still comatose, from the military hospital.

***

The next day, during Alistair's daily visit to Peter, he 'tells' him Rachel has not only made it to Europa, but also found an aquatic supra intelligent life form there. While he sits next to Peter's bed, one hand on his friend's, Alistair feels a slight movement from Peter's fingers. They seem to be gently probing his own. Although he thinks at first he must have imagined this very slight sign of life, Alistair watches Peter's fingers more closely and sees them quiver again. Encouraged, Alistair leans forward and softly brushes a strand of hair that has fallen over Peter's forehead. Noting how much it has grown recently, he tucks the hair behind Peter's ear, and as he does so, the skin of his forefinger brushes against a raised object. Curious, Alistair lifts the hair behind Peter's ear and sees the edge of a soft, skin-colored microchip sticking out of the flesh like a skin-flap.

Alistair glances around quickly to make sure the nurse has left the room, and he is alone with Peter. To avoid detection by cameras, he leans forward and continues to talk softly to Peter, just as he'd been doing minutes before. Feeling along the side of Peter's neck, Alistair can trace the full outline of the storage chip. He has no idea how to remove this, since it seems lodged firmly below the skin. Before leaving, he whispers softly in Peter's ear as he bends down to straighten his pillows, "Will bring tweezers and try to remove during next visit."

Since his friend does not respond, Alistair wonders if he imagined or merely hoped that Peter's fingers moved slightly. Most importantly, though, Alistair wonders what information the chip holds, and once he extracts it, what he should do with it. He is, after all, a ranked military officer who swore an oath of loyalty to the Ruling Cabinet. Later, in private, Robyn persuades Alistair to examine the chip very carefully before he comes to any decisions.

When Alistair arrives the next day at his usual time, a pair of scissors and tweezers concealed, he informs the nurse he is going to give Peter a long-overdue haircut. Using his body as a shield against cameras, he is able to work out the chip from the soft flesh behind Peter's ear and drop it onto the towel he's draped around Peter's shoulders. Once the haircut is passable, he wraps the towel carefully around the rescued chip and places it in the leather satchel he has brought. As soon as the nurse comes in, she laughs at the botched job Alistair has done, and hastily applies a bandage to the small cut she sees behind Peter's ear, before she asks for the scissors and skillfully repairs his haircut.

Arriving home, Alistair takes the chip from its hiding place inserts it into his own personal computer. As he slips on his earphones, he adjusts his body so anyone who might be watching him cannot make out what he is viewing.

Peter appears on the screen, standing in a classroom. Alistair gasps out loud. After a brief introduction, Peter proceeds to conduct a comprehensive lecture using images and a number of 3-D diagrams, which Alistair understands immediately to be on the creation of the two trans-humans as well as on his own innovative, scientific research in the field of human bioengineering.

Alistair removes the chip from the computer half-way through Peter's presentation and sits back with it in his hand. Although he can't understand much of what Peter has been saying, since it's so far removed from his own field of study, he knows how valuable the information would be to the Ruling Cabinet and to Tom at Ash Hollow.

As he sits quietly, pondering the position he suddenly finds himself in, Alistair allows thoughts to surface that he often represses. He knows he is a loyal supporter of the U.S. and its space colonies; he also knows he unequivocally endorses the need for a military force to ensure order and the rule of law. Alistair has always respected those who proudly and dutifully maintain the safety of others and equates them with the Rangers, the shadowy figures in his favorite books by J.R.R. Tolkien who do their work at the borders of the 'Shire' so its inhabitants can live peacefully within. However, over the years, Alistair has become more and more aware of the dark, secret world of the Cabinet in which, unlike the Rangers of the North, they operate outside of the boundaries of ethical and moral laws.

Sitting at his desk, reflecting on the path his life has taken to this day and the fundamental choice he will now have to make, Alistair realizes Peter's chip has put him at a crossroads.

Part II

2080-2100

Chapter 31
Inanna

Twenty years have gone by since I was taken to Ash Hollow and Deep Creek, and it is now impossible for most of us to go outside without protective gear. That is, except for Rajeev and me. Peter, of course, had modified our skin so it could withstand extreme levels of UV rays. Our plans to enclose the Deep Creek settlement under a biosphere, using treated glass domes and proto-cell technology to wrap the limestone cliffs around them like a shawl, has been highly successful. And I'm very glad to report that the government has yet to find Rajeev and I, even though the FBI still circulates our images from time to time on wanted posters placed publicly in all their underground cities.

I now spend my time traveling between the two settlements, both of which are currently thriving. Our dear Sarah, Peter, and Sophie's daughter, is twenty-five years old and about to marry Tom's son, Seed. Because most of us are confined to one settlement or the other, we have developed a program that will allow us to relay low frequency pictures of the upcoming wedding from Ash Hollow over to the folks living at Deep Creek.

Even though Caroline, Stefan and their mother, Mary, moved to Deep Creek ten years ago, they are still very close to Sarah and Seed and will, of course, want to 'attend' the wedding. When Caro met and married Born, Anna's relative from Norway, they made the difficult decision to live at Deep Creek rather than Ash Hollow. They brought Mary and Stefan with them to live in adjacent houses located at the bottom of the limestone cliffs near the river that keeps flowing through the creek canyon. A river that is still fed by deep, underground springs.

When I travel between the two settlements, I witness a land completely dead. The flatlands of Colorado and Nebraska have been turned into large, dried, red mud and desert wastelands - rather, I suspect, like the surface of Mars, pictures of which Rachel sent to us from her visit there twenty years ago. I suppose, at this point, Rachel must be ten years out from Proxima Centauri. Sadly, our communications with her ceased several years after she left Europa as *Persephone* moved deeper into outer space.

Our two settlements are very comfortable. In addition to the stable, human population, we've also managed to preserve a few of the animals that were natural to this habitat. We even have one old, black bear roaming around the bottom of the canyon that feeds on protocell meat we produce. The bear has become quite tame and rather lonely, I suspect, because it is without a mate.

Our food supplies are sufficient to maintain health and well-being. So far, no virulent or contagious diseases have affected our little settlement of 200+ inhabitants, although, as should be expected, a few of our older residents have died. We've buried them in the Earth outside the caves. Their bodies 'nourish' the roots of the trees and bushes, which I'm happy to say, still surround us at Deep Creek.

For the first ten years of our partnership, when the inhabitants of our settlements could still visit each other and share resources, we were a happier, more extended social group. Now that our individual communities are isolated and more in-grown, it is much more confining. However, our governing councils are fair and humane. They seem to work well, ensuring the smooth operation of our lives, keeping the peace amongst us all and equitably settling minor disputes.

In both settlements, children are born regularly and, since we see them as vital to the survival of our species, we welcome these newborns with great joy. Given the limitations of our resources, though, the number of babies allowed to be conceived is controlled; as we had planned all along, couples must now apply for permission to procreate. Hototo and Alice have a son, called by the Hopi name, Hania (spirit warrior). In honor of his mother, Hania was also given the Norwegian name, Leif. An active little boy with a mop of chestnut hair, he spends a great deal of time in the cave gardens growing flowers and food. Hania's best friend is Caro's son, Ola, who is a blonde, blue-eyed Scandinavian child. Although Hania has a stronger personality and tends to try to control Ola, he can be outmaneuvered by little Ola, who knows how to quietly get what he wants.

In 2060, when I first arrived at Ash Hollow, Tom, Rajeev, and I worked in the lab Tom had constructed for Peter's use. We were trying to understand how, exactly, we had been altered as trans-humans. Although we were able to reconstruct SOME of the formulae and technology that made us bionic, we could not completely interpret the interfaces Peter had found between our human DNA and cell structures, and the technology he inserted into our bodies.

Despite our incomplete research, I still continue to study human DNA and genetics on my own, because of my interest in it as a trained biologist. Rajeev, on the other hand, applies his training and efforts to the machinery and systems of our settlements, which keep them running smoothly. He also continues to broaden his understanding of protocell technology. I know Tom was terribly disappointed he had not been able to retrieve information on trans-human technology from Peter before he died, since he had desperately wanted to learn how to prolong his own life.

Lately, I've been completing the process of *asexual cloning* two, trans-human children within my own body. I am now very close to creating both a viable male and female child—twins, if you like. Over the last two years, I have found I can grow and develop living embryos from my own unfertilized egg cells, and because of my ability to consciously control all my body's biological functions, I can give these embryos more beneficial gene combinations.

For example, my children will be able to consciously repair breaks in their own DNA double strands as well as other DNA-related damage in their bodies associated with the highly stressful environmental conditions existing outside. They will, therefore, live longer, healthier lives. Also, by not using male sperm in the reproductive processes, I have found that genotypes of the kind I'm creating will be entirely free of the genetic diseases that occur randomly in normal sexual reproduction.

I intend to give birth to my children in a few years and will soon ask Hototo if he will take on the role of 'father.' Alice has already indicated to me she is fine with sharing Hototo with me in this way.

From the beginning of our existence as trans-humans, I wanted Rajeev to be my sexual partner and husband. Because of the super sensitive receptors in our skin that respond to the slightest human feelings and thoughts, I knew that having sex with humans would be neurologically painful and I wanted to avoid this kind of trauma. However, Rajeev has told me he is not in love with me—that he thinks of me only as a 'sister.' He has, however, agreed to be an "uncle" to my children once they are born, and I am very grateful for that.

Chapter 32
Rajeev

Unlike Inanna, Rajeev spends all his time at the Ash Hollow Settlement. Rajeev has elected to live there because he's in love with Caro and finds it painful to spend much time around her at Deep Creek, where she and her husband now live. However, he does go to Deep Creek once a month and has developed a relationship with Caro's little son, Ola, who considers him to be a benevolent uncle. One of Rajeev's joys in life is to listen to Ola, a gentle soul, carefully and repeatedly explain the process by which bees and bats pollinate flowers. Despite life as a single man, Rajeev has also played a significant role in raising Sarah these last twenty years, and he, along with Tom, both think of themselves as her 'fathers.'

Constantly experimenting with protocell technology, Rajeev has successfully grown meat using cells extracted from Creamie the goat and Buddy the horse, both of whom have now died, much to the chagrin of Caroline and all the children at Ash Hollow. In addition, Rajeev has worked with Tom to refine the electronics that run their energy and lighting systems.

As he aged, Rajeev adopted a more monk-like existence, spending all his free time practicing yoga and meditation as well as in private prayer and spiritual contemplation. Sarah loaned him her grandmother's memoir, *A Quantum Life*. She discovered Mehr's book in Sophie's suitcase, buried under her clothes. Rajeev has found her writing to be insightful and a useful guide to his ongoing spiritual studies. Though he has observed that while Sarah has enjoyed reading the memoir because it is a connection to her ancestors, she is not particularly drawn to its esoteric teachings. In fact, Rajeev has concluded that Sarah is extremely pragmatic and seems to want to experience fully the physical world she has been born into, rather than dwell on a world she cannot see. She has told him, "I am most content when I'm working with Noemi in the greenhouses, getting my hands into dirt and seeing things come to life around me".

Through the years, Rajeev has come to know Tom well. Since he regularly conducts scans and updates on Tom's private data system, Rajeev has learned Tom is still very much in touch with Weather City. Rajeev has also discovered that Tom's company is sitting on a fortune's worth of patents and research.

Tom has told him, "I continue to be disappointed in not being able to greatly extend my lifespan, as I intended to do before Peter died and was lost to us."

Rajeev has shared with him that he believes determining how to activate the 90% of human DNA currently underused, could be a second window into improving human longevity. Rajeev is fully aware that Inanna already understands and is in the process of activating her dormant DNA, as she engineers embryos within her own body. As a result, her biological offspring will live longer and be stronger and more intelligent than most human beings.

Despite his monk-like existence, Rajeev is not lonely. Having lovingly raised Sarah, he now looks forward to any grandchildren born to her. Additionally, he also loves Inanna like a sister and is eternally grateful Peter created the two of them together so they could be a family of sorts. Some time ago, Inanna approached him with the proposition of initiating a sexual relationship, and perhaps even eventually a marriage. However, Rajeev categorically turned her down. He cannot imagine an intimate life without the kind of love he considers to be necessary between a man and his wife.

Although Rajeev does not actually fear the physical intimacy of sexual intercourse in the same way Inanna does, he knows it would be very difficult to experience the fears, joys, pain, sadness and other intense thoughts and feelings of his partner through the regular touch of her skin. And he knows, because Inanna has carefully protected herself since she was very young against an intrusion of any kind on her body or mind, she would find it nearly unbearable to experience this kind of intimacy. For this reason, he feels strongly that she had ultimately chosen him, not because she actually loved him, but because he is comfortable and safe and knowable. While he was 'honored' to some degree by her request of marriage, Rajeev believes unequivocally that both of them deserve more.

Chapter 33
Tom

Over the last twenty years, Tom has enjoyed the leadership challenges Ash Hollow presented. Until 2080, he was still able to travel easily to Weather City on a frequent basis and participate in national government affairs. Despite the temperature challenges and crumbling roads, he has been able to travel frequently to Deep Creek in a titanium car and wearing a protective suit.

Tom remains disappointed they were never able to uncover Peter's research on the two trans-humans before he died. He is pleased, though, that the Ash Hollow Settlement has functioned smoothly with adequate supplies of food and reasonable social relations despite what could have been extremely claustrophobic living conditions. In affirmation of the accuracy of its design, the dome lets in enough light to ensure the environment is bright, and the floating living spaces continue to evolve in new and interesting ways as Rajeev introduces protocell technology. So far, Rajeev has created a living reef under the lakes, which now serves as a wonderful playground for the settlement's children.

Tom's oldest child, Rosie, has grown up into a compassionate, caring adult who works in the community hospital and has married one of the doctors there. His son Seed will soon marry Sarah and there will be tremendous festivities associated with this welcome union. Although Sarah and Seed have already put in a request to conceive a child, there is a waiting list of couples who want to procreate, the length of which will require they wait their turn for several years. The community leadership including Tom continues to be very careful in balancing the existing level of resources with the number of current community residents, while, at the same time, taking into account the necessity of maintaining the community's current population numbers over the next hundred years or so.

At sixty years of age, Tom hopes he'll be around for another thirty years, at least. He's still working on ideas of how to extend his life with Rajeev, but he's accepted the fact that, like all humans, he's mortal and his organic lifespan won't be more than a hundred years. Recently, because Sarah has shared her grandmother's journals with him, Tom has also become interested in holographic reality and quantum cognition. In all these studies, Rajeev, who loves to spend hours discussing the finer points of human consciousness and other philosophical matters, has been an enthusiastic partner.

Tom and his wife continue to share a close relationship. In addition to valuing all of Noemi's virtues and skills, he has been gratified to see how well her gardens and food cultivation projects are flourishing.

During his visits to Weather City, Tom meets with Alistair occasionally over a drink and feels they've finally formed an uneasy friendship. Their memories of Peter and Sophie remain their primary bond, second only to Tom's willingness to accept Alistair's brother, Neil, his sister-in-law, and wife's sister and nephew as residents of Ash Hollow.

Recently as they were sitting together in a crowded bar at one of the small tables in the back, Alistair has told him: "While this new government of ours makes sense from a survival and a security perspective, I also believe that not everyone has received a fair deal from them."

"How so?" Tom had asked.

Alistair had hesitated before he replied. "Well, you could say that most of the citizens of our new nation hardly have freedom of choice. While most of life's essentials are provided to them, they're still obliged to work in government sanctioned jobs. Their choices are narrow including where they live, whom they marry and how many children they can have. And if you include the many they left on the outside, primarily because they were seen to be less useful, it turns out to be most of them."

"We couldn't save them all my friend," Tom had told him leaning forward and covering his hand. "I think you can legitimately give your conscious, admirable though it might be a reprieve from this kind of thinking. We had to make choices to ensure some of us remained alive. Be happy that you and your family were among the lucky ones."

In fact, because of these comments, Tom has recently concluded that Alistair is naïve. At the same time, he has realized that, unlike Alistair, he has found ways to live with himself that do not include this useless second guessing.

Chapter 34
Sarah

Sarah is thrilled to be getting married to Seed. Because they grew up together and have known each other so well, she has always felt they were destined to be a couple for life. For his part, despite a cooling-off period in early adolescence when he was particularly scornful of her girlishness, Seed has come to realize she is, and has always been, the center of his universe.

Even though Seed is Tom and Noemi's second child, he is the one who will reluctantly take over his father's company when the time comes to inherit, not his older sister, who has told her father she has no interest in it whatsoever. While Sarah has some basic concept of what 'taking over the company' entails, she has deliberately distanced herself from learning too much about the business. Like her revolutionary mother and father before her, she is also extremely scornful of the kind of world that plutocrats like Tom have created—both before and after the burning years that overtook the Earth. However, on a purely practical level, Sarah also acknowledges that Tom's money and hard work have ensured the basic survival of both settlements.

Sarah's wedding will be celebrated under the larger of the two glass domes at Ash Hollow on the beach of a star-shaped island. She'll wear an altered, white, cotton wedding dress that had belonged to Noemi. For the wedding, Noemi has created a bower of yellow roses, under which Sarah and Seed will be married, and all of the flower arrangements on the wedding tables, as well as the bouquets for bridesmaids and her daughter, Rosie, the maid of honor.

The wedding guests will feast on 'Roast Buddy and Creamie,' prepared by Rajeev, as well as on a variety of fruits and vegetables, including fresh salads filled with orange and yellow nasturtiums, flowers similar to those that will adorn the bride's hair. In addition to these delicacies, the Deep Creek settlement has provided blue corn and juniper berries for the wedding meal.

Tom will serve as justice of the peace; Rajeev and Inanna will be responsible for giving the bride away as well as ensuring live pictures of the wedding are broadcast to Deep Creek so members of that settlement will be able to join in on the festivities.

On the day of the wedding, Inanna, who like Rajeev still looks twenty-five while all the other original settlers have aged considerably, has chosen to wear a dress of a butter-soft, fringed, yellow material. She's woven white roses into her long, black hair shaped into a tight plait falling down her back. Rajeev wears a white, cotton dhoti and white pants. In honor of Eastern traditions, Rajeev has also decorated Sarah and Inanna's hands with henna to symbolize both the outer and inner sun, explaining the Mehndi designs on their palms incorporate the concept of awakening inner light. When Rajeev was at Deep Creek on the day before the wedding, he had happily decorated Caro's hands in the same way as Sarah and Inanna's, so the three women could feel a special bond. Hototo and Alice are attending the wedding in person, having ridden back in the titanium van with Tom on his most recent visit.

As they sit at the head table surrounded by those they love, including those 'beamed in' from Deep Creek, Sarah tells Seed this is the happiest day of her life. When Rajeev offers a toast to the bride and groom, he invokes the memory of Sarah's parents, Sophie and Peter, and glasses of an aged, dry champagne brought back from Weather City and kept for special occasions, are raised to them. Although Rajeev does not drink, he notices Inanna, Alice, and Hototo are imbibing at one of the nearby tables, where they lean close together and laugh at private jokes. At one point, Rajeev thinks he sees Hototo lean over and kiss both Alice and Inanna intimately on the lips, but the movement has happened so quickly, he is not entirely sure of what exactly he has seen. Not allowing himself to grow regretful of what he might have had with Caro or Inanna, he focuses his attention, instead, on the newlyweds.

After the wedding, the bride and groom leave the island in a small boat that has been decorated with white roses. They sail off to begin their life as a married couple in a specially constructed greenhouse filled for the occasion with one hundred yellow butterflies. The butterflies are a poignant reference to the fragment of a poem written by her grandmother that Sarah had found on a slip of paper inserted in Mehr's memoir.

> The journey started a long
> time ago,
> before the great white bird

came. We had no magic gypsy
creating road maps
on parchment.

We could only
listen to the music of
each other's voices, and then
with fingertips trace the known
lines.

I ran
through a garden with you
let in by a secret door, holding
your hand, while all around
faces of familiars glanced up to wave,
and a hundred yellow butterflies
flew into our eyes, blinding
us with their light.

Chapter 35
Rachel

Strangely, as *Persephone* left Earth's outer solar system on its journey to Proxima Centauri, the Worldship met with some unexplained atmospheric resistance. Rachel and Yuri described it afterwards as follows: *It was almost as if the craft encountered the edges of an enormous bubble or a transparent hologram and had then been propelled swiftly through it to the other side.*

In his journal, Yuri wrote about the event in more detail: *As we approached the outer limits of Earth's solar system, we realized Persephone was experiencing some tensile resistance from an almost entirely invisible electromagnetic field. To me, it looked as if a hologram with walls of shimmering transparent plastic was completely surrounding our vessel. What flashed through my head as I became aware of this 'thing' blocking our way, was that it had the strength and perhaps inherent will to hurl us back again to Earth like a giant catapult, if it chose to do so. However, for no logical reason at all that I can think of—almost as if by someone's command or, as though we were being released from some kind of quarantine designed to keep us within our own solar system—we found ourselves cruising once again smoothly on the other side of the plasmic entity. It's still hard for me now to speculate about the reason and substance of the visible resistance we saw and felt.*

Now, however, in the year 2080, *Persephone* is long past this invisible barrier and a full twenty years into the planned thirty-eight-year flight to Proxima Centauri. Yuri has continued to improve the fuel performance and thrust of *Persephone*'s engines, so in fact, they anticipate arriving at their destination a few years earlier than expected. What is astounding to all crew members is the very real possibility of a return trip to Earth that would encompass comparatively few years if Yuri and his engineers are successful in their on-going efforts to develop a way to vastly improve on their speed.

Persephone's final destination, Proxima Centauri, is part of a star system closest to Earth including Alpha Centauri A, a yellow sun-like star, and B, an orange sun-like star that orbit each other at the same approximate distance Uranus orbits our Sun. In order to designate a planet as habitable, it must have a star-sun with a long and stable life span, so biological life has had time to emerge and evolve over time. For this reason, the crew members will be studying this star system very closely.

Once *Persephone* draws near to it, the crew will put up the ship's solar sails, creating reverse momentum drag. In doing so, *Persephone* will be in position to more slowly approach the twenty-one Earth-like planets revolving around Proxima Centauri. Research completed prior to the launch of *Persephone* indicates that eleven of these twenty-one planets have an ***Earth-Similar index*** of 0.8 – 1, meaning that life is highly probable.

As they get closer to Proxima Centauri, the team assigned to the task has been able to predict the amount of carbon dioxide present on several planets and created a database showing atmospheric variations from planet to planet. In fact, one of these planets, closer than many of the others to Proxima Centauri, appears to have better biological conditions for life than Earth itself. It may even be full of life forms crew members have never seen before.

Already identified as a potential target for resettlement by Earth's astro-physicists, this planet, which Rachel and her crew have now named Persephone 2, is older than Earth and may be involved in a perpetually renewable cycle constantly increasing its biodiversity.

Other preliminary evidence on Persephone 2 indicates the planet contains more oxygen than Earth and, as a result, a higher level of gravity. Scientists on *Persephone* are delighted with these promising conditions, which will provide a hospitable atmosphere over the long term. Most important, though, is this very large planet experiences more tectonic activity than Earth and contains a better magnetic field, both of which should result in a high degree of climate stability.

Persephone's crew members are now receiving preliminary photographs of Persephone 2 that reveal bodies of water evenly scattered across its surface as well as lakes and shallow seas. The scientists are optimistic this will serve as a welcoming habitat for humans.

Eighteen years before they were set to land on Persephone 2, and in her fifties, Rachel finally decided it was time to have a child. Using her own eggs, taken from her and frozen when she was in her thirties, she has chosen a preeminent Earth scientist, Tsung-Dao Yang, as her sperm donor. According to the ship's records, Dr. Yang holds degrees in mathematics and physics and was a Nobel Peace Prize winner. The healthy 9-pound daughter, Dha-shi-zhi, (meaning "the strongest") who is birthed after an uneventful pregnancy, has been named by Rachel after a powerful female bodhisattva.

Yuri has also fathered a child, a son called Nikolai. Although he knew it was against regulations, Yuri asked Rachel for special permission to serve as the designated sperm donor for Anna, his Somalian neighbor and monogamous life-partner. Because he is the co-captain and had shown extraordinary loyalty and ingeniousness throughout the mission, Rachel agreed to change the 'anonymous fatherhood' policy for him on a one-time basis. Once they set up their experimental colony on Persephone 2, though, Rachel knows she and her leadership team will have to decide how any new generation of children born there will be procreated.

Contrary to the practice on board ship, Rachel is in favor of choice on Persephone 2. She feels vasectomies should no longer be required for males, allowing them to be free to choose partners with whom they will have children. As for females, she hopes they will be able to decide whether a sperm donor for an unborn child will come from the sperm banks they carried on board *Persephone*, banks that contain sperm of a wide variety of human beings, or from a living male they know. Since their numbers now consist of 300 individuals, they will surely need a drastic increase in the humans on the planet in order to create a socially and genetically robust civilization. Rachel hopes the social scientists on board the ship will be able to formulate some policies around repopulation that are practical and generous. Of course, Rachel also realizes their current population statistics don't consider other bi-ped humans or forms of sentient life that may already exist on Persephone 2.

The community they've designed to ensure a peaceful and productive environment on *Persephone* has worked well over the past twenty years without any major disagreements. In fact, the only arguments that have occurred were to do with issues relating to scientific discovery, but even these areas of contention resulted from leaderships on-going requirement that any new research be defended by detailed results and open debate.

Even though Rachel hasn't chosen a 'regular' partner as has Yuri, her few careful liaisons have been with crew members who aren't in the same scientific field as she, including a Vietnamese psychologist. Rachel always makes it clear from the beginning that any partner she selects must limit his conversation only to personal and general scientific observations, and they cannot discuss specific work or relate

161

any 'gossip' about other crew members.

In all the years she's been on *Persephone*, Rachel has never found a satisfactory dance partner, even though Yuri has tried to learn. As a result, she continues to dance alone, spinning through her crystalline dwelling that reflects multiple images of a still beautiful and independent woman.

As they had planned and two years earlier than originally scheduled, Rachel and her crew successfully landed on Persephone 2, thirty-six years after they left Earth, where they began to build a new home. Fate was to determine however that Rachel was to live there for only a few years before she died of an unknown viral infection. She was buried according to a ritual the colony decided to adopt for all its members, which required bodies to be composted then 'joined' with the elements on the planet's surface.

***

Two years after Rachel's death and by the year 2100, the spacecraft, *Persephone*, has been permanently stabilized in a secure orbit around Persephone 2 where it serves as a space-station. The burgeoning new settlement includes Rachel's beloved daughter, Dha-shi-Zhi who is now twenty years old. Dha-shi-Zhi has recently coupled monogamously with Nikolai, Yuri and Anna's son, and they have produced a boy whom they have named, Centauri.

The crew members have built a small, beautiful, protocell city comprised of sand, wood, bricks, coral, trees, and plants, and is located on the shoreline of one of the planet's seas. Like the Caribbean on Earth, this ocean is a gorgeous aquamarine blue full of beautiful tropical fish and coral reefs and lined with palm trees. In the interior of the planet and behind this small, thriving city, are all manner of forests, mountains, and waterfalls.

After exploring the full interior of Persephone 2, the settlers now know a great deal of seismic activity has occurred on the planet in the past, including volcanic eruptions and Earthquakes. In fact, a group of scientists is presently observing a large, spectacular, volcanic eruption taking place many hundreds of miles away. Over the past few years, traveling parties have discovered a desert located in the center of the planet like the Sahara Desert on Earth, stretching for thousands of miles with constant storms blowing undulating sand in patterns that are like ocean waves. They have also confirmed the planet's Northern and

Southern poles contain ice and snow like the Earth's poles once did. Unlike Earth, though, their sun, the star, Proxima Centauri, is a beautiful, glowing orange.

While they've encountered animals some similar to those on Earth and some which are completely new to them, they have not found any forms of intelligent life in any way like their own.

So far, the colony functions peacefully and is egalitarian in its basic nature, with an elected body whose members will serve for three-year terms. The composition of the body must, by law, be equally divided between male and female representatives and contain artists as well as scientists to encourage disparate points of view. Members are selected to serve by ballot, based on what are considered essential categories of advanced knowledge, including math, science, biology, social sciences, psychology, music, art, and physics.

Monogamous relationships are now allowed among the settlers and, besides heterosexual relationships, include both male and male and female and female couples. 'Open marriages' among partners are not discouraged either if the practice does not lead to violence or jealousy and is conducted with mutual consent.

It has been decided that some human embryos on Persephone 2 will be implanted in artificial wombs, using the eggs and sperm that were carried on the Worldship to the planet. The children resulting from this procedure will be raised by the whole community and treated no differently than their peers who result from natural sex and human birth.

Children are required to attend a community school, which provides a learning system based not on academics but on developing human compassion firmly centered within the context of a just society. Subjects such as math, physics, biology, psychology, and history are presented in a way that supports this core idea.

While there have been no real encounters with other intelligent life forms, Dha-shi-Zhi, a physicist and biologist, has become intensely aware of the **quantum superposition** of another universe co-existing alongside their own. This universe is an alternate world in which she, herself, exists in an entirely separate form. Strangely enough, the knowledge that she is not a unique living being has not upset Dha-shi-Zhi's notion of her individuality or the understanding she has of her life as being a contained journey through space and time. Rather, she has begun to think of herself as a series of individuals. On many

163

occasions, Dha-shi-Zhi has briefly caught glimpses of this other Dha-shi-Zhi, who is an exact replica of herself.

Dha-shi-Zhi is in the process of writing about her experiences with this other parallel world from both a scientific and humanistic perspective. She is playing with the notion that, since birth, she has been entering many separate worlds and there may be multiple versions of Dha-shi-Zhi who have lived alternative lives; perhaps happier, more successful, or perhaps less moral and ethical, ones in which she has already died or suffered the loss of loved ones. Being a theoretical scientist, Dha-shi-Zhi is not averse to accepting any of these theories and realizes multiple versions of herself, while philosophically and spiritually complex, do not violate the basic laws of physics. She also realizes, that in some ways, she may need to reconcile herself to the idea the collective fate of her individual totality has already been determined—while there are many pathways of learning she can choose to get where she is going, there are still pre-determined events that, like immovable gates, cannot change.

Dha-shi-Zhi realizes it is purely by chance both she and her counterpart are located in a physical place where human life can, in fact, exist at all. For them to communicate directly with one another, though, Dha-shi-Zhi thinks they will both have to become aware of the other at exactly the same moment.

Within a few months of actually observing her other self in its parallel world, Dha-shi-Zhi's hypothesizes that the two selves might, perhaps, communicate. Together, she and Nikolai have concluded there are definitely certain circumstances in which computations performed in different universes can be combined, enabling parallel processing and, therefore, communication via spoken language and visual images. To test their hypothesis, Dha-shi-Zhi and Nikolai have attempted to establish communication with this other Dha-shi-Zhi in her parallel world. Although they haven't yet been successful, they are vigorously continuing their efforts.

Dha-shi-Zhi is still extremely sad about her mother Rachel's death, and she realizes she holds out some hope that Rachel might still be alive in this parallel universe that she has discovered. Besides nurturing the hope that she might in fact find another version of the mother whom she adored and misses terribly, Dha-shi-Zhi is also excited by the experimental nature of her work as she realizes she will be one of the first scientists to prove the quantum theory of multiverses.

Although she is unsure how contact between her two selves will affect her everyday life, she knows it will open up a whole new world of human knowledge for the members of their small settlement. What she clearly does not know, though, is her counterpart is a very different person and, in fact, lives a very different life to hers. By opening up this quantum door, Dha-shi-Zhi knows she will be exposing herself to a place of great complexity and potential danger.

Chapter 36
Alistair

Alistair continues to run the missions on Europa, Mars and the Moon. Since it has been years since he had any contact with Rachel or *Persephone*, he often finds himself wondering whether the ship has succeeded in reaching Proxima Centauri and if Rachel is still alive.

Even though he enjoys a comfortable lifestyle, Alistair has never fully adapted to living in Weather City, because despite everything done to make this underground environment attractive, he misses the direct feel and sight of the Earth's surface.

Robyn still works in genetics and is busily attempting to engineer longer, healthier lives for the plutocrats. Alistair, for his part, looks forward with a kind of perverse, sadistic pleasure to his twice-yearly meetings with Tom, at which they've come to know each other better. Alistair has easily picked up on Tom's disdain for his concern about those who have been left outside to die, and he realizes Tom sees this as weakness of character. He also understands that unlike him, Tom does not miss the Earth as it once was and is completely immersed in the challenges of keeping his small community at Ash Hollow alive and well. At each one of their get-togethers however Tom has repeatedly told him, "I'm still blown away by the fact that they lost all the data around Peter's work." This one repetitive thought of Tom's has led Alistair to think of himself as being the smarter of the two, despite Tom's wealth and advantage.

On the surface of Earth, everything in the Southern hemisphere has been reduced to a desert-like environment. The government does know, however, that in Alaska there are still some signs of forests and wetland, even though all the ice has long-since melted. Alistair assumes a few individuals who were wise enough to travel North may still have survived in Alaska, as well as those in the northernmost parts of Europe, Russia and China not submerged underwater by the rising seas.

Knowing that most food and water supplies, all information networks, and all power sources on Earth are still owned and controlled by the plutocrats, Alistair assumes the political status quo will remain in place for a very long time. Although the thought depresses him to no end, he acknowledges that, in some ways, this dynamic will ensure a peaceful, and secure world and this may be all human beings like him

166

and his family can now legitimately hope for.

As for the Declaration of Independence and the Constitution, an itemized, social contract of democratic freedom that governed the United States in the past, Alistair sees these documents as just more ideas burned on the bonfire of obsolete political ideals.

The par terraforming on the surface of Mars is continuing smoothly, with constant construction of more biospheres and the enclosing of caves and craters, making them habitable and ready for resettlement. Moon par terraforming settlements have also remained stable and able to communicate with Weather City's satellite systems.

Because its atmosphere is slowly being warmed with the addition of greenhouse gases caused by human settlement, Mars is also experiencing terraforming. Scientists hope that once the atmosphere on Mars warms up sufficiently to melt its frozen dirt and polar ice caps, the process will release carbon dioxide trapped under ice and dirt, causing liquid water to flow. At this juncture, botanists will seed the dirt with bacteria, lichens and mosses. The hope is that once plant life accelerates the production of oxygen on the surface, the planet will be able to support human and animal life outside of the biospheres.

5,000 settlers now live on Europa. As a direct result of the policy papers, he has authored over the years and Rachel's last communication with him, Alistair has been able to ensure no further encroachment by the U.S. government on the natural habitat of the Europans. Although efforts have been made to communicate with them, no one was as successful as Rachel in developing a meaningful dialogue.

***

Alistair has spent the many years since Peter died in 2060 debating what he should do with the chip he found in Peter's neck. After much thought he has locked it away in a safety deposit box, which he has placed together with a letter at the back of a desk drawer in his house.

"When Peter, my friend and colleague, who had been shot in the chest by government SEALs, was removed from life support and passed away, I decided I would not show the critical information contained on a chip I found behind his ear to anyone, not even to my wife, Robyn. My reasons for keeping this information from others is described below.

Upon careful consideration, I have come to realize if I give Peter's valuable research to Tom or to our government, neither will use it for the betterment of

167

humankind. Tom, as the head of a mega-corporation, and because of his continued collusion with our government, would likely use it to increase his vast fortune and for his benefit by trying to extend his own, personal life span. There is a risk he would reveal the whereabouts of Inanna and Rajeev and the secrets they contain. I also believe our government would most likely use Peter's technological advances to produce enhanced weaponry and super soldiers for the purposes of increasing their military domination over other potential worlds outside our galaxy, and other species within it, like the Europans.

It is my solemn belief that access to this advanced technology is dangerous since we do not yet have any of the answers as to how to establish peaceful and just societies. In some dark corner of my mind, I see Lord Sauron and Peter's one 'ring' being used to rule the other rings of power, which might indeed stretch into other galaxies, and onto other planets.

In summary, you who hold the bionic technology contained within this disk, will have tremendous knowledge at your disposal, I am, therefore, symbolically putting the 'ring' on you when fate decides the time is right.

My dream for humanity is that it will exist some day in a kinder and better world—a world in which this important information will be shared only to further the betterment of humankind.

Sincerely,
Alistair Trimmingham (aka Ranger of the North and Keeper of the Ring)

Chapter 37
Inanna

My reengineered twins, Sophie and Peter, are now five years old. Two dark-haired little things with enormous amounts of energy, they keep me happy and busy. I'm delighted to say they are exact replicas of the genetic blueprints I created for them. Since both are capable of conscious DNA self-repair, the twins will be very strong physically and disease-free. Although they have the capacity to live very long lives, the actual length will still be subject to accidents and mishaps.

With modified *alleles* for higher intelligence, the twins both have a cognitive ability of *1,000 Innate Intelligence points*. In addition, they have perfect recall, possess super-fast thinking and calculation, and very powerful geometric visualization. Interestingly, just like me, they can execute multiple analyses or trains of thought in parallel at the same time.

As part of my on-going experiment with genetic modification, I've documented how I was able to create the twins from beginning to end. With my computerized, machine-like capabilities, I first examined the human reproductive system very closely, including all the facets of human genetic make-up. I then accessed the nano chip within my brain that contains the elite gene bank on *Persephone* and what Peter downloaded before the ship departed from Earth. From there, I chose specific genetic materials I favored for my potential children, relating to height, weight, and intelligence, and duplicated this in my own children's DNA. Although in 2016, it was already possible for scientists, like Robyn to manipulate embryonic genetic material outside the womb, my process is much more advanced.

My research ultimately confirmed that, with the right training, the human female can learn how to manipulate her own and her partner's genetic creations, eliminating diseased and twisted strands of DNA. Of course, since I am an enhanced human being, I was able to create new genetic material using my own genes, reprogramming them then placing them into a live embryo, a process that non-enhanced human beings cannot yet accomplish.

As a symbol referring to the advance of human evolution, I've 'marked' both of my children with the sign of a blue serpent, meaning life and wisdom, and representing the cosmic unified consciousness of

DNA.

Hototo and Rajeev have proven to be great surrogate fathers to my twins. Leif, Hototo and Alice's son, is a caring and supportive big brother, carrying them around on his shoulders and inventing all manner of dangerous games.

Just as my friend, Sophie, predicted in our conversation as we camped near the Platte riverbed, and despite the emotional scars I carry from my past, Alice, Hototo and I have managed to weave together an emotionally satisfying relationship with each other, one that has drawn us all very close together.

Although as a trans-human, the process of making love to a human is incredibly painful for me, I have found I can temporarily stop the signals coming in from my peripheral nerves so sexual contact with anyone including Hototo and Alice can be satisfactory.

At this juncture, our Deep Creek colony has grown to 250 individuals. Of course, there have been deaths among the oldest members, as well as many births. Our 'made' environment continues to provide us with food and water. Without mates, many of the animals have become extinct. However, since we've preserved their DNA, we will be able to introduce them again when our planet becomes habitable. Right now, the Peregrine Falcons are a cause of great excitement among the community as well as other birds that have continued to breed and build many new nests in the cliffs where they raise their young.

Despite my advanced capabilities, I still have many questions I cannot answer categorically. Foremost among them are: Will our world regenerate itself? And did Rachel make it to Proxima Centauri?

From my background as a scientist, I know theoretically that the ozone layer, once it's free of the detrimental effects of fossil fuel and weather modification, can quickly regenerate itself and any holes we inadvertently ripped in our *magnetosphere* can also mend. Since no comet or asteroid has yet collided with Earth in the last millennium to cause any further catastrophes on a global scale, I am hopeful Earth will continue to survive as a home for humankind and that my twins, with their advanced abilities, will have much to contribute to this new world.

As for Rachel, I feel in my heart she reached Proxima Centauri safely. Knowing I will live for a long time, I am determined, at some point in the future, to find out what happened to her and her mission.

Chapter 38
Tom

Under Tom's skillful leadership, Ash Hollow has been operating successfully for over forty years and now boasts a slightly larger population. Still in touch with the Ruling Cabinet, Tom, at eighty, continues to travel on an infrequent basis to Weather City to conduct his business interests there. His assumption has always been that his company will re-emerge as a major international power when the ozone layer heals, and life is again possible on the surface of the Earth.

Contrary to his original thoughts on the matter, Tom is now convinced Sophie and Peter performed a vital service to the world in particular when they ended the weather modification program.

After waiting fifteen years for permission to have their first child, Tom's son, Seed, and daughter-in-law, Sarah, finally produce a daughter, Alexandra, now five-years-old. Tom sees her as a spunky little thing who has an intuitive understanding of how things work, and delights in taking everything apart and putting it back together again. As a first-time grandfather, Tom enjoys her company tremendously.

When Sarah his daughter-in-law brought Mehr's memoir to his attention, Tom actually read it and has developed, despite his usual skepticism, a partial understanding of the immortality of consciousness. He has told Rajeev, "I suppose I rather hope in some vague, way that I will return to Earth in a few hundred years as myself, and find my fortune intact, and the human species thriving in all its teaming complexity. However, to be honest since this seems highly unlikely, I would feel much more confident having my genetic code transferred into a non-biological matrix, a process I believe will be the only way for me to achieve the kind of endless, individualized, immortality I most desire."

Tom has also, without the government's direct knowledge and through an obscure and murky intellectual property clause, secured patents on the technology lodged inside both Rajeev and Inanna. Under this clause, they and all their descendants now legally 'belong' to him. In addition, he's left sealed instructions specifying that, since his company "owns" Rajeev, Inanna, and their descendants, they must be used for future research when life does resume on the surface of the planet. By taking these actions, he hopes his lasting legacy will ultimately be the vital knowledge that finally unlocks the secret of extending human life. Also, if he was to be completely honest with himself, Tom admits he is happy to have ownership over them, since he has always been afraid of Inanna and her growing power, especially now that she has successfully produced offspring almost completely on her own, and he feels secure knowing that her future is now under his control.

He has not seen Alistair, his erstwhile friend since Alistair left the protection of the bio-dome in 2090, as he explained in the letter he left for Styx and Robyn, to head North and live once more on the Earth's surface. At their infrequent meetings throughout the years, Tom had become increasingly aware that Alistair was deeply depressed about being forced to live underground. When he had begun to discuss his desire and plans to live once more on the surface of Earth, Tom had not really believed him, and had thus felt no compunction to dissuade him or encourage him to seek help.

Tom has recently told Neil, "While I sincerely regret your brother's foolish decision, I cannot help but think that it was an incredibly insensitive way to behave towards his family members and in particular his daughter, Styx."

Chapter 39
Rajeev and Caro

Because Caro's husband died unexpectedly of an undiagnosed congenital heart defect, Rajeev has spent more and more time with her and Ola. While his actual anatomical age is considerably older, Rajeev looks much younger, and his body and skin still function as though he were only twenty-five. Caro, on the other hand, is fifty-three. Despite her biological 'frailty,' she is still a very beautiful woman, in Rajeev's eyes. Ola has grown into a tall, healthy young man who, it seems, is very popular with everyone in the Settlement, especially the girls.

Over the past few months, Rajeev has discussed with Inanna his feelings of love for Caro and his intentions to propose to her. In all their extended conversations, Inanna has told him, "You must move forward without delay in telling her this." Rajeev, however, is very cautious by nature and has always kept his feelings close to his chest. Over the years, he has managed to harbor his love for Caro in silence. Now that she is at last within reach, he finds he is unable to satisfactorily articulate his feelings.

Because he is also a deeply spiritual and philosophical man, Rajeev fully accepts the notion that it is possible to love someone for a lifetime even though that love is unrequited. For that reason, he has found many non-romantic ways to express his devotion to Caro; by building strong relationships with members of her family, he has given her emotional and physical support whenever she needed it. Now that the possibility of a physical relationship with her is finally within his grasp, Rajeev is having a very difficult time saying words that will prompt Caro to examine her own feelings towards him.

In order to avoid thinking too much about Caro, Rajeev spends a great deal of time in the underground caves at Deep Creek, a place he regards as his personal 'temple.' After Hototo, Ola, Leif, and Rajeev discovered how to move deeper into the caves through flowstone-covered passages, Rajeev found a twenty-foot long and fifteen-foot-high chamber covered with bone-white, slender, coral-shaped helictites. This space, above all others, has become his hideout. Rajeev is fascinated by its translucent calcite 'draperies' shaped like caramel condor wings that grow where water runs in grooves along the 'ceilings.' He is awed by the beaded and frosted clusters of aragonite crystals and calcite, which form stunning stalactites and stalagmites, rising and falling unexpectedly from the cave's surfaces.

Around the freshwater pools in the caves that originate from deep under the Earth, Rajeev has found iron oxide-tinted stalagmites and **botryoids**. However, the rarest, most delicate and beautiful formations he has seen are the white, curving strands of gypsum flowers along the Deep River Creek bed that look like fern heads before they begin unfolding in late spring.

Walking on the dirt at the bottom of Deep Creek, as is his habit when he's sorting through diverse emotions, Rajeev focuses on mathematical and scientific inquiry, two of the enduring disciplines in his life. He has lately been transfixed by his theory that *free electrons* are transferred into the body through the soil. .

Rajeev's theory of earth-connectedness has been harder for him to extend to Ash Hollow, which is primarily a water-bound environment. However, he has concluded that, by swimming in shallow pools daily, the residents do absorb necessary electrons from the rocks and water itself. In fact, he is convinced that a healthy, overall diet, and activities based on contact with electrons, combined with a total absence of plastics in the environment, have resulted in surprisingly healthy populations in both settlements.

In tandem with his primary research on free electrons, Rajeev has also taken on two additional projects: he is developing a better ventilation system for the settlement biospheres, which he believes will prevent prolonged contact with chemical-resistant-based diseases that spread in closed atmospheres; and, because of his interest in preventing potential epidemics arising from the introduction of new viruses or bacterial infections that cannot be treated, Rajeev has taken to studying various cave microbial communities to determine how microbes adapt and survive in harsh environments.

Rajeev's scientific work during the day, followed by evenings with Caro and Ola in their small house on the banks of the Creek, keep him very happy. Although Rajeev knows Caro enjoys his company, he believes that as time passes, she will also realize he is in love with her and has been for a very long time. If that should happen, he desperately hopes she would turn out to be the one to 'make the first move,' since by now he knows he is quite unable to do that on his own.

Part III

2160 - 2165

Chapter 40
Inanna

At 120, I find myself still in surprisingly good health—my appearance can be compared to that of a forty-five-year-old and my body itself is still strong and fit. The negative consequence of outliving my human peers, though, is that life can be very lonely. To compensate for the many losses we survived, Rajeev and I have become an amiable couple who live together quietly and demonstrate great love and affection for one another. We embrace often in sympathy, and we sleep together each night, side by side, holding hands.

Preceded by Alice, Hototo died in 2120. Even though Caro's death at the ripe old age of ninety-three occurred two decades ago, Rajeev still mourns her. Painfully, my lovely daughter Sophie died in a freak accident after a fall from a ledge in one of the caves she loved to explore on her own. Although it was no one's fault, her death caused me many months of intense suffering I cannot fully explain to this day. For long periods of time, I was not capable of turning off my human feelings as I had always been able to do. As a result, I was not in my right mind and became severely depressed. It has only been through Rajeev's persistent affection and love that I've been able to fully recover, and, in some way, find value and importance in the full expression of human emotion.

Sarah's daughter, Alexandra, has also been a passionate and warm friend to me; she travels between our two camps, often with Rajeev. When her turn came up to have a child, Alexandra was already fifty-five, so, using her own frozen eggs, she gave birth to a daughter, Sophia. I am very sad that Sarah never met this little granddaughter, and my daughter never met young Sophia, either.

Sophia is a charming child with a shock of unruly, dark brown curls that are soft, yet wiry to the touch. Alexandra ended up marrying Jules, Alistair's great nephew and the grandson of Neil. Sophia is, therefore, a bi-racial child of great beauty and extreme intelligence. She isn't big but is very sturdy and compact and loves to waddle around our home babbling away and carrying things. She seems to like everything in pairs, one in each hand—two stones, two shoes, two spoons, two sticks and so on, and she screams if you take one of them away.

To my dismay, my son left the Settlement a few years ago now.

Intent on finding other groups like ours, Peter set off to develop a network of communities that could support each other politically and economically when all of this is over. Ultimately, Peter wants to begin to promote an alternative to the plutocratic governments that have been in control of Earth for so long. I suppose he's a kind of revolutionary. In order to remain in touch, we communicate directly, one brain to another. He's complex, very tough, and doesn't steer away from removing anyone or anything that stands in his way.

I worry Peter hasn't found a permanent partner yet, either male or female. Because his physical, emotional, and cognitive differences have turned him into an extreme loner, Peter will most likely find it difficult to establish the type of close relationship that exists with a partner. Rajeev, on the other hand has told me, "I'm sure Peter will find his own way eventually." Maintaining an optimism about life that I so admire, Rajeev buoys me up like a tide moving inexorably forward, always predictable, always energetic, and always life-giving and timely.

And so, we continue to await the regeneration of our Earth. Rajeev and I believe the process will occur slowly over many more years, starting in the northern-most areas of the planet, where we are hopeful there are still small communities of human survivors. Until then, our little diorama, our little three-dimensional, full-size, model world, enclosed as it is in its glass showcase, goes on surviving happily and with hope.

Chapter 41
Peter

Peter, Inanna's son, left the settlement of Ash Hollow in 2155 and has been travelling North since then to find other independent communities of survivors like the ones at Ash Hollow and Deep Creek. Since he has UV-resistant skin, a super-strong musculature for walking and running, and advanced hearing and vision like his mother, he can easily travel on foot.

Although Peter has found a number of active communities in Canada and also in Alaska that have survived, he has taken pains to avoid those few with reputations for violence and cult-like behavior. Along the way, he has listened carefully to many horror stories about corrupt, cruel leaders, cannibalism, and torture and about the worst kind of bestiality of which human beings are capable. In spite of his very real feelings of sadness and cynicism that resulted from learning about these human behaviors, Peter has become tougher and more determined to disregard any obstacles that might clutter his path.

After traveling through Canada and Alaska, Peter crosses the Bering Straits with a boat captain who operates a sketchy black market, cross-ocean, transportation system. Here he finds an independent community of over one hundred people floating under a biosphere in the middle of the sea. Consisting of approximately five miles of hills and small towns, the facility was built as a refuge for family and friends against the Burning Years by a Russian oligarch who fell out of favor with the central government. The Russian explains to Peter that, although the mag-lev train that ran under the ocean and connected Canada to Russia is still in place, it has not been operational for many years. Before Peter leaves, he also shows him the grave of 'Alistair Trimmingham', a U.S. citizen whom he tells Peter had died there of radiation sickness, shortly after he made his way to their settlement from D.C. many years ago.

From the Bering Straits, Peter travels across Northern Russia, where he learns that much of China's pre-existing coastal areas are under water, as are those of India and the rest of Asia. Although Australia has survived with only a slight rise in the sea along its coastlines, it now contains a large, salt lake in its mid-section. England

and Ireland on the other hand, are half their original sizes; London itself is gone.

Reaching Scandinavia, Peter finds many small, independent communities, most of which were created during 2025 that have survived the release of viruses from the melting permafrost. Although some of these colonies are governed by humane and wise leaders, others are controlled by rulers with cruel and unbending beliefs and ideologies.

From Southern Norway, Peter finds a Captain who operates a small, covered boat who takes him down through the North Sea and across the Atlantic to the U.S. Finally, he arrives in New Pittsburgh, where he begins to develop an organized network of the world-wide communities, he has contacted during his journey that have survived and are independent of any centralized form of government. Although Peter is not entirely sure yet what configuration this 'federation' will adopt, he's hopeful there is enough support among the disparate groups he has visited to create a strong and viable community of sorts.

Chapter 42
Alexandra

Alexandra has grown up mainly in the Ash Hollow settlement, where her mother and father lived. Throughout her life, Alexandra had always been very close to her grandfather Tom who died in 2105, shortly preceded by her grandmother Noemi.

Tom and Noemi never fully recovered from the death of their daughter Rosie. As a result of her work in the community hospital, Rosie caught a fatal case of pneumonia. Since she and her husband never had any children, Seed became the sole heir to Tom's company and all its assets.

Although Seed maintained some minimal communication with Weather City after Tom's death, he adamantly refused to sit on the Ruling Cabinet. Noemi's gardens and herbal botany remained his primary interests in life, and, in fact, when he finally died at the age of ninety-two, he was surrounded, like Remedios the Beauty in *One Hundred Years of Solitude*, by the ancestors of the yellow butterflies he and Sarah had been given as a wedding gift.

Alexandra's primary interest of study continues to be human psychology. As a student, she read intensely about all the world's great psychologists. Although she is not impressed by Freud's work, she does think Jung's theories contain a great deal of truth. While she understands that psychologists work primarily with the most troubled of individuals, Alexandra is also particularly interested in the characteristics of exemplary people. In addition, she is fascinated by Brian Weiss, a Twentieth Century psychiatrist who believed elements of the human personality survive after death, and past-life experiences influenced many of the phobias and ailments he witnessed in his patients.

Alexandra visits Deep Creek regularly and spends many hours discussing her thoughts on the human psyche with Inanna. Like Seed, she has also declined to participate on the Weather City Ruling Cabinet and is quite happy to have her husband, Jules, help run the family business from afar with her. So far, Alexandra has not resolved how she will handle the burden that, by the nature of the family she was born into, has been placed on her shoulders.

***

In September 2165, Sophia becomes quite sick. In a desperate effort to control the disease, every medicine available is tried. The illness, which came on swiftly and violently, caused fever, headaches, vomiting, and seizures. Given that Sophia is the great granddaughter of Tom, and as a final resort, Inanna advises Alexandra to contact Weather City for assistance. Although the cost of taking the child in for treatment will not be an issue, Alexandra knows the Government will be very reluctant to expose its population to an unknown disease by allowing Sophia to enter the city. Although Alexandra has assured the Ruling Cabinet that no other residents of Ash Hollow have contracted the disease, and doctors there surmise the illness must have resulted from the bite of an unknown variety of insect, Alexandra is still waiting for a response to her request.

After two days, Alexandra receives permission to bring her in. Upon arrival at Weather City, Sophia is kept in an isolation unit in the hospital for three weeks, and Jules and Alexandra are allowed to live in the hospital with her. Happily, Sophia's condition improves drastically to the point where the doctors tell her parents they believe she won't suffer any long-term effects. Despite Sophia's seemingly complete recovery, however, they are advising the family to remain in Weather City for at least the next six months so they can monitor her to ensure her condition continues to be stable. Jules and Alexandra resign themselves to following the doctors' advice.

Once six months have passed and Sophia has not had a relapse, Alexandra and Jules begin to make plans to return to Ash Hollow. It is at this point, however, that the Ruling Cabinet informs them it is highly unlikely permission will be given for them to leave the city, now that they are once more back 'in the fold.'

To avoid risking the lives and well-being of the settlers at Ash Hollow or revealing the existence of the Deep Creek settlement, to say nothing of the location of Inanna and Rajeev, they reluctantly agree to stay in Weather City without resistance. As a part of her strange disease Sophia has lost most of her memories about her past life at Ash Hollow, including most of the people who lived there. Despite being very upset Alexandra is pleased that this memory loss includes the existence of Inanna and Rajeev. Although Alexandra hates to involve her child in a web of deceit, she will not jeopardize the trans-human's safety in any way and so she decides she will never tell her daughter about their existence.

Like any group of refugees who have had to leave all they've known to help themselves and those they love, Alexandra and Jules feel a tremendous sense of loss. In the end, to assuage these feelings they decide to live near Alistair's granddaughter Europa, her husband Chris, and their three-year-old son Obi.

PART IV

2168

CHAPTER 43
Alexander, Jules and Sophia

Three years after their move from Ash Hollow, Sophia is healthy but still suffers memory loss about her time at Ash Hollow. As they had surmised, her illness resulted from an insect bite. Given the drastic changes Earth has undergone, it is highly likely other unknown insects like this, as well as bacterial and viral species, are now growing and adapting to the new environmental conditions both under and on the surface of the planet.

Alexandra has found a job teaching in the department of social sciences at the University. Although she has adapted to her new life, there are still many days when she is greatly depressed. She desperately misses the two communities of Deep Creek and Ash Hollow and is uncertain about her family's future as heirs to Tom's great fortune. To protect Sophia from the ugliness of this world, she intends to keep her away from her inheritance for as long as possible.

Recently Alexandra has had a surprise visit from Inanna's son Peter who is now living in New Pittsburgh. Peter has told Alexandra, "I'm able to relay messages safely for you to and from Inanna, but your contact with me can only be infrequent and you must tell no one about it."

After he has left, Alexandra carefully considers the dangerous activities to which he has alluded to during their meeting. He has virtually admitted that he is now the leader of a new generation of 'counter elites.' Although she completely understands and agrees with his dissatisfaction with their 'well-ordered society,' she is afraid his actions and those of his friends might unleash a prolonged period of great violence.

Despite all her misgivings about Peter and his current involvements however, Alexandra has a reason to feel happiness for the first time in a long while because he has brought her a handwritten note from Inanna, one he has asked her to destroy immediately after she has read it.

Dearest Alexandra,

We are all well here. Rajeev and I are still the two, old people on the block who refuse to die, and, as a result, have outlived all our peers! Of course, we've made new friends over the years, but we mourn our old friends and now you've left us too.

I miss you so much that it's as if one of my limbs has been severed.

Peter tells us you live comfortably in Weather City, and you've found a job you enjoy. I imagine that Jules continues to run the business and keep things in order for the time being. I can't wait to learn more about Sophia, even if it's vicariously from afar. I hope you'll send me pictures of her from time to time. Tell me, does she favor language, science, art? – I'm greedy to know it all!

Thank you for sending me a copy of Mehr's memoir. I was intrigued; it gave me hope that something positive may also wait in the wings for Rajeev and me at the end of our lives on Earth.

The section Mehr wrote on love made me consider my own attachments. As you know, for many years I loved Hototo and Alice. Losing them and then my two darling Sophies were sadness's that have been hard to overcome. And now I have to add you, Jules and Sophia to that list, so I ask myself, how much harder can life get?

Know however, dearest Alexandra, that Rajeev, my old friend, and the harbor into which I have so gratefully sailed and laid anchor, keeps my spirits up daily with his gentle and reflective humor, as well as his physical closeness and affection.

I'm also gratified to see that Peter, my beloved son, was born with a fierce commitment to social and economic equality for those who, despite all the odds, still remain on our little planet, which I understand from him, is slowly recovering in the very northernmost climes. Peter is convinced those of us living outside of the government's control will need to be prepared to resist and exercise our independence and demand our freedom. I am inclined to agree with him.

I know you've always been a reluctant heiress and you've pledged to keep Sophia away from her inheritance. However, I believe there will come a time when Tom's family legacy and long arm will be put to good use—will, in fact, be a positive factor in leveraging (a word he so often loved to use!) a more positive future for all of humankind.

So, my dearest, darling Alexandra, I leave you with these few words and thoughts for the time being and will look forward greatly to our ongoing correspondence over the next few years.

A million kisses as always to you, Jules and my beloved Sophia,
Your Inanna

THIS MARKS THE END OF BOOK ONE
THE STORY CONTINUES IN 'HOMO DEUS'

I hope that readers will take climate change very seriously and do whatever they can to help preserve our Earth. To start, I suggest you join 350.org or other important organizations, like the Sierra Club, and support their projects. Updated information on climate change issues can be found on my website https://theburningyears.squarespace.com.

In addition to supporting the efforts of action groups, there are other ways that all of us can personally combat global warming **despite what the Federal Government may or may not do**. We can do this by FOCUSING on our small local communities. By powering our homes with renewable energy; by using energy-efficient appliances; by eliminating waste and eating all the food we buy; by reducing the amount of meat we consume; by driving fuel-efficient vehicles; by using public transportation more often; and by flying less often.

The sequel to this book – *Homo Deus* – comes next, so please join me as we follow the families and characters you've already met into the year 2190, as many of them take part in the search for an ancient source of energy. A source which will help them as they attempt to form a new human civilization on Earth's surface.

GLOSSARY

Algae bioreactors— can be used to reduce pollutants such as CO2.

Alkaline Hydrolysis—is a process for the disposal of human remains which produces less carbon dioxide and pollutants than cremation. The process is being marketed as an alternative to the traditional options of burial or cremation.

Alleles—one of two or more alternative forms of a gene that arise by mutation and are found at the same place on a chromosome.

Anaerobic digesters—are microorganisms which break down biodegradable material in the absence of oxygen. One of the end products is biogas, which is combusted to generate electricity and heat.

Bio-dynamic system—treats soil fertility and plant growth as ecologically interrelated tasks.

Bio-Gas Digesters—are the latest in the Renewable Energy development. Designed to be installed as a retrofit model in a domestic environment to produce methane gas for cooking and heating. It's clean, maintenance free and delivers pressurized biogas.

Bioluminescent light sources—the production and emission of light by a living organism.

Bionic—means having artificial body parts, especially electromechanical ones *and* having ordinary human powers increased by the aid of bionic devices.

Bliss Bacteria—a cultivated bacteria that removes bad odors.

Cellular Reprograming—is the conversion of one specific cell type to another. This means cells are genetically reprogrammed to an embryonic stem cell-like state. For instance, aging can be defined as the progressive decline in the ability of a cell or organism to resist stress and disease. Recent advances in cellular reprogramming technologies have enabled reprogramming to ameliorate aging both *in vitro* and *in vivo*. Cellular reprogramming may in the future assist the development of novel therapeutic strategies to extend a healthy lifespan.

Chlorofluorocarbons (CFCs)—are nontoxic, nonflammable

chemicals containing atoms of carbon, chlorine, and fluorine. They are used in the manufacture of aerosol sprays, blowing agents for foams and packing materials, as solvents, and as refrigerants.

Chemosynthetic bacteria—are organisms that use inorganic molecules as a source of energy and convert them into organic substances. **Chemosynthetic bacteria**, unlike plants, obtain their energy from the oxidation of inorganic molecules, rather than photosynthesis.

Coronal Mass Ejection—a giant cloud of solar plasma drenched with magnetic field lines that are blown away from the Sun during strong, long-duration solar flares and filament eruptions.

Cremulator—a device to grind the bone fragments that remain after resomation into fine powder.

CRISPR Technology—involves a technique for gene splicing and editing. It has the potential to cure any genetic disease and could lead to designer babies.

Cyborg Robot—is a machine-like human whose physical and mental abilities are extended beyond normal human limitations.

Electric Universe model grew out of a broad interdisciplinary approach to science. It is not a technique taught in universities. The **Electric Universe** is based more on observations and experiment than abstract theory. It recognizes connections between diverse disciplines. It concludes that the crucial requirement for understanding the universe is to take fully into account the basic electrical nature of atoms and their interactions. Strangely, this is not the case in conventional cosmology where weaker magnetism and the infinitely weaker force of gravity rule the cosmos. Such a simplification may suit a theoretical physics based on electrical neutrality of matter in Earthly laboratories, but it does not apply in space where *plasma dominates*.

http://www.holoscience.com/wp/synopsis/synopsis-02-the-electric-universe/

http://www.nasa.gov/centers/glenn/about/fs21grc.html

Electro-pharma—uses electrical impulses, rather than the chemicals or biological molecules found in today's pharmaceuticals, to treat diseases.

Electronic propulsion—an electrically powered spacecraft propulsion system which uses electrical energy to change the velocity of a spacecraft. Electric thrusters are less powerful and typically use much less fuel.

EPPP System (External Pulsed Plasma Propulsion)— a nuclear pulse propulsion or external pulsed plasma propulsion is a hypothetical method of spacecraft propulsion that uses nuclear explosions for thrust. NASA Glenn's patented Annular Engine has the potential to exceed the performance capabilities of the NEXT ion propulsion system and other electric propulsion thruster designs. It uses a new thruster design that yields a total (annular) beam area that is 2 times greater than that of NEXT.

http://www.nasa.gov/centers/glenn/about/fs21grc.html

Free electrons—It is well established, though not widely known, that the surface of the Earth possesses a limitless and continuously renewed supply of free or mobile electrons as a consequence of a global atmospheric electron circuit.

Global dimming—creates a cooling effect that may partially counteract the effect of greenhouse gases on global warming. https://www.sciencealert.com/scientists-warn-dimming-the-sun-is-simply-too-dangerous-heres-why?utm_source=ScienceAlert+-+Daily+Email+Updates&utm_campaign=47d2a6a587-RSS_EMAIL_CAMPAIGN&utm_medium=email&utm_term=0_fe5632fb09-47d2a6a587-365884945

Graphite—is a crystalline form of carbon, a semi-metal, a native element mineral, and one of the allotropes of carbon. **Graphite** is the most stable form of carbon under standard conditions.

Heliostat—is a device that includes a mirror, usually a plane mirror, which turns so as to keep reflecting sunlight toward a predetermined target, compensating for the sun's apparent motions in the sky.

Homogametic and heterogametic sex—refers to the **sex** of a species in which the **sex** chromosomes are not the same. For example, in humans, males, with an X and a Y **sex** chromosome, would be referred to as the **heterogametic sex**, and females having two X **sex** chromosomes would be referred to as the **homogametic sex.**

Hydrobots—are very large fish-shaped robots that swim and are equipped with chemical sensors and Wi-Fi technology.

Hydroponics—is a subset of hydroculture, the method of growing plants without soil, using mineral nutrient solutions in a water solvent.

Hygroscopic materials—readily attract water from their surroundings.

Intercropping—is a multiple cropping practice involving growing two or more crops in proximity. The most common goal of intercropping is to produce a greater yield on a given piece of land by making use of resources that would otherwise not be utilized by a single crop.

Ionosphere—is the layer of the Earth's atmosphere that contains a high concentration of ions and free electrons and is able to reflect radio waves. It lies above the mesosphere and extends from about 50 to 600 miles (80 to 1,000 km) above the Earth's surface.

Liquid Lithium—s a chemical element with the symbol Li and atomic number 3. It is a soft, silver-white metal belonging to the alkali metal group of chemical elements.

Maglev guideways—The magnetized coil running along the track, called a **guideway**, repels the large magnets on the train's undercarriage, allowing the train to **levitate** between 0.39 and 3.93 inches (1 to 10 centimeters) above the guideway. Once the train is levitated, power is supplied to the coils within the guideway walls to create a unique system of magnetic fields that pull and push the train along the guideway.

Maglev Train—is a magnetic levitation train. Maglev trains float on a cushion of air, eliminating friction. This lack of friction and the trains' aerodynamic designs allow these trains to reach unprecedented ground transportation speeds of more than **310 mph** (500 kph). Developers say that maglev trains will eventually link cities that are up to 1,000 miles (1,609 kilometers) apart. At 310 mph, you could travel from Paris to Rome in just over two hours. (Taken from an article by Kevin Bonsor http://science.howstuffworks.com/transport/engines-equipment/maglev-train1.htm)

Magnetosphere—is the region surrounding the Earth or another astronomical body in which its magnetic field is the predominant effective magnetic field.

MEMS—are internal microscopic medical devices of the future with moving parts fabricated using modified semiconductor device fabrication technologies, normally used to make electronics.

More about my research on Inanna and Rajeev http://www.natasha.cc/consciousnessreframed.htm

Nanotubes—area tubular molecule composed of a large number of carbon atoms. Nanotubes could in the future replace some metal electronic components, leading to faster devices.

Natural computing—is based on taking inspiration from nature for the development of novel problem-solving techniques.

Network Sonar ability—echolocation, the power to glean <u>information</u> about surroundings by bouncing sound waves off surfaces, in a virtual environment. Although the human brain normally suppresses echoes, it perceives them when a person uses echolocation, the research showed. Bats, dolphins and porpoises use echolocation to navigate and hunt.

Neuroelectric—relates to the electrical phenomena (as potentials or signals) generated by the nervous system.

Nikola Tesla—was a Serbian American inventor, electrical engineer, mechanical engineer, physicist, and futurist best known for his contributions to the design of the modern alternating current (AC) electricity supply system.

Nuclear Subterrenes—machines that work by melting their way through the rock and soil, actually vitrifying it as they go, and leaving a neat, solidly glass-lined tunnel behind them.

Optimal Germination—For every species of seed, there is an optimal soil temperature for germination, and at that temperature, the maximum number of seeds will germinate and, in less time, than at any other temperature. For example, if you sow onion seeds at 32°F you get 90% germination.

Parabolic Hearing—ears enhanced to hear with amazing clarity, distance, and even frequencies outside normal range. Users' ears can pick up every single sound, can decipher layer upon layer of differing sounds/conversations, locate the source of noise, or pick up a sound from a mile away in a busy city.

Paralimbic lobe—In species of whale the limbic lobe, is vastly enlarged and made up of three separate lobes separated by two clefts: the limbic and paralimbic clefts. The cellular structure of the paralimbic lobe in species of whale includes many more spindle cells than the human brain. In humans these cells are associated with social organization, emotional expression and empathy.

Para terraforming—involves the construction of a habitable enclosure on a planet which eventually grows to encompass most of the planet's usable area. The enclosure would consist of a transparent roof held one or more kilometers above the surface, pressurized with a breathable atmosphere, and anchored with tension towers and cables at regular intervals. The par terraforming can be tailored to the needs of the planet's population, growing only as fast and only in those areas where it is required. Para terraforming greatly reduces the amount of atmosphere that one would need to add to planets like Mars to provide Earth-like atmospheric pressures. Para terraforming is also less likely to cause harm to any native lifeforms that may hypothetically inhabit the planet, as the parts of the planet outside the enclosure will not be affected.

Particle worms—are chemical worms.

Photo-voltaic cell— a solar cell, and an electrical device that converts the energy of light directly into electricity by the photovoltaic effect, which is a physical and chemical phenomenon.

Plutocrats—are a small minority of the wealthiest citizens who rule everybody else.

Probability—is a theory that includes random variables and events that affect our lives which can be forecast based on a set of mathematical formulas. For example, how many times do you need to throw the dice before it to lands on six?

Protocell—a self-organized, spherical collection of lipids proposed as a stepping-stone to the origin of life. A central question in evolution is how simple protocells first arose and how they could differ in reproductive output, thus enabling the accumulation of novel biological emergences over time, i.e., biological evolution. A functional protocell has now been achieved in a laboratory setting, the goal to fully understand the process appears well within reach. This will mean we can chemically construct biological processes such as animal protein, cotton clothes, animal skin (leather), etc. http://technologyofus.com/armstrong-protocells/

Quantum teleportation—is a process by which quantum information (e.g., the exact state of an atom or photon) can be transmitted (exactly, in principle) from one location or person to another, with the help of classical communication and previously shared quantum entanglement between the sending and receiving location or person.

Regolith—is a layer of loose, heterogeneous superficial material covering solid rock. It includes dust, soil, broken rock, and other related materials and is present on Earth, the Moon, Mars, some asteroids, and other terrestrial planets and moons.

Resomator—a device that dissolves bodies in superheated alkaline water (water mixed with corrosive potassium hydroxide). It's basically a human-sized metal vat—a body pressure cooker. The liquefaction process takes about two-and-a-half hours, and the resultant product is sterile and DNA-free.

Singularity—is individual human intelligence released into a computer system that makes it trillions of times more powerful than current human intelligence.

Skin that is tone-textured and changeable—is skin that is artificially enhanced and is sun-resistant, and healthier and fresher than normal human skin.

Soil Ecosystems—Soils play an important role in all of our natural ecological cycles—carbon, nitrogen, oxygen, water and nutrient. They also provide benefits through their contribution in a number of ecosystems.

Stellar Formation and Evolution—is the process by which a star, a luminous sphere of plasma held together by its own gravity, is formed and changes over the course of time. Dense regions within molecular clouds in interstellar space, sometimes referred to as "stellar nurseries" or "star-forming regions," fuse to form stars. Depending on the mass of the star, its lifetime can range from a few million years for the most massive to trillions of years for the least massive, which is considerably longer than the age of the universe.

Sterilized Cryobots—Current space missions are governed by the Outer Space Treaty and the COSPAR guidelines for planetary protection. Forward contamination is prevented primarily by sterilizing the spacecraft and its equipment like cryobots. A

Cryobot or Philberth-probe is a robot that can penetrate water ice. A **cryobot** uses heat to melt the ice, and gravity to sink downward. The difference between the **cryobot** and a drill is that the **cryobot** uses less power than a drill and doesn't pollute the environment.

Symbiosis—is a close and often long-term interaction between two different biological species.

Synthetic biology—is an interdisciplinary branch of **biology** and engineering. The subject combines various disciplines from within these domains, such as biotechnology, evolutionary **biology**, molecular **biology**, systems **biology**, biophysics, computer engineering, and genetic engineering.

Ubuntu Principles—include a philosophy based on absolute equality and abundance for all and Unity Consciousness.

Weather Geoengineering—is the deliberate large-scale manipulation of an environmental process that affects the Earth's climate, in an attempt to counteract the effects of global warming.

Whole Body Navigational Grid—future brain-machine-interfaces (BMIs) implanted in the brain that allow humans to use cortical activity to control artificially enhanced limbs at will. Includes a nano-engineered spinal communication system.

ACKNOWLEDGEMENTS

My sincere thanks to JoAnn Deck my former agent and editor. My thanks also to Paul Butler the editor of the last books in the series. Paul has improved my writing considerably. Also to Susan Hoffman Fishman https://www.susanhoffmanfishman.com whose generosity and extraordinary eye for detail strengthened *The Burning Years*.

Also, my thanks to David Miller whose generosity and line editing was so valuable. Also, kudos to Bill Hern for researching my unique and crazy family history, and for giving me his advice and help to get this series published.

My profound thanks to Andrew Sparke and his team at APS Books who took me on as one of their authors. APS has published over 1000 titles by 100+ authors and photographers including the best-selling alternative history series 'An Extra Knot' by Hugh Lupus, and rare photography collections like 'Duran Duran En Scène'. www.andrewsparke.com

I would also like to thank Susan Toy https://islandeditions.wordpress.com/about-susan-m-toy/ for taking the time to be a first reader for my books, and cheer me on.

A shout out to my son-in-law Arthur Vallin who has helped me develop my book trailer and provided a visual interpretation of my characters. https://www.arthurvallin.com

My love and thanks also to my husband, Chris who have given me encouragement and support in my writing over the years. To my two daughters Alexandra and Sarah who have also supported me and made the resources of their company available to me. www.Harleyandco.com

Particular thanks to Richard Nelson who was inspirational, and without whose help and support I could not have developed the characters and plot of these books. His eclectic and varied library located in Merlin's Cave were invaluable to me as I conducted my research.

In addition, my sincere thanks to Dr. Rachel Armstrong, a frequent contributor to TED https://www.ted.com/talks/rachel_armstrong_architecture_that_repairs_itself, and Professor of Living Architecture, who graciously read this book and helped me to understand many of the scientific facts outlined in it. Rachel also spoke to me about science in a highly poetic language, which appealed to my love of metaphor. With Dr. Armstrong's permission, the character, Dr. Rachel Chen, uses a direct quote from Dr. Armstrong when she talks to her crew about the importance of soil. Rachel Armstrong kindly offered the following advice to me:

"I would like to suggest that their colony is successful as they have figured out how to make soil ecosystems. The trouble with current approaches - like the one used in the Martian - where the protagonist poops in the Martian sand ... is that it lacks a complex micro organismal set of networks ...

The thing that makes soil successful is the tiny ecosystems that live in it which benefit from the matrix of air, water, and nutrients ... and of course structural shelter ...

Hydroponics is not enough ... it's not a 'compost elevator' ... it does not allow organic matter to be decomposed and returned to the world in a new body or set of relationships ... by trying to reduce the idea of soil into a hydroponics system we increase fragility and eliminate the idea of regeneration.

So, if your colony on Mars figured out what these relationships are ... and there is no reason why a 'worm system' could not be based on protocells rather than annelids ... so they act as subtractive and additive printers that transform matter in the process ... we have biological worms on Earth - why not chemical ones on Mars ..."

My thanks also to Wallace Thornhill www.holoscience.com/wp/, professor of physics and electronics, who graciously took the time to assist me in my understanding of warm nuclear fusion. His advice to me:

"And the latest thing (needed for interstellar travel because it uses no fuel) is http://finance.yahoo.com/news/nasa-latest-tests-show-physics-230112770.html. Also, you could assume that it would continue to accelerate beyond the speeds of ion plasma thrusters."

Thanks also to author Peter Levenda who took the time to seriously consider many of the questions I asked him about the nature of consciousness itself, and the relation of consciousness to immediate social and political problems. His answers included serious questions back to me that I should consider as I developed my novels, such as, "What does spiritual growth look like in communities that are undergoing persecution and which are threatened with extinction?" and "If Marx was right that religion is the opium of the people, what does that imply for consciousness studies in the 21st century?" "Do socially constructed fields such as gender and race

affect determinations of consciousness, and/or spirituality?" "Do political systems represent spiritual constructs and, if so, what are the implications?" "What is the link between fascism and occultism? How does the one influence the other? Why are there no Marxist occultists? Or fascist atheists?"
https://peterlevenda.substack.com/p/unholy-communion-

I also want to bow a knee to Whitley Strieber, Linda Moulton Howe, Jacques Vallee, Klaus, Kelly Chase, Cristina Gomez, Ross Coulthart, Richard Dolan and Diana Walsh Pasulka and many others whose writing, podcasts and research have considerably assisted me as I developed this series.

Finally, I extend my thanks to Naomi Klein for her enlightening book, *This Changes Everything*, which provided me with the impetus and inspiration to write this series.

And last but not least to Bill McGibben for his untiring work in the field of climate change – thank you.
https://billmckibben.substack.com

THE AUTHOR

Felicity Harley is a public speaker, published journalist, and writer. She holds an undergraduate degree in Social Sciences which includes the study of economics, political science, human geography, demography, sociology, psychology, anthropology, and history. Active in political and social affairs her whole life she is currently the President of the Community Foundation for Saint Vincent and the Grenadines www.cfsvg.org

Along with her career as a nonprofit executive, she served for twenty years on the board of Curbstone Press, an internationally recognized indie publishing house that focused on social activism and social change.

Her work has been published in an anthology called *Gathered Light – On the Poetry of Joni Mitchell,* alongside writers such as Wally Lamb, Kim Addonizio, Fred Wah (Poet Laureate of Canada), Larry Klein, Susan Deer Cloud, Cornelius Eady, and others. In celebration of the 65th Anniversary of the Universal Declaration of Human Rights and on behalf of Poets for Human Rights, Felicity was the winner of the Anita McAndrews Award. In 2014 she was commissioned by Hartbeat Ensemble to write the play "Transplant." This was directed by one of the nation's 25 premier young directors, Steven Raider Ginsberg.

In 2015 Felicity's book of short stories *Portraits and Landscapes*, was published, and is now available.

The Burning Years is the first book in a quintet series called *"Until This Last"*, the title of which has been taken from an essay about economic inequality written by John Ruskin. An essay that also became a major inspiration for Mahatma Gandhi

Made in the USA
Middletown, DE
18 May 2024

54410436R00116